VALKYRIE

VALKYRIE

CHOOSER OF THE SLAIN™ BOOK ONE

MICHAEL ANDERLE

DISRUPTIVE IMAGINATION®

LMBPN Publishing
PMB 196, 2540 South Maryland Pkwy
Las Vegas, NV 89109

Version 1.00, August 2022
eBook ISBN: 979-8-88541-685-6
Print ISBN: 979-8-88541-686-3

THE VALKYRIE TEAM

Thanks to our Beta Team
John Ashmore, Kelly O'Donnell, Rachel Beckford

Thanks to the JIT Readers

Christopher Gilliard
Deb Mader
Dave Hicks
Diane L. Smith
Dorothy Lloyd
Wendy L Bonell
Peter Manis
James Caplan
Zacc Pelter
Jackey Hankard-Brodie

If I've missed anyone, please let me know!

Editor
The SkyFyre Editing Team

PROLOGUE

Gray water faded to mist, and mist faded to sky, infinite and lit from everywhere at once. Waves crashed against sand and stone as the ocean breathed.

Long, slender boats slid out of the distance and sliced across the water, leaving rippling V's in their wake. The prows were curved, high, and proud. Oars rose and dipped into the water, steady as the beat of drums. Steady as the beat of her heart.

Time slipped past in confusion. Blurry days, months, and years passed as ragged traders and raiders became settlers and camps became towns.

The raucous scream of a raven cut through the mist, and she turned away from the busy little place of men. She drew back out to the beach, to the place where land met the moody sea.

A lone figure walked along the shore, the long shaft of his spear thumping in time with his steady footfall. He was tall, taller than the waves, taller than the sky. His face was shrouded in shadow and mist. Birds followed him like a dark halo.

He came to her, and she slid to her knees. The coarse sand was rough on her bare skin.

"You have come." His voice was like the grinding of millstones, although there was a softness that felt almost like affection. "You've slept for so long. I've missed you."

Slept? Confusion. Thoughts slid in and out of her, muddled. *But I've barely closed my eyes, Grandad.*

Was that sound chuckling, or was it the rumbling of the ocean? Or were they both the same?

The understanding came to her all at once. She wasn't sleeping. She was Valerie, and though she might still be safe and warm between her sheets in an apartment in Virginia, this wasn't a dream.

"Awaken, Val Kearie."

The mist swirled. The sea, the distant longboats, and Odin dissolved into the flutter of dark wings.

"Awaken."

CHAPTER ONE

Viking Inc., Business Division
Manassas, VA
Monday Morning

"Do we really have to have these meetings so early?" Nathanial Hawker—Hawk to his friends and "that sharp-nosed" bastard to his enemies—tipped back in his chair and stifled a yawn. Pre-dawn light hadn't yet begun to creep in through the front window of the Viking Inc. Manassas office. The Keurig on the side table gurgled as it went through its warm-up routine.

"What do you mean?" Jasper Taggart gave Hawk a pitiless smile. A thin sheen of wax on the old man's bald pate indicated he had already showered, which meant he had already run his daily 5k. "It's almost five a.m. The day's half over!"

Hawk popped a coffee pod into the machine and bit his tongue. It was no good cussing out the boss before the meeting had started. Jasper was in his fifties, a good ten

3

years Hawk's senior. As a colonel in the Marines and later as a freelance contractor, Jasper had headed up more covert ops than Hawk could name on a good day. The man commanded respect, even if his scheduling habits didn't.

The office alarm system beeped as someone came through the back door and punched in her ID code. A middle-aged woman swept into the front office hauling a big blue handbag over one shoulder and a bakery bag in her fist. "Sorry I'm late. I decided to run a few surprise drills down at the Lakeland facility. Rogers sprained an ankle and I had to get it sorted with insurance."

Hawk checked his watch. Three minutes to five. To Charlie, early was late. He appreciated that.

Jasper had a less positive outlook. "Another goddamned injury? Christ, the Kyiv fuckup was bad enough. Quit sending my recruits to the hospital. They need refreshers on basic comms protocols, not midnight obstacle course drills."

Charlie Evans dropped her bakery bag into the office mini-fridge. She was a small woman with a dark pixie cut beginning to silver at the edges. Johnny-on-the-street might look at Charlie's horn-rimmed reading glasses and large, colorful bags and see a high school art teacher trying too hard to be quirky. They wouldn't see the former middleweight boxing champion and special forces Major still rippling beneath her yellow raincoat.

"It was an emergency comms drill," she said. "Rogers got all excited and forgot how to put one foot in front of the other. He fell down the stairwell trying to get to the server room before the buzzer."

Jasper groaned and rubbed his temples. He looked at

the ceiling and murmured, "Talent... Odin, please, send me someone with *talent*. But if basic competence is the best you can manage, I'll take that."

"Amen," Charlie replied ironically. None of the senior staff were what you'd call *Ásatrú*, but when you called your organization "Viking Incorporated" and named your ops divisions after the Norse gods of war, foresight, and knowledge, it was easy to fall into the habit. The rookies had taken to calling the three of them jarls.

"Your prayers are answered." Hawk dropped a stack of folders onto the table. "Not by Odin but by Heimdall. Here are the recruitment files you asked for."

Jasper eagerly picked up the files. "Fresh meat."

"Don't get your hopes up."

Jasper flipped open the top folder and glanced over the bio page. "First guy. Twenty-two-year-old former Marine, private first-class, two tours of duty in Lebanon... Dishonorably discharged for drug abuse and gambling problems." Frowning, he dropped the dossier into the circular filing bin.

"Next up: ten-year veteran with the San Francisco PD. Two years as detective. Not bad. Terminated on six charges of use of excessive force. Holy shit." Jasper stared up at Hawk. "Her union didn't even back her up?"

"We're fighting a bit of an image problem, boss," Hawk observed. "People hear 'independent military contractor,' and they think we take the thugs who can't get hired anywhere else."

Jasper sighed. "I know we have to build our own talent base, but I'd like to at least start with people who are not actively addicted to meth. *Former* addicts, *maybe*."

"Check the next file."

Jasper obliged and scanned the final dossier thoughtfully. "A network engineer who's been running a Search-and-Rescue team out of Montana during tourist season. So he's got some tech know-how and survival grit." He flipped the page. "No criminal record?"

"One count of underaged drinking, expunged when he turned eighteen."

"Fantastic," Jasper scoffed bitterly. "Charlie, give the man a signing bonus. Make sure he keeps up on his medic training. Maybe he can splint up Rogers' ankle for us."

Charlie nibbled the tip of a ballpoint pen and scratched something into her notebook. "I'll get in touch with the guy. See if he's a good fit."

"And that's all she wrote?" Jasper gestured at the measly three files.

"I'll have more files next week. I'm working on talent scouting," Hawk replied stiffly.

"Oh!" Charlie sat up straight. She leaned across the office space, tugged open the mini-fridge door, and drew a clear plastic clamshell from her bakery bag. "I've been doing a little scouting myself."

Jasper watched Charlie pop open the shell to reveal a perfect creamy yellow wedge. "Jesus… *Another* one? What's this now?"

Charlie grinned and drove her fork into the pie. "Lemon meringue cheesecake. I made it to the bakery before closing last night. Can you believe they were about to throw this thing into the trash?"

Jasper held out a hand. "Hand it over. Let me try."

She drew the pie closer to her. "You going to give me that raise we talked about last week?"

"No."

"Then buy your own damn pie, boss." Charlie turned her attention back to the pie.

"You're going to get sick on that stuff." Hawk watched dispassionately as Charlie popped the first bite and thumbed a crumb of cheese from the corner of her mouth.

"Or fat," Jasper added darkly.

Charlie smirked and flicked him a view of her middle finger. "You're just jealous, old man."

"You said you'd been scouting," Hawk interrupted. "Did you have something for us, or are you showing off your unnatural metabolism?"

"Nothing unnatural about it. Just good old-fashioned iron pumping, six days a week." Charlie set aside the plate of half-eaten pie and kissed her muscular upper arm. "But yeah. I've got the new recruit right here." She shuffled through her bag and came up with a plain brown folder. She dropped it on the desk between Hawk and Jasper. "I've got a good feeling about this one. The CV got my big toe a-twitching."

Jasper was eyeing Charlie's pie, so Hawk flipped open the file.

"Well in *that* case... 'Kearie, Valerie L.,'" he read. "Strategic tech and market consultant with the firm Asher and Asher, right here in Manassas. How convenient." His tone grew contemplative. "Postgrad student at the University of Virginia."

Charlie snatched her plate from under Jasper's nose and took a spitefully large bite. "On hiatus. She's taking some time away from her active studies to do a little traveling, put some of that fabled real-world experience under her belt. The postgrad program is holding her spot open for her. UVA doesn't like to do that, so her department must think she's something special."

Abandoning his hopes for a stolen bite of pie, Jasper swiveled in his chair to read over Hawk's shoulder.

"Her department..." Hawk flipped through the file until he located the academic records. His semi-permanent frown deepened. "History."

"Middle Ages European history specifically," Jasper clarified. He gave Charlie a puzzled look. "What do we need a history nerd for?"

Charlie scooped the last lonely lump of meringue with her pinky finger and licked it clean before depositing her empty clamshell into the garbage. She opened her mouth, but Hawk cut in. "Students of history can be particularly adept at identifying and predicting long-term social patterns," he mused. "Nothing wrong with a history nerd. UVA is a good school."

Charlie nodded and leaned back with her hands folded behind her head. "Knew you'd appreciate that."

Jasper sniffed. "Egghead. That's all fine, sure, but we're looking for field operatives. Not another pencil-pushing consultant."

"She has a black belt in jujitsu." Charlie bit at the corner of her mouth, privy to some secret joke.

"So does my wife's shithead nephew," Jasper pointed out. "He's seventeen and bought it at a strip-mall dojo run by a guy who spends his summers doing caricatures at Six Flags."

Hawk quoted from the dossier, "Family connections: Hank Kearie, Brother. Navy SEAL, ten years, six tours of duty, one purple heart. Philip 'Puck' Kearie, Brother. Captain, US Army, six years, nine commendations, based in Fairfax."

"Too bad military training isn't passed through genetics." Jasper folded his arms.

"It may not be, but…" Hawk flipped over the report and read the back. He let out a low whistle. "Father—David Pearson."

"Holy shit." Jasper's stubborn reluctance had melted away. "The army general who ran those Kuwaiti ops a few years back?"

"Looks like the children took their mother's surname," Hawk guessed. "I didn't even know General Pearson had kids."

"They're trying to keep the nepotism to a minimum." Charlie sounded pleased with herself. "The family is big on self-reliance. You're an only child, aren't you, Jasper?"

"I am." Jasper shifted his weight uneasily. "Of a single mother. I appreciate self-reliance."

"There's more than one school of hard knocks." Hawk closed the file and dropped it onto the desk. "Growing up with a single working-class parent is one, and growing up in a military family is another. I'm guessing Miss Kearie didn't learn her martial arts from your strip-mall dojo."

Jasper nodded slowly. "This girl's got a nice pedigree. I'll give you that. I say, if she comes sniffing for a job we think about trying her out."

Charlie shook her head. "I don't think we should let this one get away, Jasper."

"Because of the toe?"

Charlie sighed. "We bring her on as a consultant." She lifted a hand to halt Jasper's protest. "We've got plenty of consultants, sure. But we bring her in to test her out on a couple of jobs with the potential for going hot. See how much mettle a military brat really can pick up by osmosis. If she's got the grit, we put her in ops training. I bet she flies right through it."

"It looks like a close-knit military family," Hawk noted. "Despite the conflicting surnames. We'll need to watch Miss Kearie and see if she shows any potential positive action-based leanings."

Charlie and Jasper shared a rare glance of commiserating confusion.

"Potential positive action-based leanings," Jasper repeated slowly, working through the term. "Is that another way of saying they like to kick ass and take names?"

"Yes."

"Then why didn't you just say it?" Charlie pushed.

Hawk straightened the untidy folders. "Look. In today's society, you learn to guard your tongue. Everyone is ready to misquote you at a moment's notice. I can't lower my guard, or the Twitter trolls will be so far up my ass they'll be cleaning my tonsils with a toothbrush from the wrong entry point."

"Twee-tar?" Jasper drawled the word out, turning it over like he'd never heard it before. "Is that one of the newfangled glowing boxes all the damn kids are staring at these days?"

Charlie snickered. "You worried one of us is going to go

misquoting you to the media, Hawk?"

"Not you, no," Hawk snapped. "But I'm getting into the habit. You two had better learn the new doublespeak, too. The world is changing." He huffed and fussed with the recruitment files. When his temper had cooled, he conceded. "We can give Miss Kearie a trial run. But we're opening ourselves up to some nasty lawsuits if we expose her to danger that she's not equipped to handle."

"Not to mention a decorated army general might get a little salty if his baby girl gets kidnapped or killed on what's supposed to be a Shanghai cakewalk," Jasper noted.

"That's exactly the kind of good-old-boys-club crap we need to cut out," Hawk asserted. "Senior management at a paramilitary contractor calling an accomplished post-graduate professional 'baby girl'? You're a PR nightmare waiting to happen, Taggert."

Charlie opened her mouth to make a quip, then seemed to think better. Joking was one thing behind closed doors, but you should only push the envelope so far. This wasn't the office Christmas party.

Jasper seemed to take the admonition to heart and nodded. "Let's say we're all perfectly politically correct about it. What kind of liability are we exposing ourselves to if we send her on a job and she gets killed?"

"Same as we are with any other ops agent who signs the waiver and NDA," Charlie pointed out. "A big insurance payout to her beneficiary. I think she'll do it, boss. I think she'll jump at the chance."

"Why do you think that?" Jasper gave her a long side-eye. "Don't say it's an omen from your big toe."

Charlie smiled a mischievous smile. "Miss Kearie's got

adventure in the blood. My guy in Central Intelligence tells me they've been wining and dining her for months. She hasn't signed over her soul yet…but she hasn't said no."

Jasper and Hawk exchanged startled glances. Leave it to Charlie to save the sharpest hook for last.

"The CIA wants her?" Jasper leaned forward to rap his knuckles impatiently on the brown file folder. "Well then. We've got to have her."

Cowabunga Coffee Co.
Manassas, VA
Mdday Monday

Valerie Kearie's thumbs hovered over the send button on her MeadFeed app, but she drew in a breath and forced herself to set the phone down. She took a long sip of cappuccino and waited for her temper to settle. She counted to ten and looked at her unsent message again.

No, you damned sot-brained Neanderthal! Mead and wine are not the same thing.

She hit delete and typed:

Wine is created from the sugars of fermented fruit. Mead is fermented from honey. They are similar but fundamentally different things. It's easy to get confused.

She frowned as she studied the message. She debated

adding a smiley emoji and decided it would be too conde-scending. Finally she hit send and forced herself to turn the phone facedown on the café table. *No more phone during lunch,* she promised herself. *Certainly no more MeadFeed debates.*

When she got going, she could scroll for hours, debating brewing methods and comparing different melomels with her growing number of followers. Mead lovers loved ValLovesMead. But she had to be back in the office in thirty minutes, and it would be nice to at least *taste* her lunch.

A bell tinkled as a tall woman in a yellow raincoat swept into the café carrying a mist of midday rain with her. Val sighed and scooted her chair out of the draft.

"Oh, you don't have to make room for me. I'll sit right here."

Val froze, staring as the woman pulled out the empty chair across from her and sat.

The stranger had a mane of brassy blonde hair and the kind of massive dark sunglasses you only saw in movies from the early nineties.

"The name's Sally." Raincoat Woman held out a hand and smiled. Her teeth were too big for her skull. "Sally Snow. Do you have a minute?"

Valerie set down her egg burrito and wiped a bit of cheese from the corner of her mouth. She did not shake the outstretched hand. "Are you here to make me an offer I can't refuse?"

Sally's broad smile flickered. "What do you mean?"

Valerie frowned, sat back, and looked over her unex-pected lunch companion. "Where do I begin? You just came in out of the rain. Your jacket has a hood but you weren't wearing it.

"Why would you bother? You don't care if your hair gets wet, because that's not your real hair. It's a wig. You're wearing dark shades on an overcast day, presumably to obscure your face. Are those three-inch heels on your boots? Don't see many of those outside of a strip club."

Valerie flushed and silently cursed a tongue that had a habit of racing ahead of her brain. "Uh, that's just an observation, though." She held up her hands. "No offense. I think they're pretty cute. Your boots."

The grin returned to Sally's face. "I knew I should have put in the colored contacts instead. You get a lot of spooks joining you for lunch, Miss Kearie?"

"Actually yeah." Val didn't bat an eye at hearing Sally speak her name. "I think I've been interviewed by an average of four federal agents a year since I was in ninth grade and my brothers started applying for clearance jobs."

"But I hear most of the agents are coming after *you* these days." Sally set a large handbag on the chair beside her and pulled out a steel thermos.

"I don't think they like you bringing your own drinks in," Val observed. Sally chuckled as she sipped.

"So what are you?" Val straightened and nudged her lunch aside. There was only a heel of empty tortilla left. "NSA or Homeland Security? I haven't heard from them yet."

"Neither." Sally smacked her lips in satisfaction. "I represent a private contracting firm that runs intelligence-gathering operations on behalf of the federal government."

Valerie's eyebrows arched. "Mercenaries."

Sally drew herself up, offended. "Spies."

"Spies that trade valuable information for money," Valerie specified.

"Miss Kearie, *everything* gets traded for money somewhere down the line. People gotta eat, after all. We go where Uncle Sam can't. Or where he doesn't want to be seen. Moscow, Pyongyang, Urumqi, northern Syria... We go in, set up a few information networks, tag a few servers, grease a few wheels so it's easier for the official diplomats to do their jobs. No, we're not Uncle Sam. We're his punk little sister, Sal." Her cheek twitched, which Val took to mean that Sally had winked behind those black glasses.

Sally finished, "At the end of the day, we're all family."

It was such an absurd and unexpected comparison that Val couldn't help but snort. She swirled the dregs of cappuccino to give herself a moment to consider. "That's a more interesting pitch than the CIA gave me," she admitted.

"*They* wanted you stuck behind a desk at Langley analyzing social media trends in northern Italy. How boring."

Valerie snapped to attention. The cheap wig and sunglasses had been a painfully obvious disguise, but anyone who had ferreted out the contents of her initial CIA interview must have had some serious intel connections. What game was this woman playing?

Sally Snow smiled again, teasing from behind her sunglasses. "We're looking for a consultant, too. More along the lines of information management than social media trends. Plus we like our consultants to work on location, wherever that might be."

"Oh." It was all Valerie could think to say. For the first time since she had sent her application to the State Department and triggered this gauntlet of covert job interviews conducted by humorless men in business suits, she felt *excited*. She knew better than to let it show, however. Daddy hadn't taught poker to no fool.

Her poker face must have done its job because Sally kept talking. As she did, she reached into a pocket in her jacket and drew out a small black business card. "We're no MI6, but we take care of our own. I've got to run, Val—can I call you Val?—I've got to be across town in twenty. Here's my number." She placed the card facedown on the table and slid it across to Val.

One of the baristas was clearing tables and drawing closer to them. Sally grabbed her contraband thermos, slung her bag over her shoulder, and rose to her feet. She tapped her fingers across the card and mouthed, *text me*.

Before the barista could reach them, Sally had turned and was dashing back into the rain, running like she'd been born in those stripper heels.

"Did she buy anything?" the barista asked, fastidiously wiping nothing off Val's table. Valerie smiled stiffly and waited for the barista to move on before flipping over the card. It was blank, save for a ten-digit phone number and two words.

Viking Inc.

CHAPTER TWO

Offices of Asher and Asher
Manassas, VA
Monday Afternoon

Crysta, Mr. Asher's personal assistant, bumped into Valerie as she was climbing the stairs to her second-floor office. Glancing over her shoulder to make sure they were alone, Crysta leaned in close to whisper into Val's ear, "Watch your ass, honey. Mr. Lech is sniffing around your office again."

Val ground her teeth. "Asher needs to get a damned HR department."

Crysta gave Val a sympathetic smile. "His name's on the building, Val. Even if we had HR, reporting him wouldn't get you anything but a pink slip."

Val glanced at the door and sucked in a steadying breath. "You're right. Breaking his nose will be far more satisfying anyway."

"I'll pretend I didn't hear that." Crysta clicked down the narrow staircase, hips swaying in her pencil skirt.

Val pulled her phone from her pocket, dismissed seven new messages from MeadFeed, and turned on the camera's record function. A little bit of insurance could only be a good thing.

She steeled herself and climbed the last few stairs.

Laurence Asher stood in the empty hallway, leaning against the wall outside Val's office like the Fonz in a three-piece suit. He saw Val and smiled a small I-know-a-secret smile that might have worked if Val were in a bar looking for an easy hookup. *If* she didn't know Laurence Asher.

He straightened as she drew closer. "Valley Girl! I went over your analysis of the Glendale project. I'm impressed. Your eye for detail is—" He made a chef's kiss.

She kept her tone neutral. "Thank you, Mr. Asher." Val pulled out her office key and started to slip it into the lock. She frowned when the door swung open.

"I took the liberty," Laurence remarked offhandedly. "I wanted to talk to you in private."

With casual swiftness, he put a hand on her waist, ushered her into the room, and shut the door behind him.

Jeez, liberty sure is one word for it, Val thought. She eased away from his sweaty palm and set her bag and phone on her desk. It was a small desk, appropriate for a tiny office that had been converted from a janitor's closet. She turned to see Mr. Asher, or Mr. Lech, as the rest of the office called him in private, leaning against her door with his arms crossed. Boxing her in.

"You're a tough nut to crack, Val." Laurence studied her

from beneath his heavy brow. "So competent, and yet so solitary. Stoic. Icy, almost. All of us around here have been wondering when you'll open up and let us get to know you better."

Val spoke deliberately, careful to pronounce each word clearly. "Mr. Asher. Please don't touch me. Open the office door. You are making me uncomfortable. If you wish to talk about my performance, I'd be happy to schedule a meeting with your father and the three of us can work it out."

Laurence rolled his eyes. "Dad's been a wreck since Uncle Gil died. He doesn't want to be bothered about this kind of thing. He leaves the matter of office morale to me."

"We all miss the other Mr. Asher," Val agreed. "He was a real *professional*. We're sure that someday you'll step up and fill his shoes."

Laurence's lazy grin faltered. He moved forward, shrinking the already narrow gap between them. Forced to choose between standing still or backing into her desk, Val stood her ground.

"Come on." His voice was quiet, almost friendly, as he slipped a hand onto Val's waist above the band of her dress pants, brushing against the hem of her blouse. "Loosen up. Try to be friendly. It'll be good for your career. Think of your future."

"My future?" Val's eyes went wide. "Oh. Okay."

Quick as a snake, she grabbed Laurence Asher by the future.

She twisted hard enough to make Laurence squeak. "Let me think."

"Jesus Christ—" Laurence slapped her wrist, but like most men, he wasn't well-trained in what to do when someone had you by the balls. She jerked viciously, and he went rigid. A vein popped out of his forehead as he sucked in air. She didn't need to say it: one wrong move and she'd pop his testicle like a balloon.

She stepped forward, forcing him to shuffle awkwardly off to the side. "I've thought about my future." She guided him from the doorway until his back was against her cheap IKEA bookshelf. "You are *definitely* not in it."

She drove the knuckles of her free hand into his guts and let go. He doubled over, wheezing and cradling his offended future. "Bitch," he rasped as she snatched up her bag and phone. "You're fired. You're fucking fired and I'm calling the police. I'm calling my lawyer. I'm calling—" He groaned and doubled over as a fresh wave of pain rippled through him. "Oh. God damn."

"You go ahead and do that." Val left her office and slammed the door shut behind her. "You take this job and shove it, and I hope the corners catch!"

A few junior associates poked their heads out of their offices as Val stormed back to the stairs. She descended to the ground floor, where Crysta was back at her station in front of the closed office door of Merrik Asher.

Crysta took in Val's expression and disheveled hair. She scrambled from her seat to throw open the heavy wooden doors to the senior partner's office before Val could beat them down with her bare fists.

Merrik Asher sat behind a wooden desk about as big as Valerie's entire office, talking into his phone.

"I'm gonna have to call you back, Jerry." He cut his call as Val stormed in. "Miss Kearie, what—"

"I'm here to tender my resignation, effective immediately."

"Resignation? You kicked butt on the Glendale project, what—"

Val silenced Mr. Asher by slapping her phone onto the desk. Staring him in the eye, she pressed the *replay* button.

Like his dearly departed brother, the elder Asher was a reasonable, professional man. He listened to the staticky audio in contemplative silence. When he heard Laurence invite himself into Val's office, his expression deepened into a frown.

Stomping sounds echoed from the stairwell, and shouts came from the waiting room beyond Mr. Asher's office. Val-on-audio was politely but firmly asking Laurence to keep his hands to himself when the man burst through his father's doors in the flesh. His jacket was disheveled and his skin was an interesting shade of nauseated green.

"Call a goddamned ambulance," Laurence panted. "And the cops—" His eyes fixed on Val standing beside his father's desk. "That bitch assaulted me!"

Merrik Asher reached forward and stopped the playback. "Get out of my office," he told his son.

"She attacked me—"

"If you need a doctor, get your sorry ass to a hospital," Mr. Asher roared. "Or call an ambulance. I don't care. Nobody's bringing the cops into this. I shut out the rumors because I didn't want to believe them, Larry, but Jesus *Christ,* I guess you had it coming."

Laurence gaped at his father, too stunned to speak.

Then, limping a little, he turned and shuffled out of the office. Crysta snapped the doors firmly shut behind him.

"Nobody's going to call the cops," Merrik repeated more quietly. "Right, Miss Kearie?"

Val gave her soon-to-be-former-employer a long, hard look. She slipped her phone off the table and back into her bag as she carefully chose her next words. "I want to retain my full signing bonus. And my commission from the Glendale job."

Mr. Asher nodded. "You were off probation on Friday. Of course, the bonus and commission are yours in full."

"In my bank account by the end of the day."

Mr. Asher didn't bat an eye. "We're sad to see you go, Miss Kearie. If you're ever interested in working consulting again, please reach out."

Val shouldered her bag with a snort. "Don't you worry about me, Mr. Asher. I have plenty of prospects."

Pearson and Kearie Residence
Manassas, VA
Monday Evening

The clouds had rolled away and the morning rains had faded into a muggy-hot summer night. Val sat at the patio picnic table, frowning over a crappy pinochle hand as Puck manned the grill. Tonight's menu was burgers and Grams' potato salad—Val's favorite.

The Kearie kid with the biggest sob story got to pick the menu for their summer cookouts. It was a silly old tradition, but nobody complained.

"You better back up that audio onto a secured server, Val." David Pearson tipped back his pint glass and downed the last of his red ale. "In case you ever decide to press charges."

Val rolled her eyes. "Already done, Dad." She played an ace, taking the trick. Across the table from her, Grams nodded approval. "I'm twenty-six. Not sixteen."

Hank played a ten on Val's next queen. "You should press charges anyway. The sooner, the better. Only way to weed out crap like that is to nip it quick. I'm betting the other girls in the office don't have your self-defense experience."

"Leave Val alone," Grams muttered. She threw a worthless nine onto the pile and rearranged her hand. "She doesn't owe anyone anything. Puck? Are you making burgers or jerky over there, boy?"

"Salmonella kills over four hundred people a year," Puck answered as he flipped the row of burgers a final time.

Val tried to hide her grin. "You get shot at for a living."

"You know what sucks more than getting shot?" Puck picked up the platter of burger buns and started dropping patties onto bread. "Getting shot because you were too busy squatting in a bush shitting your brains out to watch your six. Clear your game off the table. Food's coming."

"I got diddly squat anyway," David grunted and dropped a fistful of low cards onto the pile. He consulted the scorepad as Hank and Val swept the cards aside. "Ninety-seven to twenty-one. Let's go ahead and call this one for the girls."

"*Again*," Hank grumbled.

"All right, Val." Puck scooted into the empty spot beside Gram and passed out the paper plates. "So you punched the owner's son in the stomach, squeezed his balls to stop him procreating, and quit your job. Now what? You got another position lined up?"

"Not…exactly." Val took a bite of potato salad to buy herself time to think. "I'm considering a few options."

"What kind of options?" Hank asked.

"Consultant stuff."

"What kind of consultant stuff?"

Val shook her head.

"Oh," Puck responded. "*That* kind of consultant stuff."

"What's the agency?" David asked. His tone was suddenly all business as he studied his daughter. A lifelong Captain America type, David Pearson had strong opinions about shady government agencies with three-letter names.

"Private outfit," Val explained. "Viking Inc."

Under most circumstances, hearing that one's daughter had turned down a chance to work for a federal agency in favor of a private contractor would not have comforted anybody. But David Pearson felt relief and relaxed about three graying hairs.

"That's Jasper Taggert's operation," he told her.

"You know him?" Val asked.

"Only by reputation. Good officer. Haven't heard much about his outfit but in that line of work, no news is good news. No scandals or war crimes that I'm aware of."

"So it's no Blackwater." Hank's voice dripped irony as he bit into his burger. "But I don't know, Val. That kind of work tends to be very temporary. Is it going to pay the bills?"

"I'm not worried about money," Val asserted quickly. "At least not for a while. I'm interested in the experience. I want to test out the consultancy market. Do some networking. Maybe think about opening my own firm someday."

Across the table, Grams gave an approving nod.

"That can be a dangerous line of work," Puck warned. "You don't have any real combat training."

Val kicked him beneath the table. "What, growing up with you doesn't count?"

"You watch your mouth or I'll give you a swirlie for dessert." Puck remained straight-faced. "Just like when we were little."

"All right, asshole." Valerie bared her teeth in a fierce grin and pushed away from the table. "You and me. Right now. Let's go. I'll give you a mud pie for dessert."

"Guys!" David was dismayed. "In the middle of supper?"

"Hush," Grams admonished her son-in-law. She stared up at Val and Puck with bright, eager eyes. "I want to see."

"You heard the woman." Puck sighed and dropped his napkin on the table beside his plate. He hopped down the patio steps to join Val on the grassy lawn. "Come on, Valley-Girl," he taunted as he tugged his wifebeater over his shoulders and tossed it aside. "Let's dance!"

Something shifted inside Valerie. Maybe it was the last of the dying daylight flashing off Puck's dog tags, turning the world into a flash of white. Maybe it was Gram's sharp whistle of encouragement, like a gambler rooting on her favorite horse. Maybe it was hearing her old nickname on Puck's lips, echoed off the Lech's ugly mug earlier that day.

She'd been wearing manic good cheer like a suit of

armor since walking out of the offices of Asher and Asher that afternoon. Now it funneled out of her, draining out of her feet and running onto the grass. She was empty as Puck pounded his chest and came in for a tackle.

She fell into a crouch and ducked below his arcing fists. Before he could re-adjust, she rose and drove her knee into Puck's guts. He let out a great gasping wheeze and stumbled, clutching his belly. Val didn't pause to think. She wove her fingers together and brought the club of her fists down onto the squishy part of Puck's back.

He let out a curse that would have made even Grams blush, overbalanced, and collapsed into the grass.

Laughter exploded from the patio. Hank doubled over, slapping his thighs, and Grams shook her fists in the air. David buried his face in his hands and shook his head slowly.

Val's thoughts came crashing back all at once and she dropped to her knees. Her heart slammed in her chest. "Shit. Puck. Puck! Are you okay?"

Puck was trembling. She was afraid she'd busted one of his ribs, but as he turned over onto his back she saw that he was laughing—if a touch ruefully. "I shouldn't have had that beer."

A clod of dirt clung to his cheek. Val brushed it away and hauled him to his feet, chuckling uneasily. "Yeah, that's what it was," she agreed. "The one beer. It took the fight right outta ya."

"You got the drop on me." Puck patted her shoulder with only the slightest hint of condescension.

Val snorted, thinking, *Yes. Yes I did.*

"Quit bullshitting," David called gruffly. "Come eat the rest of your dinner before it gets cold."

Later that night, after the dishes had been washed and Grams had gone to bed, Val sent a text to the ten-digit phone number on the Viking Inc. business card.

Hi, Sally. This is Val. When can we meet?

CHAPTER THREE

Viking Inc., Business Division
Manassas, VA
Tuesday Afternoon

"Sally!" Val grinned and extended her hand to the short but powerfully built woman who came from the back room to greet her. "Is that a new haircut?"

Sally Snow had shed her wig in favor of a dark pixie cut. Her polite smile broadened into genuine amusement as she shook Val's hand. "It's Charlotte Evans, but you can call me Charlie. Glad you could make it, Miss Kearie. You can take off your coat."

"You look like a Charlie." Val nodded approval as she put her jacket on the hook beside the front door. The lobby was small but warmly appointed with a thick rug and an old sofa with a hand-carved wooden back. Like most of the buildings in the business district, the Viking Inc. office was a re-purposed brownstone, almost stuffy compared to

Charlie with her big jangly earrings and artfully styled hair.

"I'm glad you got me in so quick," Val stated. "About thirty minutes after our meeting yesterday, I decided I could really use a change of scenery."

"That wouldn't have anything to do with the call for a private ambulance to the offices of Asher and Asher yesterday afternoon, would it?" Charlie wondered.

Val turned, surprised to see two more men entering the lobby. The first was an older fellow, bald with a short, silvering clean-cut beard and pale gray eyes. His tight athletic shirt defined his cut edges and bulging arms. The man over his shoulder was tall and lean, wearing a sports jacket. He straightened his tie and looked down at Val over his beak-like nose.

"Ah—" Val's smile wavered and turned a little sheepish. She supposed that if she was seriously going to pursue a career in intelligence, she should get used to being surrounded by people with big noses. "There was a kerfuffle," she admitted as she added her messenger bag to the hook. "It…was a long time coming."

Charlie gestured at the men. "Miss Kearie, these are my associates. Jasper Taggert, Chief Operating Officer, head of the Tyr division and founding member of Viking Inc."

The shorter man held out a hand. His palms were hot and sweat gleamed on his exposed skin. He was fresh from a workout. He took her hand in an iron grip—not crushing or painful, as was the way of insecure men, but uncompromising and unapologetic. "Colonel Taggert." She met his eye and returned a firm shake. Grams had taught Val that if she had no hope of matching a man's physical strength, the best thing she could do was stare him in the eye and declare that she would not be dismissed. "My father says you have an impeccable service record. It's good to meet you."

"Glad to hear someone remembers." Jasper spoke gruffly, but Val thought he looked quietly pleased as he stepped back to make room for his associate.

"This is Nate Hawker," Charlie introduced the taller man as he held out a hand. "Head of our Heimdall division."

"Oh, I know that name. The Norse god of foresight," Val interjected cheerfully. "I suppose that makes you the Spymaster, Mr. Hawker."

Hawker's thin lips quirked into a frown. He had a strong grip, but his hands were cold and almost clawlike. He shook stiffly.

"You wanted a nerd, Hawk." Taggert pointed out.

"You called it a kerfuffle, but I didn't notice any police calls to the offices of Asher and Asher," Nate Hawker mentioned. It took Val a moment to fall back to their earlier line of conversation. Hawker studied Val narrowly. *Hawk*, Taggert had called him. Val always thought it was terrific serendipity when someone's surname spun so appropriately into a nickname, like a wink and a nod at destiny.

"No, Mr. Asher wanted to call the police, but Mr. Asher —senior, I mean—talked him out of it," Val explained.

"Is there a blooming legal matter we need to be aware of?" Nate Hawker asked.

Val hesitated. It was a fair question. If the company wanted to send her out on field assignments, she couldn't afford to get bogged down with subpoenas and legal procedures. One more reason to hang on to her recording of Laurence and let the matter die for now. Finally, she answered. "No. The younger Asher has a problem with his female colleagues. If the job is good, I can ignore a couple of suggestive remarks from the man signing my paychecks. But then he put a hand on me and…" She shrugged.

"The ambulance was called but here you are with nary a scratch," Charlie observed. "I hope Mr. Asher learned his lesson?"

"I caught the whole thing on my phone," Val explained. "I'm not going to press charges, but if there are ever allegations of more misconduct in the offices of Asher and Asher, I'll turn over my evidence."

Taggert grunted. She felt jittery, knowing these people were judging and appraising and analyzing everything she said in this interview. Was Taggert's grunt a sound of approval or disgust? She couldn't tell.

Somewhat dryly, Taggert asked, "You get into a lot of fights?"

Val felt her ears go pink. "Exactly as many as are necessary, sir. My mom wasn't around when I grew up. I have two older brothers and a military dad. They treated me like one of the boys."

"Indian rug burns, contact football, and fart jokes?" Charlie guessed.

Val huffed a little laugh. "More or less. I could hold my own all right until Hank and Puck hit puberty and got those first shots of testosterone. I broke an arm wrestling Puck for the last freezie-pop. Dad whacked him good for that and said they had to be gentle with me from then on."

Charlie snorted.

"I didn't like that," Val stated. "Been doing jujitsu ever since."

"Where men have the edge in strength, we gotta lean on technique," Charlie agreed, holding out a closed fist. Val stared at it blankly for a moment before understanding came. They fist-bumped.

Hawker folded his arms, unimpressed. "We're not the Marines, Miss Kearie. If you're getting in hand-to-hand fights in this job, then something has already gone very wrong."

"Right!" Val opened her hands wide. "The job. Tell me about it."

Taggert and Hawker exchanged a glance so brief that Val might have missed it if she had not known to look.

"Let's back up, first." Taggert wiped his brow with the back of his wrist and sank onto one of the chairs. Hawker slipped onto the couch and produced a file. Without waiting for an invitation, Val seated herself across from Taggert.

Apparently, the gauntlet wasn't run yet. Val wasn't surprised. She'd expect nothing less than deep skepticism and doubt from a couple of professionals with well-established careers and extensive military training. In their eyes, she was probably a woman in her mid-twenties—barely more than a girl!—with a liberal arts degree and a sense of legacy entitlement stemming from her daddy's reputation.

That was fine. She was used to proving herself. The trick wasn't only to meet challenges, but to meet them *cheerfully*, and with her teeth out.

"What's your experience with firearms?" Taggert

flipped through the file. Charlie settled beside Hawker, making the old couch look very small. She reached under the seat and pulled out a thermos.

"Proficient with sidearms," Val replied. "Target shooting is a family pastime. We go out to the ranges a couple times a year. I haven't owned a firearm since leaving home but I keep my licenses up to date." She smiled faintly. "Makes Dad happy."

"Beyond sidearms?" Taggert pressed.

Val's eyebrows arched. "If getting into melee combat means the job's gone bad, then the job's gone *really* bad if I need to pick up a rifle."

Charlie snorted into her drink. Taggert looked up, face stoic, and Val realized he expected a real answer.

"I've picked up a couple of long barrels, but not since high school."

"What languages do you speak?" Hawker asked.

"English, mostly. My German is conversational, and my Dutch is…basic. My Latin is pretty good."

"No one speaks Latin." Hawk spoke almost reflexively, as if he had caught Val in a trap.

Val stared at him for a moment. "Okay, technically I don't speak Latin. I can read and write it just fine. I thought this was a job interview. Do you want me to give technical answers or thorough answers?"

Charlie rolled her eyes. "Be thorough. Don't mind him. He's a professional asshole."

Val nodded slowly. "If we're talking languages, I've held certifications in Java, SQL, C++, and Python."

"Held?" Taggert's gaze was hard. "Past tense?"

"I'm current in Java and C++. Haven't needed the others

in a couple of years, but I brush up quick. Stuff like that is like riding a bike."

Taggert's brow pulled into a thoughtful frown. "Up to date on your shots?"

"You mean vaccines? Of course."

"Got a valid passport?"

"In a file in my apartment," she confirmed.

"I'd get in the habit of keeping it on your person, Miss Kearie. Are you free tomorrow for a trial assignment?"

"Sure," Val agreed readily. "Since my abrupt resignation from Asher and Asher, my schedule is suddenly wide open."

Taggert nodded at Hawker. "Give her the file."

Hawker sighed and reached for a second, smaller folio. He handed it to Val across the coffee table. She flipped it open, expecting to see a brief on some local businesses dealing with hackers or maybe a private courier assignment. A fetch quest, in other words, to see how this liberal arts major stood up to a real-world scenario.

The location at the top of the first page made her eyes bulge.

"Spain?" She managed to keep her voice even.

"Seville." Hawker leaned back. He looked a little too self-satisfied at her surprise as he folded his arms behind his head. "Plane leaves at oh four twenty. Should be a three, four-day job, tops."

"Vikings don't waste time," Charlie put in. "Gallagher Solutions is an American-owned company. They're dealing with a combined ransomware and brute-force network attack. We think someone's trying to do more than make a fast buck off them. The plane was supposed to be undergoing maintenance until Thursday, but we pulled a few strings to have her flight-ready sooner. Every hour of downtime is killing Gallagher's bottom line."

Val spared a second to study Charlie. She hadn't shared her title or position within the company, but she must have been more than a talent scout. The three of them had this job sorted and ready to go before Val had arrived at the office.

"Ransomware," Val muttered, thumbing through the Gallagher file. "You want me on an IT issue?" The thought made her nervous. She was no technical slouch, but that was a tall order.

Hawk snorted. "No. We've got a trained cybersecurity expert to handle the tech."

Val didn't let her relief show.

"We want you to tag along with him and find out if there are any moles sandbagging the Gallagher organization from the inside. Find out what groups are conducting these attacks and who they're using to do it."

"Groups." Val turned the word over slowly. "You're thinking hackers? Terrorists?"

Charlie nodded. "Gallagher works with Spanish banks and corporations to streamline compliance with the recent international anti-money laundering laws."

"Making it harder to funnel money into sanctioned organizations," Val mused. "So...probably some kind of extremist group, yeah. But why doesn't Gallagher have in-house experts to deal with an IT problem?"

"They aren't a tech company, and it's beyond their outsourced IT people," Taggert answered. "It's why we're sending in our expert. He'll handle the system problems while you sniff out any moles and track down the culprit. Between the two of you, it should be a cakewalk."

"Cakewalk. Sure." Val snapped the folder shut. "I'll take the rest of the afternoon to look over the file and prepare." She shot Charlie a quizzical glance.

Charlie nodded. "You can call or text that same number if you have any questions. I'll email you the onboarding paperwork. I'll need it back by seventeen hundred, *capisce?*"

Val glanced at the clock, translating the times. It was already almost three p.m. They wanted her at an airstrip in less than thirteen hours, and already her plate was full.

She nodded at Charlie, then flashed Taggert and Hawker a broad grin. She stood, slipped the file into her bag, and slung the strap over her shoulder. "Got it. If you'll excuse me, gentlemen. I have work to do."

Val was six blocks down Franklin Street before her heart rate started to slow. She plucked her phone from her coat pocket with a flourish and dialed the first number on her contacts list. David Pearson picked up on the second ring.

"Valerie!"

"Hey, Dad." She let out a long breath, and her father chuckled.

"Post-interview yips? You still get those?"

"Never stopped," she confessed. It had been a joke between them since Val was in high school. Valerie Kearie could go into an interview for a cutthroat Ivy League school, compete in front of nationally ranked jujitsu judges, or debrief federal agents about her own brothers and never say boo—until she was five minutes out the door. Once the deed was done, all the postponed anticipation caught her from behind.

"They're sending me out on a trial assignment tomorrow."

"No kidding?" Dad sounded surprised, but cautiously pleased. "Congratulations. Where?"

"It's in Spain."

The silence stretched long enough that Val checked her phone to confirm she still had a connection.

"What the hell kind of operation sends a new recruit overseas on her first assignment without a single day of training or orientation?" Dad's tone was pleasant, but she could hear his teeth grinding. It was his someone's-being-a-dipshit-but-I'm-trying-to-stay-professional voice.

"Viking, Inc., apparently." Val swallowed. "Don't go all helicopter on me, Dad. I'm going as an adjunct to a senior operative. They want to see how I handle the field, and this is the job available."

"What's the job?"

"I'm gonna have to read my NDA's before I start gabbing details. I'll send you what I can later. I've glanced over the file and I don't think it's dangerous or anything. Taggert called it a cakewalk."

Dad grunted. "You've still got that tracker app on your phone, right?"

"I'll be gone for three days! We probably won't even leave the office building."

"Valerie—"

"Yeah, I've still got the app." Secretly, Val was pleased. Gallagher Solutions might be having problems with some terrorist group, but if Val was only doing some fact-finding, then her part in the job would be over long before the time there was any chance of it getting hot. Still, it was nice knowing that General Pearson and the Kearie boys would turn over every sod of earth between here and Seville to find her if she went missing. "Listen, my plane leaves early, and I've got a lot to do. I'll text you when I'm off the ground."

Her father sighed on the other end of the line. "Stay safe, Val. Good hunting."

CHAPTER FOUR

Pine Glen Apartments
Manassas, VA,
Wednesday morning

Val stood in the front lobby of her apartment building, staring out into the gloomy darkness of another rainy Virginia morning. With her alarm set to go off at six a.m. sharp every morning, Val considered herself a respectably early riser by any reasonable standards. Getting up at three-thirty a.m., however, was downright unreasonable. Oh, sorry. *Oh three thirty*. Viking used military time, not civilian.

She took a long drink of too-hot coffee from her go-cup and checked her phone. Charlie had texted her a tracking link for her ride, like some off-brand Uber. She watched the little white dot slide down Sixty-First Avenue and looked up, sighing into the pre-dawn gloom. She debated running back to her apartment for one more cup of instant joe and decided not to risk making her ride wait.

Not a good look for her first assignment, even if she had been up until ten p.m. packing her go-bag and filling out one damn piece of paperwork after another.

A silver two-door BMW pulled up to the door of the complex, its headlights low and glowering in the gloom, its windows black and obscure. Val blinked and checked her phone. The white dot blipped in front of Pine Glen.

"Okay, not an Uber." She shouldered her bag, snatched up her roller suitcase, and darted. The BMW's trunk popped open and she deposited her bags before hopping into the passenger seat, out of the rain.

"Valerie Kearie?" the man behind the steering wheel asked as she pulled the door shut behind her. He held out a hand to shake and was left dangling as she fumbled at her seatbelt. "Hi, I'm Jacob Pinkerton."

"Seriously?" Val spluttered. She poked around the sleek dashboard for a cup holder and set her coffee down. Flustered, she turned to take his hand. "Pinkerton? Like the PI firm?"

He grinned. "Investigation is a family business. I'm your partner for this assignment."

Jacob Pinkerton was too big for his own car. He hunkered down in the seat like a linebacker crammed into a VW Beetle. He was all square jaw and thick forearms rippling beneath a polo shirt about half a size too small. Shoulders for days. Handshake like a gorilla. She was too tired and startled to turn and look him in the eye properly.

"You don't look like a techie," Val remarked as Jacob shifted his car out of neutral and pulled onto Sixty-First.

"Yeah, I never quite got into the habit of living behind a screen 24/7 after leaving FORECON." Jacob consulted his onboard computer and turned left at the next light. The car growled as they took the on-ramp to the interstate.

"FORECON?" Val stared at the unnaturally sharp lines of his crew cut. Had he come straight from a midnight foray at a barber shop? "The Marine special forces?"

Jacob nodded. "Corporal. Seven years. Comes in handy when I'm bodyguarding skinny little blondes doing their first overseas assignments."

Val stared blankly at the passing mile markers for a minute before realization dawned. "A bodyguard? Do I need a bodyguard?" She felt both offended and concerned. She glanced down at her phone, wondering if she ought to tell Dad that apparently, the Vikings thought she needed not only a senior operative but a babysitter.

"Oh, don't take it personally, Miss Kearie," Jacob said amiably. "The company always sends a bruiser like me to protect people like you on foreign assignment, at least until you've cleared basic training."

"Basic training? Charlie didn't say anything about basic." Val's frown deepened. She was in excellent physical shape, and though she didn't live it daily since she'd left home, she still had basic military discipline written in her bones.

Jacob shrugged and pulled off a lonely exit leading down a road lined with private airstrips. "Like they say in the Marines—even the cooks know how to shoot." He slowed at a security gate, rolled down his window, and pressed his hand to the access panel to give it a clear reading of his palm.

"I can shoot." She tried her best to sound puzzled instead of defensive as the chain-link fence rolled back and they approached a small hangar. "Can you be more specific about this training?"

Jacob chuckled gruffly. "Not my department. Shit, it looks like they've already got the GIV gassed up already."

A small Gulfstream IV stood alone on the runway, the lights on her wingtips flicking through a prep sequence.

Val thought it was too early in the morning to parse through this. It was too early in the morning to sit in this warm car with its leather seats and new-car smell and wonder what the hell kind of cologne her new bodyguard was wearing.

She shook herself hard as Jacob parked in a car bay at the side of the empty airplane hangar.

"Up and at 'em," Jacob greeted her cheerfully as he undid his seatbelt and slid from the BMW. "Are you coming, Miss Kearie, or should I call a Lyft to take you back home?"

Hotel Sevilla Center
Seville, Spain
Wednesday Evening

Filip Yardman was a small olive-skinned man with a nervous tic. He never stopped fiddling with the tip of his necktie. Val would swear that the fabric was faded near the bottom from all his agitated fingering.

Filip sat across the table from Val and Jacob in the Hotel Sevilla restaurant. By Val's internal clock it was barely past noon, but at six p.m. local time, it was the wrong time of day to begin an investigation. The branch manager of

Gallagher Solutions had agreed to meet them for a working dinner instead.

Filip's demeanor calmed considerably when their waiter brought a bottle of house wine and offered each of them a glass.

"Thank you for getting out here so quickly." He spoke English with a faint Spanish lisp that Val found endearing. "I only got promoted to branch manager at the end of last year. I barely had time to orient myself when…boom." He mimicked firing a gun and chuckled nervously. "All systems under attack."

"Tell me about the problem," Val urged. "I read the file but I want to hear your take." Plus she wanted to keep a sharp ear out for any inconsistencies.

Filip took a steadying sip as the waiter placed a tapas tray between them. When the server was gone, Filip leaned forward. His voice was low and intent. "Yesterday morning, first thing. My people in finance come in early to take care of the monthly payroll. They report serious lag time on the network and say programs are not responding as they should. Sounds like spyware or something to me. I don't know. I'm not a tech guy. I'm on the phone with IT back at the home office in Boston when the whole network freezes up. Popups on every computer. Demands for money. Ten million euros."

"Typical ransomware pattern." Jacob prodded at the olive salad with his fork uncertainly, as if expecting one of the orbs to grow legs and scuttle off the plate. He saw Val staring at him and coughed into his napkin. "Hackers get some annoying bug into the system and hold it hostage."

Filipe snorted softly and picked up one of the olives

with his bare fingers. He tapped the oil off before popping it into his mouth. "Ten million euros is half my entire operating budget for a year. I don't have that kind of cash lying around. Even if I were inclined to negotiate with terrorists." His dark eyes narrowed. "I'm on the phone with Boston for hours. We try everything. We can't get anything back running. They've locked me and every single one of my staff out of our own network."

Val glanced at the wine menu and saw a small selection of meads from a local meadery. She felt a pang of regret, but her first day on the job wasn't the time to indulge the MeadFeed habit. She promised herself that if the assignment went well, she'd take a quick detour north before her plane departed for Virginia. The followers would love it.

"That does go beyond the typical cyber attack," Jacob admitted. Determined not to be outmanned by *Señor* Filip, he took the plunge and grabbed the fattest green olive on the plate. He popped it in his mouth and looked instantly regretful.

Filipe spoke grimly. "*Sí.* I'm under a lot of pressure to get this fixed yesterday."

"Then why are we meeting here?" Jacob forced himself to swallow the olive as he glanced around the hotel restaurant. He lifted his wine glass to his nose and sniffed deeply before cleansing his pallet with a long sip. "By our clock, it's barely past noon. There's plenty of daylight left."

"Office is closed for the evening," Filip explained softly. "A few people were willing to stay past close, but with the networks down there's not much anyone can do. I sent everyone home. I don't want anyone messing around with the system and maybe getting us into deeper trouble."

Val nodded in appreciation. She wrapped a thin slice of Manchego from the tapas plate around a black olive. "Not a problem. I had some time to look over the file on the plane ride here, but there's still plenty of research I can do up in my room. We'll go over what we know now, then meet you at the office first thing in the morning to see for ourselves."

"Right." Filip drained his half glass of wine in one gulp. "According to the ransom demands, the hackers call themselves *Hijos Del Solitario.*"

"*Hijos Del Solitario…*" Val worked the moniker over as she chewed. "Something like…'Sons of the Loner'?"

Filip nodded.

"Never heard of them," Jacob grunted. He eyed the plate warily before deciding to brave another attempt. He forked a thin slice of *jamón* onto some bread and sniffed.

"I haven't either," Filip stated. "Closest I know is *El Solitario.* He was arrested in '07 for bank robbery and the murder of two Spanish civil guards."

"Hacking and wire fraud," Val mused. "Bank robbing for the modern age."

Conversation paused as the waiter returned to take their orders. Val and Filipe asked for a portion of the chef's nightly paella. After ponderous consideration, Jacob ordered the seafood pasta. "But just the squid and clams, please. No prawns." Filip graciously translated.

A picky Marine, Val marveled. She'd have to tell Puck. He insisted such beasts did not exist.

"This *Solitario.*" Jacob speared a slice of cheese on the end of his fork once the waiter had gone away. "Who gave him the name? Media?"

Filip shook his head. "He stood up in court and addressed all of Spain through the cameras. He called himself that and said he was liberating the people from the banks or something like that."

"So what was he?" Val inquired. "Some guy looking for his fifteen minutes? Or maybe a Basque separatist?"

"Or Islamist," Jacob murmured.

Val frowned but said nothing. She was pretty sure jihadis wouldn't be naming themselves after Spanish bank robbers, but some people saw terrorists in every shadow.

Filip shook his head. "Anarchist. I think. I didn't follow the trial very closely. Someone like a Robin Hood type, yes? Steal from the rich, give to the poor."

"These Robin Hood types rarely get around to the second part of that mission statement." Jacob's voice dripped with skepticism as he arched an eyebrow. Filip shrugged.

Val typed a quick note into her phone. Something else to investigate when she got back up to her room. "So you're under attack from a hacker, or group, naming themselves after a single bank robber from the mid-aughts," she confirmed.

"That doesn't make sense," Jacob pointed out. "Gallagher's not directly involved in the Spanish financial sector, right *señor*?"

Filip hesitated. "We do work directly with the banking system, but we don't handle any of their money. We only help them come into compliance with the new financial regulations."

When the waiter came around to refill the water and

wine, Val requested another round of tapas. She hadn't eaten on the plane, and if this place held true to European tradition, it might be another forty minutes before the mains came out.

"With more of that bread and ham," Jacob added sheepishly. The waiter listened to Filip's translation and nodded. Jacob turned back to the others, all business. "These regulations are meant to stop money from funneling down into extremist cells and terrorist groups."

Filip nodded.

"So you don't actually have a massive cash flow compared to other operations, and you're not directly involved with the nitty-gritty of the banking system. What you are is a pain in the ass for the extremist groups who want to keep the money flowing," Jacob concluded.

Filip nodded again and forced himself to sip water before starting on his wine again.

"Gallagher Solutions is an American-owned company." Looking pleased with himself, Jacob forked the last thin slice of ham off the tapas plate and swallowed it whole. "*Solitario* has to be a front for one of the groups you're bothering with these new regulations. Boko Haram, ISIL, one of them."

Valerie frowned. It wasn't a bad line of reasoning, but she disliked the impulse to label everything that went wrong in the modern world as the work of some brown-skinned Allah-worshipping terrorist. Besides, according to her understanding, terrorist cells founded on radical Islamic principles generally hadn't yet joined the twenty-first century when it came to warfare—but no one ever got ahead by underestimating the enemy.

"It's a possibility we should at least keep in mind," she agreed reluctantly. "While we explore all avenues."

Filip shook his head. Val noted that the more wine he drank, the steadier his hands became. Was it simple nerves that had the man reaching for a little liquid courage? Or did his dependence run a little deeper?

"Filip?" she asked. "You look like you disagree."

"One of my accountants was digging around the systems earlier today," Filip muttered.

Jacob set his glass down sharply. "You've had amateurs digging through the systems during a cyberattack?" He sounded pissed, and Val appreciated that. She was glad to see they shared some common sense as far as the job went. "That's as likely to make the problem worse—"

Filip held up his hands, cutting the big American off. "I know. I know. He promised me he didn't mess with anything, only found the name of the virus attacking our system. It's called Cleopatra."

Val and Jacob exchanged baffled looks.

"The queen of Egypt?" Jacob sounded as if he hadn't heard correctly.

Filip nodded. "My guy grabbed a few screenshots before I made him shut it down. I don't know what any of it means. I'll send them to you."

"Now, please, if you have it," Val requested. Filip snatched at his phone, all nerves once more. As Filip fiddled with the files, Val and Jacob looked at each other thoughtfully.

"Hackers naming themselves after a Spanish bank robber, utilizing a virus named after an Egyptian queen from before the birth of Christ," Val murmured. "Doesn't exactly scream *jihadi* to me."

"Nothing says that this group is the one that developed or named the bug." Jacob set his jaw stubbornly. Their waiter delivered the second plate of tapas and Jacob snatched up a slice of Manchego, presumably before all that gross olive juice could get all over it.

Val's phone vibrated. She'd received a new email with screenshot attachments. "Thanks," she told Filip. "Are there any newer hires on your staff, *señor*?"

"Eh?" Filip frowned.

Jacob picked up the ball and ran with it as Val chewed another olive. "It can be stupidly easy to get ransomware into a closed network," he explained. "That opens the doors for the kind of brute-force takeover we're looking at. All it takes is one careless associate popping the wrong thumb drive into the wrong port."

"Or one compromised employee opening your system up to outside attack for the right price," Val added.

Filip's face fell even lower, as if Val had cut away his last shred of hope for humanity.

"Money talks, and nobody's immune to bribery," Jacob claimed.

Val felt bad for Filip. "Sorry. But anything is possible. I'd like to see employee files for everyone who's joined your branch in the last twelve months."

Filip drained his second glass of wine before nodding. "It's a strange, sad world we're living in. I suppose anything is possible."

CHAPTER FIVE

Gallagher Solutions
Seville, Spain
Thursday Morning

The Seville branch of Gallagher Solutions was in an office building that a coastal American might have called modern, and any traditional Spaniard would have called an eyesore. Industrial-chic foyers constructed from arcing steel and massive glass windows, and sleek, ultra-simple wooden chairs and desks in the lobby. It made Val long to crawl back to her hotel, which was older than most buildings in the United States, and spend the afternoon steeped in Spanish history.

Filip met them in the lobby at five a.m., a few hours before most of his staff would show up and begin the day. He gave Val and Jacob guest passes on lanyards.

"I've cleared my schedule for the day," he informed them. "Helping you get this mess sorted out is my top priority. You speak Spanish?"

Jacob made a see-sawing motion with his hand. "Only what I remember from school."

"Just Latin," Val answered. "We'll appreciate the translations."

Filip nodded. He had sobered, Val noted. Gone was the twitchy, anxious mess of a man. Here stood a hollow-eyed fellow who, though he clearly had slept roughly, was all business.

"All my employee files are digitized." He shepherded them from the lobby down a wide corridor lined with glass-walled conference rooms. "So I called up the main office in Boston and the IT head there walked me through setting up a secure connection to the home server. Something isolated from the local network. It's in here."

To Val's relief, Filip did not expect them to conduct their investigation in one of those glass-walled zoo enclosures lining the hallway. Instead, he led them into his private office, where a laptop sat open on his desk beside the desktop monitor.

Jacob cracked his knuckles and settled into Filip's fancy office chair without waiting to be invited. "I'll make sure that connection is secure." He got to typing.

"Have any of your employees been out sick recently?" Val inquired. "Or taken unscheduled vacations?"

"This is Spain, *señorita*. It's strange if somebody *doesn't* take off a few random days in the month."

Val sighed. Damn these Europeans and their weeks and weeks of legally mandated paid time off. She pressed on. "All right. You said you've got your whole staff coming in as scheduled. But with the networks compromised, how much work are they really getting done?"

Filip shifted his weight. "Not much," he admitted.

"That's good." Jacob pushed the laptop across the desk toward Val with a nod. "This connection is good to go, but don't go opening any strange emails."

Val snorted and slid into one of the empty chairs. "May I?"

Filip nodded and leaned over to type in his password.

"Good man. Let's take a look at this ugly bitch."

"Jacob's going to scout the lay of the digital landscape," Val told Filip as she scrolled through the list of employee files. All in English, thank god.

"Good. My people are going crazy with nothing to do. The sooner we get this fixed, the better."

"I'm not fixing the system yet, *señor*," Jacob corrected. "This is recon. Figuring out how sophisticated this incursion is."

"Not fixing it yet? Why not?"

"You're not in immediate danger," Val assured him. "You're being hamstrung. If Jacob starts reclaiming the systems from this attack, the perpetrators are going to jump ship. Right *now* is the best window for narrowing down our list of suspects."

Filip sighed. "All right. I'll tell Boston you're going to be a while. They can't blame me for that. They're the ones who sent you over."

Val nodded. "It looks like I've got about sixty files to sort through."

"Whoever did this doesn't have to be any sort of computer whiz," Jacob cautioned. His gaze remained fixed on Filip's dark screen. "Looks like a classic incursion to me. Anybody could have introduced this bug into the system so long as they knew where to shove a USB drive."

"Give me about an hour," Val requested, looking up at Filip. "Then we'll want to start interviewing a few associates."

Filip agreed, though he did not look happy. "I'll have my secretary clear a conference room for the interviews. You like churros? I'll go pick up breakfast."

"Can you tell me about your job, Emilio?"

The man in the gray custodian's uniform frowned down at the long stretch of conference table between himself and Valerie. His mustache twitched from side to side as he leaned down, dug into the cleaning kit at his side, and came back up with a bottle and rag. He started to talk in Spanish.

"I come in most nights right before closing," Filip translated. "I put on my uniform and I load up my cart. I do my rounds around the building. The restrooms first, then the offices. Tuesday nights I mop and polish the floors. Mondays and Thursdays I clean all the windows, unless there was rain, then I do an extra wash."

Emilio frowned beneath his wide-brimmed cap and squirted some lemony-scented oil onto the table. He started polishing the surface in small, careful loops.

"What's he—Why—?" Val glanced at Filip, who shrugged and continued translating as Emilio spoke.

Emilio spoke softly, hunched over the table as he

moved the rag. "Once or twice a month I try to polish all the tables but...I'm sorry, Mr. Yardman, I—" Filip stopped and straightened, looking startled. "He says he must have missed this table last week. *No problemo Emilio. Gracias, no problemo.*"

Emilio grunted.

"So you spend a lot of time around the offices at night by yourself," Valerie probed.

Emilio cocked his head, listening to the translation, and nodded.

Valerie glanced over the security logs Jacob had ported over from the Boston branch, confirming that Emilio's badge had been used Monday night before the attack began. She pulled up the file from the previous Monday, checking for discrepancies in the logs.

"Did you notice anything unusual Monday night when you were here? Anything out of the ordinary?"

Emilio shook his head. Val double-checked the time stamps on the security logs. They weren't similar—they were *identical*. Flipping back further, she saw Emilio had visited the same set of rooms, in the same order, every Monday as far back as the logs went. Every other day of the week stuck to the same pattern of cleaning, as well.

"Can I go home, Mr. Yardman?" Emilio shifted his weight in the chair. He had a haggard look about his face, and fatigue tugged at the ends of his mustache. "I'm real tired."

Filip told Val and Jacob what Emilio said.

"He's normally clocked out before eight a.m.?" Val confirmed. Filip nodded.

"One more thing." She turned back to Emilio. "Has anyone ever asked you to plug something into one of the computers here at Gallagher?"

Emilio's brow knit into a frown. "No, *señorita*. I see something unplugged and I leave it that way unless it's the vacuum or polisher."

"It would be pretty small." Val indicated her thumb for comparison. "Like this, or smaller."

Filip translated Emilio's answer. "Oh, you mean a thumb drive? I've seen some of the day folks plug those in from time to time."

"Did you see anyone do it recently? In the last few weeks?"

He shook his head.

"And you never fiddle with the computers?"

"I don't touch that stuff. Mama said I had a thick thumb. Might break something important. *Señor* Yardman tells me to write a report if anything looks out of place when I'm working, and I do. No reports since last August when *Señora* Morales in accounting left a banana on her desk over the weekend and it sprouted flies."

"Emilio's got quite a memory," Val observed to Filip, who shrugged and vaguely indicated the side of his head. "He's a good custodian," he insisted quietly. "Good memory, reliable, doesn't overthink."

"I'm real tired," Emilio repeated.

Val couldn't help a tired smile of her own. Jet lag was doing her no favors, either. She handed a business card to him across the table. "All right, Emilio. You call me or *Señor* Yardman if you think of anything, okay?"

He put his rag and polish away and took the card. "I write a report if there's anything out of place," he muttered. "I write a report. But I didn't write a report, because there was nothing out of place."

He went on for a few more sentences as he gathered his things and shuffled to the door, but Val didn't need a translation. She recognized anxious grumbling when she heard it.

"His pattern holds down to the minute," she observed, glancing at his security log a final time once the door had shut behind Emilio. "Autistic, maybe?"

"Probably. I don't ask. As long as he's doing his job, it's none of my business."

Val nodded and gestured for Filip's secretary to send in the next interviewee.

"David is one of the top performers in the marketing department," Filip noted as the next man approached the door. "He speaks good English, but I'll sit in here just in case."

Val nodded and gestured for David to sit.

She couldn't help but note that David Velasquez was a handsome man. One of those stereotypical swarthy Spanish fellows you expect to see in a daytime telenovela with his black hair artfully tousled, no tie, and the top button of his shirt undone.

"I come in to work early." He smoldered with offense as Val inquired about his unusual clock-ins. "I stay late to finish my files and make sure the department is on track. I work hard. I *earn* my salary. This place, it needs me."

After David, a pencil-necked woman from the services

department came in. "I get up, I work, I go home, I make dinner and play with my kids," she insisted. "Honestly. Who has time for all this?" She gestured vaguely at the frozen computer screens lining the edge of the conference room.

"Not me. Now I can't get my assignments done on time, and maybe I have to work next weekend? No. No, *Señor* Yardman. I will not. I must take care of my kids. You call me once the computers are working again."

"It's a bit funny," admitted the next employee, a man from finance who leaned lazily back in his chair. He chuckled. "This big modern building. We are a modern company, no? Cutting-edge strategies? But we get shut down by a little computer bug?"

He shook his head in mingled contempt and amusement. When Filip popped out to use the restroom, he leaned forward and suggested quietly to Val, "Really, I think *señor* stopped paying the monthly fees for antivirus protection. He is a cheap bastard."

"Do I see anyone acting odd?" demanded Mr. De Leon. He was also from marketing. "*Sí*, all day. Every day. They fiddling on their phones, playing games, browsing Facebook." His lip curled. "I don't have time for the nonsense. I work directly with clients. Many clients. Important clients. You must fix this problem. I don't care how. You must fix the problem. My clients are growing impatient."

On it went. Employees greeted Val's questions with wariness, disinterest, and frustration. None dropped any overtly suspicious answers—not that she expected to have her culprits handed to her on a silver platter. Doing this

groundwork, ruling out the busy parents and the compla-
cent middle-managers happy to have a steady paycheck,
was part of the job.

Still, by the time they broke for lunch, Val regretted her
decision not to swing by the meadery.

CHAPTER SIX

Gallagher Solutions
Seville, Spain
Thursday Afternoon

"How did the interviews go?" Jacob glanced up from the screen as Val slipped back into Filip's office. She flopped into the empty chair with a sigh. "Combing through all these employee files is a pain in the ass. No screaming red flags yet, but there are a couple worth keeping tabs on. All single men in their twenties."

"The janitor?"

Val shook her head. "A good thought but I think it's a bust. Man's a bit slow but leans hard on the rules. He reports to Filip if someone leaves a lunch box in the break room fridge over the weekend."

"So who do we have flagged?"

"The two guys in marketing, Velasquez and De Leon, are definitely ambitious. You can see the Euro signs in their eyes. Working in the marketing department gives them easy access to all sorts of people. A guy in finance, Perez, has an expunged criminal record and some family members in trouble with the law. I'm having Filip dig more into the records to see if any of them have had recent financial upheavals that would make them prone to bribery."

"What kind of religious affiliations are we looking at?"

Val sighed. "First two guys marginally Muslim. Fil says they both do the daily prayers but will smash a nice *jamón* sandwich in the lunch room a few days a week." Jacob gave her a puzzled look, and she mouthed "*ham.*"

"So not Muslim enough to keep *halal*. The finance guy is listed as Catholic."

"What about Cleo?" Val was ready to change the subject. "How's she treating you?"

Jacob frowned and turned away from the computer. He tipped back in Filip's chair and studied the ceiling thoughtfully. "She's got their whole network tied up pretty tight," he admitted. "I think it's a custom bug. Similar to other brute-force protocols I've seen, but not a perfect match for anything in my files." He gestured at the external hard drive he had plugged into Fil's computer. "It's a weird choice for a program name, too. Hackers tend to like thematic names—or stuff that sounds so mundane it loops back again to sinister. I don't get the Egyptian queen reference." He put a hand over his mouth and stiffed a yawn.

Valerie rose and poured herself a tiny cup of Turkish coffee from the carafe Filip had left on the sideboard. She knew she was kissing goodbye any hope of adjusting to the time zone. Her internal clock was all messed up. "Cleopatra. What do we know about her?" She poured a second cup and spooned in sugar.

The chair creaked as Jacob sat upright. "Smokin' hot babe who killed herself by snakebite when Caesar and Marc Antony both ditched her love triangle drama, right?"

Val handed one of the tiny cups across to Jacob, who tossed it back in one gulp and yelped like a man who had plunged unknowingly into an ice-cold swimming pool.

"You know how I *like it*." He grinned and licked up the undissolved sugar inside the rim.

"I saw you dumping in the sugar on the plane." Valerie sat back, sipping her coffee more slowly to adjust to the mouth-punch that was pure Turkish mud. "And not really. She *was* involved with the two most powerful men in Rome, but the snake stuff was probably Shakespeare's embellishment. She was generally a popular queen who kept Egypt a relevant player on the world stage at a time when Rome was..." Val gestured vaguely. "Doing the Roman thing. Even some older Islamic scholars refer to her as a wise ruler, if a godless hussy." She quirked her lips in a faint smile.

"Okay, so a moderately decent ruler whose penchant for drama got played up by people long after her death."

Val shook her head. "I wouldn't say she didn't have a flair for the dramatic. Not death-by-snakebite flair, but the woman *did* rake in an obscene amount of wealth. Something like half of all Egypt's worth funneled through the royal coffers at some point. She liked to dress in these ridiculously elaborate costumes to shore up this idea that she was the living avatar of the goddess Isis." Her warning look at Jacob dared him to draw a connection to the Islamic State. She was pleased when he only sat back and watched her patiently.

"She married both of her brothers to preserve the purity of the royal bloodline, and later had each of them killed."

Jacob coughed and reached for some water to wash down the coffee. "At, uh, different times, I'm guessing?"

Val only smiled.

"So she did like to be the center of attention. And you said she was wealthy," Jacob mused.

"In the same way that Jeff Bezos is wealthy," Val specified. "I think by modern standards we're talking a net worth of about a hundred billion US dollars."

"So I can see naming your two-prong ransomware attack after an ancient emblem of obscene riches," Jacob reasoned. "Either as a criticism of the banking system as a whole, or—"

"As an aspiration," Val finished.

"Maybe." Jacob seemed displeased.

Val finished her coffee and set the empty cup down with a firm clank. "You're not still barking up the jihad tree, are you?"

"The choice to attack *this* company is too much of a coincidence to dismiss, Miss Kearie."

Exasperated, she requested again, "Please. Call me Val."

He turned back to the computer. "There are a hundred other firms in Spain that could pay these *Solitarios* a higher ransom if all they're after is money. There has to be an ideological motive here. Which brings me back to the question: Why would they name their weapon after some greedy fratricidal pre-Islamic woman?"

The question left a bad taste in Val's mouth. She wanted to tell Jacob that he was looking for facts to fit his narrative and not the other way around, but stopped herself. She was new to this, and Jacob had over a decade of experience. He might know something she didn't.

"Egypt is over ninety-percent Muslim," she relented. "Like I said, she's well-thought-of by some Islamic scholars."

"She had wealth, power, and wisdom," Jacob mused. "That's all anybody really wants, be they bank robbers or holy warriors."

"Or it could be a red herring," Val pushed gently.

Jacob gave her a long side-eye. "You run down your rabbit holes, Miss Kearie, and I'll run down mine."

Val nodded, accepting this for what it was: a difference of opinion that shouldn't halt the investigation, no matter which way it led. "If you say so, *Mr. Pinkerton.*"

Jacob made a face. "Oh. I don't like that at all."

She gave him a toothy smile.

"All right." Jacob twisted his head side to side to crack his spine, then stood. And kept standing, it seemed to Val. She hadn't gotten used to how *tall* the man was. He unplugged his external drive and threw his bag over his shoulder. "Let's head down to the server room and see what this old Egyptian tart has to say for herself."

Gallagher Solutions
Seville, Spain
Thursday Afternoon

Filip's nervous tics had returned. He stood in front of the bank of monitors with his arms folded, bouncing on his heels. Val glanced at the clock. Afternoon already. Was *Señor* Yardman overdue for his meds?

"This is Rosa." Filip gestured at the middle-aged woman sitting at the server bank. "Closest I have to a network admin. Her English is—" He made a so-so gesture.

Rosa glanced over her broad shoulders and graced Val and Jacob with the flat, unimpressed stare of an *abuela* who was too old for this shit. Val consulted her notes. No flags on Rosa's file. She nodded at Jacob.

"Perfect." Jacob set up his tools again, plugging various bits and bobs in to the Gallagher network. "Go knock on Cleopatra's door, would you, *Señora*?"

Rosa muttered under her breath and turned back to the bank on her creaking and groaning chair. She typed an execution command into a prompt window.

Every computer screen in the server room went dark.

"They've got a flair for the dramatic, too," Val murmured, leaning in close to squint at the nearest screen. A cluster of pixels flared to life near the center of the screen, growing as if it were rushing at them from far away.

In this age of photorealism and immersive VR, Val was always startled to see old-school dot-matrix-style artwork. A pixelated chariot charged toward the viewer. Its wheels were chunky and square, and they rotated awkwardly, out of synch with the monochromatic ground rushing past. The chariot drifted and stopped, revealing the driver. A two-dimensional woman in a serpent tiara and a stereotypical Egyptian tunic blinked. Her mouth opened and closed with as much grace as that of a ventriloquist dummy.

Words scrolled across the screen beneath her.

You are vanquished and now my prisoner...

"Is that it?" Filip shifted his weight. His tone was almost petulant. "I used to have old Atari games that looked better."

"It's deliberate," Val agreed. "That old-school animation style. It screams 'signature.'"

"That it does," Jacob murmured. He had opened his laptop beside Rosa and was hard at work scrolling through lines of code. Val recognized none of it, assumed it was some obscure programming language, and was glad this was Jacob's wheelhouse, not hers.

Jacob forced a long whistle through his teeth. "Wow. Um. Okay."

"Something wrong?" Val asked. She was watching one of the side-screens, where Cleopatra's two-dimensional face had frozen with her mouth hanging grotesquely open. Something about that bothered her, and not only the lazy depiction. She paced the darkened room. Nothing about this suggested religious extremism to her, but Jacob had made a good point. Why would hackers target *this* company instead of a hundred others that could afford a higher ransom?

"Oh, the state of the economy, the price of gas, the melting ice caps..." Jacob punched a few experimental codes into the command prompt. "And, um, my brain. Apparently." He threw up his hands and turned to Rosa. "Any of this look familiar to you, *Señora?*"

Rosa grunted and shook her head. "All Greek to me," she mumbled.

"It's Greek!" Val whirled back to the computers with a shout that made poor Filip jump and clutch at his chest. Jacob spun on Val, eyes wide.

Rosa took a bite of her granola bar.

Val pointed breathlessly at the lines of code. "It's Greek. Cleopatra was Greek."

"She was definitely Egyptian," Jacob argued. "I don't think Shakespeare made that part up."

"No, I mean, we've been looking at this wrong. Cleopatra may have been the queen of Egypt, but she was a direct descendant of Ptolemy I Soter—he was one of Alexander the Great's generals," she explained. If she expected this to clear up any of Jacob's confusion, she was disappointed. "The point is, she might have had some Egyptian blood, but she was *Greek*, fundamentally and ethnically. She spoke about a dozen languages, but her mother tongue was—"

"Greek." Jacob's face lit up like he'd solved a particularly tricky Sudoku. He grinned at Val, a sharp one full of teeth. Val had seen that grin many times—on her brothers when they talked about some dangerous mission that had gone exceptionally well. Grams wore it when she drew a killer hand in pinochle.

Val had seen it in the mirror.

"We need to change how we're looking at this," she proposed.

Jacob whirled back to the computer bank. "All right. Who here speaks Greek?"

CHAPTER SEVEN

Gallagher Solutions
Seville, Spain
Thursday Night

As it turned out, Filip's brother-in-law Nicholas was a Greek expat. He was at a football match but would come by the office as soon as the game was over. Until then, the three of them made do with a rough marriage of Google Translate and a few Greek primer PDFs that Val dug up from her undergrad days when she'd taken two semesters of antiquities studies.

The workday wrapped up, and the Gallagher employees trickled away. Rosa headed up the pack, grumbling about babysitting her grandkids. Once Nick arrived and Jacob ran a preliminary background check on him, the four of them set up camp in the server room and got comfortable, working in shifts. Nick, a gregarious young man with chest hair curling out above the neck of his shirt, treated the whole adventure like a slumber party and brought sleeping bags for anyone who needed to catch a nap.

They worked in pairs: Val and her Greek primers with Filip on one team, Jacob and Nick on the other. Val was glad they had agreed on two-hour shifts. It sounded like a short work stint, but translating an unfamiliar language into complex code made her vision swim. The jet lag made everything worse.

Around ten p.m., Val and Filip handed the reins over to a bleary-eyed Jacob and went to the back of the server room to decompress. Filip had ordered catering. The empanadas had gone cold, but they were still delicious.

Val needed a break from the cramped little room. Between Jacob and Nick, she could practically smell the testosterone. When Filip saw her moving toward the first-floor restrooms, he caught her arm. "Emilio's working on the downstairs toilet still," he explained. "Don't throw off his groove. Head upstairs. There's another restroom off the main hall."

Val thought little of it until she exited the server room and let the door click shut behind her.

Dim emergency lights dotted the long hallway, casting it in an eerie patchwork of shadows. Distantly, Val heard the slosh of a mop on tiles as Emilio went through his nightly routine. *No music*, she noticed. For some reason, that struck her as odd.

She strolled down the hall toward the main foyer, where a wide staircase climbed above a double-stacked row of broad windows. Glare from the nearby street lamps made it hard to see through the glass. She felt like she was in a cage, exposed and visible to whoever might be lurking in the darkness.

She caught movement from the corner of her eye. She turned, but the foyer was silent. Empty.

As she climbed the stairs, she checked her pocket and realized she had left her phone back in the server room. It shouldn't have mattered—it wasn't like she planned on leaving the building or needed Facebook to keep her company on the pot—but it made her feel suddenly vulnerable, like she had forgotten to put on pants before leaving the house.

She scoffed at herself. *What, were you gonna text your bodyguard to come escort you to the pisser?*

Val hadn't needed a nightlight or security blanket since she was six. This was only new-job jitters getting to her.

She made it to the lavatory at the end of the second-floor corridor and did her business without fanfare.

As she was about to leave, the door swung open and crashed into Val's forehead with enough force to make her vision swim. She staggered back, too surprised to shout.

Must be some mistake, she thought dazedly, gripping the edge of the sink for balance. *I was going out and someone was coming in and we collided. Against all odds. In an empty office building.*

Then a pair of strong hands clamped around her throat, and the world came into sharp focus. She was being attacked. She was being attacked by a man in gray coveralls and a balaclava. His eyes were perfect pale circles, like white eye sockets in a grinning black skull.

The man shoved, crushing Val's spine into the corner of the sink with a painful crunch. That pain, more than the hands around her throat, turned her shock and confusion into pure indignant, primal rage.

No. No way was some random asshole going to break her fucking *spine* as she was coming out of the toilet. Not gonna happen.

She gave him a left hook and slipped on the slick floor as her knuckles connected to the side of his face. He let go and dropped her with a startled grunt, and she scrabbled on the tiles to find her footing as blood rushed back to her head.

"Help," she croaked. For all her pounding rage, the sound came out weak and strangled.

The masked man found his footing and spun in the cramped space. He flung his shoulder into Val and shoved her roughly toward the toilet. She slipped again and made a raspy scream as her elbow connected to the porcelain throne. He lunged forward, reaching again for her neck.

Val's senses clarified. In the instant before he reached her, she saw everything in slow motion: the flecks of pinkish spit spraying from his lips, the seams of his inside-out custodial jumpsuit, and the way he put all of his weight on his right knee as he fell after her.

Val braced herself against the toilet and twisted her hips. She felt her muscles tear as she drove her knee into her attacker's solar plexus. The white disks of his eyes grew larger as he let out an almost comical wheezing noise. He teetered, clutching his middle.

Val pushed to her feet. She had pain in her hip, real as thunder, but it was also distant and irrelevant, at least in the heat of battle. She snatched for the man's balaclava.

"Who are you?" she heard herself babbling. *"Who the fuck do you think you are?"*

Even in his wheezing agony, he seemed to understand what she wanted. He slipped into a defensive posture, clutching the cuff of his mask with one hand and knocking her arm aside with the other.

She punched again, putting her fist in the side of his skull. He stumbled backward and grasped behind him for the door.

"No!" She threw her entire body behind her elbow to drive it at the man's face.

With a squawk of pain and rage, he ducked to the side. Her blow only skirted his shoulders. It would leave a bruise, but nothing more.

He flung the door open, grabbed it by the handle, and smashed it into Val like a riot shield. The doorknob caught her in the gut, knocking the wind out of her. By the time she got her bearings again, the man had become a dark shape running down the hallway.

"Jake—JACOB!" She screamed and staggered from the restroom. "Stop him!"

She got her feet under her and broke into a run. Ahead, the masked man grabbed the stair rail in both hands and launched himself into the foyer, dropping out of sight. His feet hit the tile below with a muffled sound.

She reached the stairwell in time to see her attacker pick himself unsteadily off the floor and sprint for the emergency exit. She heard a door slam, and the hallway light turned on. It spotlighted the man as he shoved out of the door. No scream of sirens—security systems were down.

Jacob sprinted into the foyer, cursing as he met Val at the base of the stairs. She was clutching her gut. "You okay?"

She pointed at the emergency exit. "*Get him*," she insisted. Jacob nodded and ran, filling the doorway as he pursued the masked man into the night.

"*Señorita!*" Filip's face was waxen as he darted to Val's side. He held out his arms but she brushed away his support as she limped toward the server rooms.

"Where is Emilio?" she demanded. "And Nick? Everybody check in, right now—"

She froze when she saw Emilio leaning out of the empty lounge across from the server room. His broad face was knit into a concerned frown.

The server room door swung open and Nick poked his head out. He waved his phone uncertainly. "Ey... I call the *policía*, no?"

Val deflated, feeling the adrenaline trickle out of her fingers and toes, leaving her dull and tired and aching. She became aware of the sharp bite of pulled muscles in her hips and the twinge of pain where she'd backed into the sink.

She swallowed and shook her head. Behind them, the emergency door slammed shut. Jacob hurried down the hall, securing his sidearm under his jacket. "He's in the wind, whoever he was," he informed them grimly. His eyes swept the scene. "Are you injured, Miss Kearie?"

"Just a few pulled muscles, I think," she muttered. "And *call me Val*, goddammit."

"*Joder*," Filip hissed. He waved frantically to Emilio, who shrugged, straightened his cap, and went back to vacuuming the conference room.

"He was wearing one of the custodian jumpsuits," Val reported once she slid into a chair in the server room. Nick bought a can of chilled cola from the vending machine, which she pressed to her sore hip gratefully. "Tried to corner me in the bathroom." She touched her neck with a faintly trembling finger, wondering if she would bruise.

"You have security cameras, don't you?" Nick looked at Filip nervously.

Filip shook his head. He'd begun to sweat, although the building was cold. "Not since the network attack began." He pulled his lips into a humorless smile. "Cleopatra locked us out of all that. No telling who's been prowling around the offices."

Gallagher Solutions
Seville, Spain
Friday Morning

Val woke to the smell of fresh coffee and sat up. The door was open, and natural light flooded in from the hallway. She'd been napping on one of Nick's sleeping bags in the darkest corner of the server room. Filip and Nick stood by the door, setting cups of coffee and bags of breakfast sandwiches on the side table.

"Hey, you're awake," Jacob observed, turning from his workstation. He had bags under his eyes, but he seemed pleased.

Val checked her phone and saw that it was almost seven a.m. "Why the hell did you let me sleep all night?" She scrambled away from the sleeping bag, combing fingers through her disheveled hair. "We were supposed to take shifts."

"Take it easy there," Jacob suggested mildly. "Best thing for muscle injury is bed rest, I always figured. Besides, we were making good progress on Cleopatra without you."

Val had jet lag, throbbing bruises on her back and hip, and a massive headache. She did not like hearing that the others were doing fine without her on her first field assignment.

She grumbled and staggered to the side of the room, where Nick offered her a coffee and a wide grin. He had changed into a tracksuit somewhere along the way.

"There's a first aid kit." Filip nodded at a small box beside the bag of *bocadillo*. "And some painkiller. *Señor* Pinkerton said to let you sleep."

"Thanks," Val replied, though she did not feel at all grateful. She tossed back four pills, washed them down with scorching hot coffee, and turned. "Where are we at? What did you say about Cleo?"

"We've nearly got the bitch dethroned." Jacob stifled a yawn. "It's some wonky code, but once we got a handle on the Greek it was just a matter of untangling it from the network. I think we—"

He was cut off by the opening guitar riff of an eighties power ballad. He checked the screen on his phone. "It's Hawk."

"You called home office?" Val asked. *And you set Hawker's ringtone to* I Want to Know What Love Is?

"Yeah." Jacob accepted the call and gestured at Filip,

who led Nick from the room. "I asked him to do more digging on our persons of interest. Good morning, jarl—you're on speaker."

"It is *not* a good morning," the man on the other end of the line grumbled.

Val did some quick mental math. "Good...middle-of-the-night," she corrected.

Hawker sniffed.

"Location secure," Jacob relayed once the door had shut behind Nick and Filip.

Hawker got straight to business. "I ran the names you sent me through Interpol and a few other sources. Raul Perez has an expunged criminal record from when he was a minor. Some minor larceny stuff. Couple of cousins involved in some street gang activity in Barcelona but no sign that he's contacted any of them in the last ten years. His wife was recently unemployed and they were late on a couple of utility bills."

"They're having money trouble?" Val leaned in closer. That was new information, and a possible motive.

"Maybe," Hawk replied. "But it looks like *Señora* Perez took a new position with a land management company that pays better than her old job."

"What about the other two?" Jacob consulted his file. "David Velasquez and...Jamal De Leon, the guys in marketing. They're both relatively recent hires."

"Cleaner than a stripper pole in a nunnery. De Leon's family has been in Seville since around the time of the Inquisition. All mid-level managers, accountants, farmers, stuff like that. First in his family to go to university. Never left the country. About the same for Velasquez."

"Nobody's *that* boring," Jacob objected.

Val resisted the urge to snap something rude at her senior partner. Neither the painkiller nor the caffeine had kicked in.

"There is one thing," Hawker mused thoughtfully. "Velasquez has a half-brother working in software development for CERN. Some real big-brain stuff. Some classified stuff."

"Does he have any connection to Greece?" Jacob asked. "Or Egypt?"

"I'll check."

"It's worth looking into," Jacob added when he saw Val's look. "This Cleopatra bug is pretty sophisticated, and I don't know of many people who like to code in Greek."

Val sighed but nodded.

Jacob leaned in closer to the phone speaker. "There's one more thing, jarl. There was an incident last night."

Val felt her cheeks grow warm. It was perfectly reasonable to report her encounter with the masked man, but she didn't like being reminded that someone had almost got the better of her. She listened in silence as Jacob gave Hawker a quick summary of the situation.

"You in one piece, Miss Kearie?" Hawker asked when Jacob was through. His tone was professionally concerned but not exactly alarmed.

"I'm fine," she confirmed stiffly.

"Do you feel compelled to file a report with the Spanish police?"

Val hesitated, sensing a test. "Not at this juncture. I'm hoping we can handle the matter in-house. I'll file a report with company insurance if you want but I don't think any of these injuries are serious."

Hawker grunted a noncommittal grunt. "I'll get back to digging. Keep me posted, Pinkerton."

"Yessir." Jacob killed his phone.

Val pointed at the screen behind him. "What's that?" Unlike the mess of complex code she'd been staring at, the compilation on the prompt box looked sleek and efficient.

Jacob spun in his chair, tossing back the last of his coffee with a cheerful flourish. "*That* is our exterminator code."

"It's ready to go?" Val's heart started to race. "Well, go on. Run it."

"Don't get ahead of yourself." Jacob studied his phone, grinning obliquely as he tapped through apps.

"What's the holdup?"

"All Gallagher employees have a company app on the phone for easy reporting of expenses," he explained. "I got permission from Filip to tack a little bonus function onto the app for a couple of star employees."

She understood at once. "De Leon and Vasquez."

He rolled his wrist in a mock bow. "And Perez," he added graciously. "Because I knew you'd ask."

"You're tracking them."

"I am! Right now, they're all in the break room across the hall, warming up with the first coffee of the day." He waggled his phone in front of her with his thumb on an execute button. "What's the bet that when we send Cleo ass over teakettle, someone bolts?"

CHAPTER EIGHT

Gallagher Solutions
Seville, Spain
Friday Morning

Jacob pulled the tracking program up on his laptop and slid it across the desk to her. "I was able to regain access to the security cameras, too. They weren't on the main system, so it had to be a jammer. Found it, disabled it, and now we can monitor any unusual activity across the whole building. Once Cleopatra goes down in flames, I'm guessing whoever smuggled her here in a rolled-up carpet will get cagey."

Val gave Jacob a startled look. "You know about the carpet?"

"I looked up some trivia on our Greek queen when I was on the crapper."

"That is…too much information."

Jacob smiled and waved Val closer. "One more thing,"

he added, reaching into his bag. He rotated, blocking the line of sight to the hallway as he handed Val a small pistol.

"Hawk said I better keep you armed after what happened last night," he reported softly.

Val turned the sidearm over, checking the safety and chamber out of habit. She swallowed hard. Sparring, wrestling, and kicking ass in self-defense was one thing, but there was something so terribly *final* about a bullet. It wasn't supposed to subdue a threat. It was to end it, permanently and irrevocably. She didn't know if she could look at a human being from down the barrel of a gun and make that decision. Her reluctance to end another human's life was what ultimately kept her out of the family trade.

"So, how many illegal firearms did you smuggle onto Spanish soil?" She tried to mask her unease with a quip.

He checked that his firearm was secure beneath his overcoat. "It's only illegal if you get caught."

"Not the way that works." She considered a moment before securing the holster to her belt and covering it with the long hem of her blouse. The fist-sized lump on her hip wouldn't stand up to a second glance, but at least she wasn't flaunting it openly.

"What's our A-plan?" she asked.

"A-plan?"

"Yeah." She gestured at his pistol and to hers. "This is the backup, right? We can't go waving around guns as a first resort unless we want every *policia* and reporter in a hundred miles on our asses. This isn't Texas."

Jacob scratched his thick neck. He needed a shave, Val noted. Or maybe not. She supposed there wasn't anything wrong with the two-day shadow he'd cultivated since they'd left Virginia. It gave him a nice rugged look to offset the unnaturally sharp lines of his haircut.

"Fists, I suppose. Or blades. You're right. We can't make too much noise."

"Blades?" Her eyes went wide. "Shit. Do they teach knife fighting in FORECON?"

"Yeah." He gave her a blank look. "They don't cover it in your basic self-defense classes?" He reached into his bag, and for a half-second, she was afraid he'd pull out an eleven-inch Crocodile Dundee–style pig sticker and hand it to her. She grabbed his wrist.

"No! Knife fighting is *disgustingly* lethal," Val hissed. "And painful, and messy, and bloody. Fuck, I'll shoot someone before I get close enough to let them turn my stomach into pretty red ribbons."

"Good call," he replied amiably. "Probably best to avoid the knife fighting until we get you some training."

"Is *that* the basic training you meant?" She was horrified.

His grin broadened. "Or until we get you a sword."

"A sword?"

"Yeah. Longer range." Jacob spread his arms in case she was unfamiliar with the general dimensions of a sword. He winked. "So you can stab people *before* they get close enough to turn your belly into ribbons."

"You're fucking with me." She fought to keep her face straight. She probably shouldn't be swearing this much at her senior partner on her first mission, but some things were beyond the pale. "Are you guys actual paramilitary professionals or are you just LARPers with a private plane?"

Jacob tipped his head back and laughed. It was a rich, full sound that boomed around the close walls of the server room. Val grew unaccountably warmer, and against her better judgment, she smiled.

"There you are," he teased, seeing her relax. "I was worried that tussle last night had you spooked for good. You've been cranky ever since you woke up."

Her flush deepened. "I'm not a morning person. You handle the knife fighting, *señor* bodyguard. I'll put in a requisition request for a taser, collapsible baton, and some bear spray when we get home."

"Sure." He handed her a switchblade from his pocket. "But keep this on you just in case. No good Boy Scout leaves the den without a knife, Miss Kearie."

She took it. "*Please* call me Val. Are we ready to do this?"

She glanced over her shoulder and saw Filip pacing circuits down the hallway. When Rosa arrived in the office, he became animated and waved her back to the server room.

"Yardman's getting cagey again," Val commented. "We need to get him his network back."

Rosa muttered, "*Buenos dias,*" and ambled to her usual chair at the server bank.

Jacob nodded and took the earpiece Filip offered him. The manager handed a second earpiece to Val and showed her how to tap the line. That would give her direct, hands-free contact with Filip and Jacob. Then Jacob turned to the bank of computers and gestured for Val to monitor the laptop. "You watch the suspects. Let's do some coup."

The server room was silent but for the barely audible electric hum of machines and the industrious *clickity-clack* of keys as Jacob and Rosa initiated the ransomware counter-program. Filip lingered over Val's shoulder, his eyes glued to the security camera feeds. She could smell the stale coffee and whiskey on his breath.

She scrolled through the camera feeds, watching the main foyer where the desk attendant chatted with a delivery man, the glass-walled conference rooms where pairs of employees reviewed hard-copy files of old jobs, the rapidly emptying break room, and the second-floor main office where people worked in rows of padded cubicles.

Rosa muttered something in Spanish.

"What's that?" Jacob demanded sharply.

"I try to input the code," Rosa grumbled. "The program doesn't recognize the new code. Is bad code."

"It's not *bad code*," Jacob snapped and pushed himself up to lean over Rosa's shoulder. He stared at her screen. "I don't write bad code."

"What's going on?" Val consulted the tracker screen. All the white dots were accounted for, safe where they were supposed to be. She expected someone to jump or break from the pattern any second now.

"It looks like someone is actively resisting the changes we're trying to make to the system," Jacob explained. "Hold on, Rosa. I have some tracer code." He shuffled through his notes and handed her a sheet of lined paper covered in code. "Initiate this. Eyes sharp," he ordered Val. "Someone is actively fighting our efforts *right now*."

Val cross-checked the tracker screen against the camera feeds and shook her head. "Perez is sitting in a conference room reading hard copy. De Leon and Velasquez are both at their cubicles, but I don't have clear shots of their computer screens." She glanced across the other cameras, searching for suspicious activity from any of the other employees. Had they put their eyes on the wrong guys?

"Resistance is coming from the local network," Rosa confirmed as she ran Jacob's tracer code.

"The call is coming from inside the building." Jacob sounded downright giddy as his fingers flew over his keyboard.

"My network—" Filip started.

"We're getting your network back, *señor*. Whoever this asshole is, he can't keep up with me."

Val checked the parking garage camera on the off chance someone had set up a vampire tap on the network. Other than one black SUV parked crosswise in the handicap zone on the ground floor, there was no activity. A glance at the tracer feed indicated no network activity in that sector.

"Come *on,*" she murmured, scrolling through the feeds again. Everyone was sitting at their desks, looking downright bored. Everyone was doing what they were supposed to be—

"Hey!" Filip pointed. Val froze with her finger hovering over the scroll. Someone was walking down the second-floor corridor. More like swaggering, and with his shirt unbuttoned and his dark eyes smoldering.

He seemed to be in a bit of a hurry.

"Shit," Val whispered under her breath. She checked the cubicle farm feed and saw De Leon's desk was also empty.

She jolted to her feet. "Shit!"

"Shit?" Jacob demanded. "What's shit?"

"Good thing I didn't take the bet, is what's *shit.*" Val

laughed a little hysterically. "I've got eyes on Velasquez and De Leon. They're both on the move."

"No more fighting from the other side," Rosa observed, cucumber-cool as she went about her work.

"That's all of my cleaning code." Jacob slammed the return key and got to his feet, checking his holster. "Cleo's down and her retainers are retreating." He gestured at Val and the door, but she didn't need to be told. She was already rushing for the hallway. "That's our cue, Val Kearie."

Gallagher Solutions
Seville, Spain
Friday Morning

They rounded the corner out of the server room into the main corridor as the elevator doors at the end of the hallway began to slide shut. Val met Velasquez' eyes in that narrowing gap. They were wide and dark and glowering. She felt a kick in her gut and wondered if those eyes had stared at her from behind the balaclava. If they were the eyes of a man who had tried to strangle her with his bare hands.

The door snapped shut, but Jacob didn't miss a beat. He pivoted and sprinted toward the stairwell. "Looks like they're going for the garage, Yardman," he reported into his earpiece.

"There's an SUV idling in the parking garage near the exit," Val panted, following Jacob through the stairwell door. "Right across two handicapped spaces."

"Sounds like the perfect getaway vehicle," Jacob observed grimly. "I want to get down there and see if they pick up any more cohorts." He glanced at Val. "You understand? We're going in for recon only. Watch and learn, unseen."

Val nodded.

"*Sí*." Filip's voice through the line was high and tight. "I see the SUV. You're going to want to take the second door to the garage. It comes out closer to the exit."

"Is it sheltered from view?"

"Should be." Filip sounded slightly less confident. "Rosa says she parked her van right there. It's very big—"

"Can you tap into the other garage security cameras?" Val huffed. She had to take the steps three at a time to keep up with Jacob. "So we can watch them without risking exposure?"

Filip replied, "No. It's a shared garage. They're managed by a separate company. I don't have easy access to that system."

Jacob swore under his breath. "Eyes on the ground it is, then."

They reached the bottom of the stairs and sprinted past the first parking garage exit. The door farthest from the elevator had no window, so Jacob pressed his spine to the door and pressed gently, pushing it open a crack. Val caught a whiff of stale diesel air and held her breath. Silence. No echo of running feet, no rumbling engine.

"*Shit!*" Jacob hissed. He shoved through the door, moving with surprisingly little noise for such a big man. He ducked for cover behind a nearby panel van and Val darted after him.

She saw, almost too late, what had alarmed him so much. Down the aisle, the light above the elevator doors flicked off with a ding that echoed too loud in the quiet garage. The doors started to slide open.

Shit indeed.

Val dropped to the concrete beside Jacob as David Velasquez and Jamal De Leon came into the garage. They had a crystal clear view of the aisle, including the panel van between them and the darkened SUV beside the traffic arm. They were going to stroll right past, and Val and Jacob were exposed. They wouldn't get much spying done if they were made about five seconds into this operation.

Val caught Jacob's eye and jerked her head toward the van's cab, questioning. He hesitated a split second before waving her onward. Jamal and David's footsteps were growing louder as they drew close. Val ducked around the corner of the van as two man-shaped shadows swept across the cement wall. She sidestepped to make room for Jacob between the grille and the wall, and turned.

Jacob was fast and quiet, and if Jamal and David had focused on the SUV facing daylight at the end of the aisle, Val and Jacob might have gone unnoticed. But as she got her first clear look at the men, she saw that their heads were pivoting and scanning every angle of the garage as they moved. Jacob crept into the shadows, but too late. Jamal spotted his movement and skidded to a halt, shouting something in Spanish.

He and David turned, facing the van. Knives appeared in their hands.

Jacob and Val made eye contact. It was brief, less than half a second, but in that instant they exchanged as much information as they had in their whole relationship up until that point. They went from being near-total strangers to understanding one another perfectly on this single point: this had quickly gone from a spy job to a fight.

David and Jamal split and broke into a run. Jamal went directly for Jacob while David circled the other side of the van.

"Stay here and get the drop on him," Jacob whispered.

He did not wait for her to acknowledge how stupid crazy this plan was or protest his hypocrisy. With his pistol in one hand and his knife in the other, he crossed one arm over the other for stability and surged to his feet. He stepped into the aisle, squarely between Jamal and the exit.

"*Alta!*" Jacob barked. "*Deja de correr!* Stop running!"

Jamal skidded to a stop. His eyes grew wide as they took in Jacob's bulk and the pistol in his hands. It took a special kind of person to stare down the barrel of a gun and gamble that the man pointing it at you was only bluffing. Unfortunately for Val and Jacob, they *were* bluffing.

Who the hell are these guys?

Jamal lunged for Jacob with his knife hand outstretched. Val felt the air shift behind her and whirled, coming face-to-face with a startled-looking David Velasquez. His shock at seeing Val morphed into anger, then pain when she brought up her knee and sank it into his groin.

The pulled muscle in her hip twinged, but the pain was distant and irrelevant compared to the rage she felt remembering how someone, possibly this bastard, had cornered her in the bathroom.

David made a nauseated retching sound. He stumbled

but managed to keep his footing. Light glinted against metal as a knife appeared in his palm. He met Val's eye and lunged.

Val had felt more adrenaline rushes in the last few days than in the six months she'd worked at Asher and Asher. It was becoming a familiar, welcome feeling. It made her warm and fuzzy and downright giddy as time slowed and synced up with the beat of her heart.

She ducked and the knife went whizzing over her head. To her side, she saw Jacob swaying from side to side, neatly sidestepping and ducking every wild swing Jamal took. *Like he's danced this dance before. Like he knows it by heart. Like it's a game.*

Motion in the corner of her eye caught her attention, and she hopped back and bent around David as he slashed at her. She wanted to laugh. She wanted to scream. What she really wanted was a shield. A sword wouldn't be amiss, either.

"Defense!" Jacob barked. He grabbed Jamal by the collar and shoved him into David. The two men crashed into the side of the van, triggering an old-fashioned *aWOOO-ga* car alarm that struck Val as downright surreal. She laughed, overbalanced, stumbled, and would have fallen if not for Jacob grabbing her and hoisting her to her feet. He met her eye for the briefest moment. "Do me a favor. Don't die."

Val nodded and lunged to the side to avoid a two-point charge from David and Jamal. She went low, tucking her chin and falling into a tumble. She hit the concrete hard, but the roll was stable and she flipped to her feet and spun, elated.

Her exhilaration faded into indignant rage as she saw

the black SUV swerve and pull into the exit lane. The back hatch was swinging open. Jamal and David had left her and Jacob in the dust and were sprinting. They lunged into the back of the vehicle as it rolled toward the exit. Tires screeched as the driver hit the gas and smashed through the parking arm. The entire vehicle rocked onto two wheels as it swung onto the narrow streets of Seville.

"No!" Val screamed. She stepped forward, ready for a chase, but something grabbed her arm. Jacob's thick fingers pressed against her sleeve. She gasped, all that adrenaline and battle-hunger suddenly waylaid.

"Let them go," Jacob called over the wail of the car alarm. He was staring at his phone screen. "The trackers are still active. My guess is they're running home to daddy."

"*Daddy?*" Val resisted the urge to tear away from his grip. She didn't want to wait. She didn't want to let them go. She had the prey in her sights and she wanted to hunt. She wanted to—

"No way these dumbfucks are the brains," Jacob grunted. He shoved her back toward the elevator. "They're pawns. We let them go, and they'll lead us to their handlers. Let's get out of here before someone comes to investigate the noise. You hurt?" he inquired, almost as an afterthought.

"I'm fine! These are armed and dangerous individuals," she insisted. "You're right, the ransom they wanted isn't big enough to justify all this work. They're not in it for the money, which means they're most likely in it for principle. That makes them even more dangerous."

Jacob eyed her as he jammed the button for the elevator

door. "Oh, if only someone had suggested from the beginning that we were looking at the work of some political or religious extremists!"

"Bite me." Val bared her teeth as the door slid open. She stepped into the little box beside Jacob, grateful to be escaping the obnoxious wail of the car alarm. Her pulse had begun to slow. The rush was fading. Jacob was absorbed in his phone, and it seemed he trusted her not to chase an SUV on foot through the streets of Seville. He let her go and she rubbed her arm. The man had an unsettlingly strong grip.

"Both targets are moving up Main Street," Jacob observed. "Come on. Let's get to the server room and make sure Yardman has his network back in hand. Then we'll hunt down our terrorists."

"I said it might be an ideological thing," she protested, jamming the elevator button impatiently. The floor lurched beneath them. "I still don't think we're looking at Jihadis."

"You wanna bet, Val Kearie?"

Val flushed. He was teasing, but she kind of liked the sound of her full name on his lips. It sounded like *Valkyrie*, and that was appropriate if she was going to work with Vikings. It was certainly better than *Miss Kearie*.

Don't get sucked into the LARPing, she warned herself. *Next thing you know, you're going to be calling the bad guys Grendels. And if Hank ever finds out, he will never, ever let you live it down.*

"Tell you what," she replied. "I'll take that bet. There's a little meadery outside of town. I intend to stop by once the job wraps up. Gonna need something to celebrate outing these bastards. If they're religious terrorists, I'll buy the drinks. If they're anything else, you're buying."

"A meadery?" He gave her a bewildered look.

"Like a winery or brewery, but for mead."

He made a face. "That's a thing? Mead is honey wine. It's a girly drink."

"And you call yourself a Viking!" Her face split into a grin as the elevator door slid open and they returned to the office of Gallagher Solutions. "You're not afraid of a little fermented honey, are you Pinky?"

After a quick check-in to verify Filip and Rosa had Cleopatra well in hand, Val and Jacob grabbed their bags and booked it for the little rented Volkswagen they'd left parked in front of the Gallagher Solutions building.

CHAPTER NINE

En route to Parque de Negocios la Empresa
Seville, Spain
Friday Morning

"You should let me drive," she requested impulsively as they neared their car.

"You ever driven in old Europe before?"

When she didn't answer, he gestured for her to get in the passenger side. "Then leave this to the experts for now. We're on the clock." He grinned. "I'll give you driving lessons later."

Jacob's phone started ringing as he pulled out of the garage. "*I want you to show me. I wanna feel what love is. I know you can show me...*"

Val couldn't hold her tongue. "You are going to have to explain your ringtone choices to me, Pinkerton."

"Hush." Jacob slid his phone into the console and answered, "You're on speaker with me and Val. Talk to me, jarl."

Jacob swung the car onto the street to a chorus of honking horns.

"What the hell is that noise?" Hawker demanded.

"Ahh...the friendly drivers of Seville." Jacob glanced over his shoulder, saw he had the requisite two inches of clearance necessary to merge, and changed lanes.

More honking.

"I swear to god, Pinkerton, if you get into another pursuit that doubles our auto insurance—"

"You get into car chases?" Val demanded. She was gripping the door handle hard enough to turn her fingers white.

"Not in like two years." Jacob turned onto a side street. It was narrow, as only a street in an old European city could be, but it was blessedly empty. He grinned behind his sunglasses.

"You said you were the expert!" Val protested.

"I am. We're tracking our targets, jarl. I assume you didn't call with the weather."

"I've run more searches on Velasquez and his half-brother. He's not working directly for CERN but through a software developer with high-level contracts. The developer is based out of Seville."

"In the *Parque de Negocios la Empresa*?" Val guessed, scanning the GPS display shifting across the dashboard. The part of her mind thinking in foreign languages for the first time since her senior year of college gave a little hiccup. *Parque de Negocios la Empresa?* She considered. *The Business Park for Businesses?*

People were strange.

"Yep. Yosef Velasquez is an older family guy, couple of parking tickets a few years back. Unless he's part of some senior delinquent gang set on annoying Seville parking enforcement, he's clean."

"Or he got greedy," Val suggested. The trackers were leading her and Jacob directly toward *la Empresa*. At this point, ignoring the link between David and Yosef would be pants-on-head stupid.

Beside her, Jacob let out a heavy sigh. She was increasingly open to the possibility of a religious or political extremism motive, but there was something fun about watching Jacob roll his eyes.

"Could be." Hawker sounded distracted. "But this is more interesting. The business park itself? Property is owned by a wealthy Saudi named Salim al-Habib. His cousin was arrested last year as part of Operation Polygamy."

At the sound of that name, Val's smile vanished. Suddenly this game wasn't fun at all. "Human traffickers," she remarked under her breath.

"What was that?" Hawker asked.

Val swallowed hard. "Those were the al-Qaeda traffickers who lured foreign Muslim women into Pakistan, promising to marry them to honorable young freedom fighters. Then when they get to the holy land, they were..." She gathered herself. "They weren't treated well. A lot of those women wound up as suicide bombers."

Because a quick ticket to Heaven was preferable to the reality of their new lives.

She remembered the faraway look on Hank's broad

face, all his customary good cheer drowning in whiskey and memories he couldn't bring himself to share with his kid sister fully. *"They did it on purpose,"* he had slurred, bleary-eyed in the small hours of the morning soon after he'd come back from overseas, when they huddled in Dad's darkened kitchen like they used to do when they were kids sneaking slices of leftover fridge cake.

"It takes a broken person to put on a bomb vest. And they were in the business of breaking those women," Hank had told her.

Jacob's glance was flickering rapidly from Val to the GPS to the narrow streets. "Details on that operation are still classified. How do you know about it?"

Val cleared her throat, trying to shake away the memory of Hank's distant gaze. "I know a lot of military types. Some of them get stupid after a few drinks." Her eyes narrowed as she did some mental math. "Hang on. You were out of the Marines well before that op. How do *you* know about it?"

"Ah, look at the time!" Jacob turned hard left onto another street. "We're almost at *La Empresa.*"

"What's the plan?" Hawker asked. Val blinked. She'd nearly forgotten they were still on the phone.

"Val and I are going to monitor the building for activity. Keep tabs on our boys. Can you call Filip and have him tell Rosa to keep monitoring Cleo's activity? We locked her out of the system, but last I knew, someone was still trying to counteract our programming. Best keep an eye on the fucker. He could still be at large."

"Will do."

"Beyond that?" Jacob swung the car into an empty

parking space outside the building. "Get in, neutralize, get out."

"Copy." Hawker cut the call with no further fussing, leaving Val and Jacob alone in silence.

Jacob took the key from the ignition.

"Neutralize?" Val repeated warily. "That's a pretty, uh, aggressive term."

"Hey." His grin was more tooth than humor. "They attacked you. As your bodyguard, it's my job to make sure they don't do that again."

"Oh...kay." Val bit her lip and busied herself adjusting her earpiece. She was jittery, and not in a post-interview-yips way. She felt hot under her skin, eager. Jacob's vague comment about *neutralizing* a threat should have rung some alarm bells in her head—and in a way, it did. But those bells were quiet and somehow muffled beneath her own hot pulse. There was something else, too. Hank's midnight whisper: *"They were in the business of breaking those women."*

If these bastards were connected in any way to Operation Polygamy...

A little voice piped up in the back of her mind. *You told Dad this was a cakewalk. This was supposed to be safe. This was supposed to be easy.*

She'd been attacked twice in less than twenty-four hours. The job was anything but safe. Yet somehow it was still easy, although not how she'd expected. She thought of the masked man reaching for her throat and the knives in David's and Jamal's hands. Those memories made her feel alive.

Alive, and hungry for payback.

Parque de Negocios la Empresa warehouse
Seville, Spain
Friday Morning

"It's a newer place," Val observed, searching for some way to break the silence as Jacob fiddled with the tracker program on his phone.

Jacob parked in a secluded corner of the business park lot, between a hedge of olive trees and an unmarked brick wall that Val assumed hid dumpsters and loading doors for cargo trucks. Like the offices of Gallagher Solutions, it was a modern complex made of large windows and small bricks, but Val thought it showed a degree of restraint that the Gallagher building, with its two-story foyer and grand glass staircase, lacked. This complex would have been at home in the wealthy suburbs of any American metropolitan area.

To Val's mind, that made it boring. *A Saudi-owned business complex in the heart of historical Spain that looks like the location for the office of Dunder Mifflin. The world is getting too small,* she thought wistfully.

Jacob slipped his phone into his pocket and reached into the back seat to grab his duffel bag. Thanks to the tiny interior of the car, Val got an intimate waft of his armpit as he reached past her, and she wasn't quite ready for the face-slap of sweat and deodorant.

Coughing, she reached into her messenger bag for the pistol. She checked the chamber and safety.

"That's the second time I've seen you do that," Jacob

observed as he riffled through his bag. He was a big man, and there was something almost comical about the way he crushed himself behind the wheel with his big man-purse.

"Shooting is a family pastime," she explained. It was a repeat of the line she had given the jarls during her interview, but something about it bothered her. Had she always been this diligent about guns, back when she went to the range with Dad more than twice a year?

"It seems like the right thing to do," she muttered, checking the weapon. "Going into a potentially hot situation. Got to make sure your tools are in working order. Right?"

If she thought too hard about it, she might get uncomfortable with how comfortable she was.

Jacob wasn't listening. She looked over to see what he was pulling from his magic bag and yelped.

Sitting in the seat next to her was a six-foot-four, two-hundred-and-forty pound linebacker of a clown with dead-white skin, a garishly painted red grin, and a thin tonsure of fire-engine red hair.

"Hey, hey, kids!" She could barely make out the motion of Jacob's lips behind the thin slit of the mask's mouth as he spoke in a perfect, if muffled, imitation of Krusty the Clown. "It's clobberin' time!"

He flicked a wrist and dropped a second pasty-white latex mask in her lap.

"What the *fuck?*" She could only stare as he piled on a baggy brown overcoat and what appeared to be a thigh holster.

"Suit up." He dropped the Krusty voice as he shrugged

into his own massive windbreaker. "We don't need anyone inside IDing us."

Val wrestled into the overcoat and stared, horrified, at the mask. It had tufts of bright green hair sticking out of its rubbery ears. It smelled like the inside of a gym sock.

She could only think of one thing to say. "Good guys don't wear clown masks and smuggle guns into office buildings on a Friday afternoon!"

Jacob stopped adjusting his underarm holster to consider. "It does sound kinda fucked when you put it that way."

"What the *fuck*," she repeated, glaring at him for an explanation.

"Look." Jacob cinched the strap to secure his pistol. "You've got some brass balls, kid. I'll give you that. After last night and this morning, you're still here chomping at the bit to bring down the bad guys. We Vikings run ops a little loosey-goosey, but we do have our rules. Protect civilians. It's right there at the top. Damage control is up there, too. You know what's near the bottom of the list?"

She didn't respond, but he didn't seem to expect her to. He popped the car locks and opened his door. As he put one foot on the pavement, he answered for her. "Image control. I'd wear a Donald Trump mask and walk into the front lobby naked, waving around my balls and singing Limp Bizkit if it got the job done. Now, are you coming?" He threw up the hood of his jacket, which made his synthetic orange hair stick straight out in front of him. "Or should I call a Lyft to take you home?"

Not only did the mask smell like an old gym sock, but it

was hot as hell and the soft edges chafed at her lips and under her chin.

Val huddled behind Jacob, peering around the corner of the blank brick wall. He had chosen his parking spot well. The low body of the Volkswagen provided near-perfect cover from any pedestrian strolling through the lot.

Val was half right. No dumpster enclosure behind the wall and no freight door, but there was a single garage door flanked by double-wide industrial doors she assumed led to the building's maintenance department, or perhaps a storage warehouse.

She waited in the shadows as Jacob strolled up to the door, thumbing his phone like a paper pusher checking his texts on break. He drew a small round device from a pocket, which he casually pressed to the door. He slipped his free hand into his hood and fiddled with his earpiece.

Val frowned. She'd taken the earpieces to be standard Bluetooth headsets, but Jacob was clearly synchronizing his to the device he had stuck to the door. She didn't recognize it but could only guess it was some kind of eavesdropping tech. Certainly not standard issue. Maybe the Vikings did a lot of intel-gathering jobs.

She made a mental note to do a little more digging into Jasper Taggert when she got home.

After a minute, Jacob nodded and slipped the eaves-dropper back into his pocket. He waved Val closer, holding up four fingers. Four suspects behind that door, and by the way he was loosening the strap of his shoulder holster, Jacob expected to go in hot and outnumbered.

At least we have the element of surprise, Val thought as she slipped up behind him. He glanced at her over his shoulder and started to speak when he was cut off by the grinding whir of a motor. Beside them, the freight door jerked and started to rise.

Jacob threw up an exasperated hand, slammed his shoulder into the door, and vanished into the building.

Val's heart skipped a beat—but only one, and only until she heard the first shout of alarm.

She ducked under the opening freight door and entered a shadowy pit of chaos.

A black SUV, the same one from the parking garage, sat inside the warehouse with its back hatch open. The warehouse itself was mostly empty, save for a cluster of folding tables stacked high with wires and cables and monitors. A man in a canvas jacket ran from the table, carrying a stack of CPUs toward the SUV as three men with baseball bats attacked a clown in a trench coat.

Val watched the scene unfold like it was something from a movie. Jacob's coat flapped like a cape as he ducked beneath one swing and grabbed another bat in his massive palm. He yanked, pulling Jamal close with one hand and bringing the other closed fist up in a right hook that sent blood spraying from his mouth.

With the same fluid motion, Jacob heaved and tossed Jamal over his shoulder, directly into David's oncoming attack.

The garage door had opened all the way. The man in the canvas jacket, an older guy with a graying beard, tossed another load of computer equipment into the back of the SUV and slammed the hatch. He babbled a mix of Spanish and Arabic over his shoulder, probably telling his friends to get in the damned car, and hurried for the driver's door.

He didn't see Val surge out of the shadows until it was too late. She pivoted to throw all of her strength into a kick that connected the heel of her sneaker to the base of his throat with enough force to send him crashing into the car. He slid, stunned, to the floor. His car keys went skittering halfway across the warehouse.

You stay down! Val wanted to howl and scream, but in that moment, her body didn't feel quite her own. It was its own thing, primal and powerful and moving on pure, rage-fueled instinct.

She kicked the man again in the side of the head, and his eyes fluttered shut as he fell unconscious.

Nearby, Jacob let out a bellow that rattled the metal rafters overhead. He was holding his own remarkably well, but he could only do so much against three determined men with baseball bats. Jacob was undeniably on the defensive.

Before Val could analyze the situation, she was charging to Jacob's rescue—with a pistol in her hands.

Of course, she wasn't going to *fire* the pistol. That would be stupid! It would be noisy, and there was a non-zero chance she'd hit her partner.

Instead, she charged David Velasquez from behind and slammed the butt of her pistol right into the back of his beautiful, magazine-model head of hair a split second before he swung at Jacob's exposed spine.

David dropped like a sack of potatoes.

Val heard herself yelling nonsense above the shockingly loud thud of her pistol connecting to David's head again. "Fuck you! And your balaclava!"

She might have turned his skull into mush if he hadn't

dropped below her line of sight, and if she hadn't had more active hostiles to worry about.

"The keys!" Jacob shouted. Val looked up sharply to see Jacob grappling with Jamal, but he was pointing to the corner of the warehouse.

The fourth suspect was middle-aged and dark-haired, the world's most generic Spaniard. He held a set of car keys. Behind Val, the SUV beeped softly, followed by the low rumble of the engines. It took her a moment to understand what was going on.

The SUV had a remote start, and the last suspect was sprinting for the driver's door.

"Fuck!" Val whirled and charged, but it was no good. The man was closer to the SUV. He reached the door a few paces ahead of Val, flung it open, and threw himself into the driver's seat.

She got close enough to grab the man by the arm through the open door before he hit the gas. Val screamed, her grip tightening on the man's arm with the half-mad idea that she would pull him out of the car, but it was no good. She staggered and stumbled, barely avoiding eating cement as the SUV roared into the sunlight.

A flash of harsh sunlight glinted against blackout windows as an arm reached from the driver's seat and pulled the door firmly shut. The vehicle swerved to the left and roared out of the parking lot.

Fuck, Val thought again. Reality came back to her like a crashing wave as she returned to the shade of the warehouse. She stood over two unconscious bodies, dizzy and exhilarated. The SUV had gotten away, and the freight door hung open, spilling brilliant daylight into the warehouse. In the shadows, Jacob held a knife to Jamal De Leon's throat.

The wayward employee of Gallagher Solutions decided, quite wisely, that his best bet for survival was to hold still.

"Call the boss," Jacob ordered Val as he patted Jamal down for weapons. He found a second switchblade in one of the man's pockets and threw it well out of reach. "Ask him for a cleanup. No, don't take the mask off, dummy," he snapped when she started to peel away the latex. "Jesus, is this your first time?"

Val huffed and turned away, fumbling for her phone. Boss meant Hawker, she was sure. As she tapped through her contacts, she thought, *Boss. Not Hawker or Hawk or jarl, because Jamal speaks English, and we're not giving more away than we already have. He knows our faces, sure, but he doesn't know who we work for.*

The phone rang once before Hawker came on the line. "Fill me in."

"Three suspects in custody," she murmured. "One escaped via SUV and it looks like he took a lot of his computer gear with him. We need a cleanup at *La Empresa.*"

"Got a tracer on the SUV?"

Val winced. Behind her, she heard the vicious rip of tearing duct tape as Jacob went about securing the suspects with alarming expertise. "Negative, but maybe you can pull its license number from the security cams back at Gallagher."

"I'll see what I can do, but I'm guessing they'll dump the vehicle ASAP. Yardman tells me Cleo is well in hand and the network attack has ceased. You two head back to the airstrip and await further instructions. Cleaners are ten minutes behind you."

"Copy that," Val confirmed hoarsely. The line went dead, and she turned to see David, Jamal, and the other man neatly trussed and gagged with duct tape. From the family resemblance, she assumed the third man was David's half brother, Yosef. Despite their welts and bruises, they'd come around, and David was glaring daggers at her.

She wasn't sure how she felt about that. These men had tried hard to kill her, but she didn't want to be responsible for the death or permanent maiming of another human.

Not yet, at least. Not with the adrenaline fading away and leaving her feeling edgy and empty.

"T-ten minutes," she informed him. "We need to clear out."

"Got it." Jacob straightened, waving for Val to follow him back to their car. "What are you waiting for? Let's scram."

"Looks like I owe you that drink." Val's voice was breathless as she peeled the sweaty latex off her face. They were back in the car and it seemed she could not crank the AC up high enough. Her hands were still trembling as she scrolled through her phone. "Good news! The meadery is on our way to the airstrip."

"You're still on about that?" Jacob rolled his eyes. He'd shed his own disguise, and they were cruising down the main streets of Seville on their way out of town. *His* hands, she noted, were utterly steady after getting into a life-or-death fight with two-to-one odds. His voice was calm, almost bored.

What a bastard.

"Yes," she insisted firmly. "Don't roll your eyes. It's one of the oldest forms of alcohol known to humankind. Liquid ambrosia. Nectar of the gods. Fucking Valhalla, you heard of it? *Mead* hall." She swallowed hard and, after a moment of awkward silence, she added in a small voice, "And I could really use a drink right about now."

CHAPTER TEN

Sabor Del Cielo
Seville, Spain
Friday Afternoon

Sabor Del Cielo was a tourist trap, Val decided, but one crafted with so much heart and sincerity that it looped back around to being utterly charming. It was built in the style of a traditional Viking longhouse, all heavy raw timbers angled into a severely sloping roof, and heavy doors of banded wood and iron.

"God, please tell me someone here speaks English." Jacob stuck to her side as she strolled up the hillside toward the front door. His shoulders were hunched. He kept checking his six.

"This is Spain," Val teased. "Here, we speak Spanish. My god. You're more jittery now than you were—" She glanced around, saw an old tourist couple taking pictures near the rune poles lining the front walk, and quickly changed what she was about to say. "—this morning."

He cast her a dark look and opened his mouth to speak but was interrupted as a man in a maître d's coat swept out of the front door, his arms open wide. "*Buenos días*! Welcome. You are visitors to Spain, yes?" he guessed, noting Val's pale complexion and shock of blonde hair. "You are from the UK?"

"Close enough." Jacob relaxed visibly.

The maître d' tapped his forehead knowingly. "American. It's the accent. Welcome to *Sabor De Cielo*. We are just opening. I'm Miguel. Are you here for the tour, or would you like to go straight to the tasting room?"

"Tasting room," Jacob answered at the same time Val firmly replied, "Tour."

Miguel heard what he wanted to hear, smiled at Val, and shepherded them toward the building.

"*Sabor Del Cielo* has been a fully-operational functioning meadery for nearly four hundred years, but my family, we've been making all of Seville's mead since the early 900s AD." He paused at the threshold to point at the runes carved above the door. "The family motto. 'Our Fathers in Sweden, and our Hearts in Spain,'" he translated.

He waved them through the door into the dimly lit hall. A small seating area was lit by oil lamps. A row of glass display cases hung on the wall above the line of benches, showing off rusted spearheads, fragments of ancient armor, and little information placards. The sight of them made Val's heart swell. This was no tourist-trap shlock.

"900 AD?" She fell into quick step beside Miguel, careful not to miss a word. "Holy smokes. Ironside? You're descended from the Ironside expansions?"

Miguel beamed and gave a little flourishing bow. "So

says the family Bible," he admitted as Jacob sidled up to read the plaque beneath the display case. Out of the corner of her eye, she saw his lips moving, struggling to parse out Spanish with his high school education. She grinned.

"*Ironside*," Jacob mouthed. He turned to Val and Miguel. "Uh, who?"

"Björn Ironside." Val tripped over herself to get it out ahead of Miguel. "Kind of like the Swedish Viking version of King Arthur. A real person, but with so many stories and legends built up that he's, like…mythical. Under his rule, Vikings went, well, *Viking* all around Europe and the Mediterranean, including a raid on Seville. But it was called Isbiliya back then."

Miguel gave Val an appraising look and nodded. "Some of the Vikings came to like Spain's nice warm weather and better food, so when their brothers went back home to Sweden, they stayed behind," he explained. "Integrated into the community. Learned some Spanish customs, taught the locals how to make good honey wine."

"*Mead isn't honey wine!*" Val exclaimed. She laughed, partly self-conscious, and partly at Miguel's comical double take. "I'm sorry, *Señor*. I get excited."

"Don't you *dare* question Val Kearie's knowledge of mead," Jacob suggested. He sounded gruff but he had a playful glint in his eye. "Apparently, she's a bigshot expert." He waved his phone, letting Val catch a brief glimpse of an app she knew well: MeadFeed. "Got a few thousand followers and everything."

"Hey!" She tried to snatch the phone away but he held it out of reach. "Are you *stalking* me, sir?"

"Just getting to know the new girl," he teased.

"Val Kearie?" Miguel repeated. His face lit up. "Oh, *señorita*! Are you ValLovesMead? I'm HoneyGuy6!"

"No shit!" Val clasped his hand and shook it heartily, feeling a little like she had already hit the booze. "Yes! I loved that article you wrote on honey variants in the fermentation process. Do you have any of that buckwheat stuff? I'm *dying* to try it."

"Come on, come on," Miguel insisted. He shepherded them both toward the tasting area at the back of the building. "I've got samples for you, Val. I've got so many samples you *must* try."

Val fell in love with *Sabor Del Cielo*, and hard. It was the scent that got to her: fresh straw and ripe fruit. It was perfect and clean, and it made her feel at home in a way she had never expected. Here was a wonderful mesh of cultures. After over a thousand years of integration into the local population, Miguel's family couldn't have shared more than a passing whiff of DNA with their Swedish ancestors anymore, but they clung to the traditional methods of brewing, with honeycomb in the wort and all. At the same time, the tasting room served plates of simple but perfect tapas: fat juicy olives, perfectly cured cheese, and crusty breads that paired remarkably well with the half-dozen samplers of mead Miguel brought to the table.

"Eat your grapes and cheese," Val instructed, watching Jacob pick carefully around the olives. She picked up the sampler glass of pale clover-honey mead and held it out to him. "We have done battle! A little bit of celebration is in order."

They sat across from each other at a long wooden table with a plate and many sampling glasses between them. Miguel stopped by every few minutes to freshen the water and offer another sample. Val would have spent the whole afternoon talking his ear off if not for the after-work crowd filtering in, needing the attention of a maître d'.

"I thought your focus was on the fall of Rome or something." Jacob sniffed the offered glass and sipped. He considered, shrugged a "not bad" shrug, and tossed back the rest.

Val frowned, chomping on a fig wrapped in thin *jamón*. "The collapse of the Empire and what came right after, yeah. Not so much the Nordic stuff." Then she shrugged. "I'm sure there was some Vikings 101 class in there somewhere. Or maybe I was a huge Viking nerd in a past life."

The soft sounds of a Foreigner song played nearby, and Jacob frowned and checked his phone. His eyes widened. "Shit."

He gestured for Val to wrap up and surged to his feet. "Hey, jarl! Yeah, yeah, we're on our way to the airstrip right now—"

Shit indeed. Val surveyed the remnants of their conquered lunch; the half-drunk samples of buckwheat and chestnut and orange meads, not to mention the remaining ham and cheese. She regretted that asking for doggie bags was not done in Europe. Given the way Jacob was hustling from the building, their festivities were being cut short.

Val reached for her wallet and flagged down the nearest waiter. "Check!" She pointed at the half-empty glass still in front of her. "And a bottle of this stuff. For the road."

Two minutes later, she was chasing Jacob back to the

Volkswagen, frantically stuffing a heavy bottle into her messenger bag.

"That was Hawker on the phone?" She gasped and fell into the passenger seat. "Where's the fire?" He had the engine running and the AC cranked up to max, and didn't wait for her to buckle in before throwing the car into gear.

"The fire's in Al Hoceima," he clarified grimly.

It took her a moment to piece that together. She rubbed her eyes. "Morocco?"

Jacob nodded. "We got word from another consulting company. Cleopatra's at it again."

"Already?" Val was dismayed. She'd hoped their perp would have at least waited to catch his breath before going on the offensive again. She double hoped it wasn't the same guy who'd fled in the black SUV that morning. The guy they'd let get away. The guy *she* had let get away.

He tossed his phone into her lap. "Call ahead to the airstrip, will you? Tell the pilot to start the takeoff sequence. I want wheels up in twenty minutes."

"Fuck," she whispered. The screen swam in front of her. She was unsteady from a mix of jet lag, adrenaline drain, and, well, maybe a *little* booze.

"Double fuck," Jacob agreed. "'Cause we gotta stop at Customs on our way into Morocco."

"What for?"

"Your modesty," he informed her dryly. "Gonna have to cover up your ass and legs if we're gonna be working in an Arab country. Unless you happened to pack along a billowy, ankle-length skirt?"

Val dropped her head against the headrest and groaned. "I *hate* shopping for clothes."

En route to Global Ventures,
Al Hoceima, Morocco
Friday Evening

"I also hate you shopping for clothes," Jacob decided as Val hurried from the airstrip's tiny duty-free shop. He waved for her to follow him to a parking area. "I've got the car ready to go. What the hell took you so long?" The trunk of a red Renault Clio swung open as they approached.

"I'm sorry!" Val flung her suitcase into the trunk and fussed with the wide sleeves of her new kaftan. "But I'm not wearing a leopard print *djellaba* on the job. *I* wouldn't even take myself seriously. I had to wait for them to dig something halfway tasteful out of the back room. I guess they're used to tourists who will buy any old cheap crap."

Jacob rolled his eyes as he pulled the car onto the road.

"Don't give me that," she added sharply, pointing at the clock. "I spent less time in there than you did screwing with the stereo system on the Gulfstream before takeoff."

Jacob wisely decided not to argue further. When his phone bleated Foreigner again, he nodded at Val. "Can you get that?"

"Good news," Hawker snapped when she accepted the call. "I tracked down the license plate of the black SUV. It's a Budget rental."

"How is that good news?" Val wondered.

"It's good because the idiots who rented it didn't pay cash, and I managed to trace the credit card info. It was rented by one Salim al-Hadid. Owner of *La Empresa* business park."

"I guess that really seals it," Val conceded grimly. "He is behind this."

"Well, no. Salim himself has a real good alibi."

"What's that?" Jacob asked.

"He's busy giving an interview on the Saudi oil market. I'm watching him on Al Jazeera right now. Guy's got friends and family, though. Forced to guess, I'd say we're chasing his stepson, Aahil. Guy's a well-known firebrand in more conservative Muslim circles. Also, his mother was born in Casablanca."

"There's the Moroccan connection." Jacob frowned. "But I'm still not seeing the Spain connection. What has any of this got to do with Sons of the Loner?"

"Al Hoceima was built mostly by Spaniards around 1925," Val suggested, but she had her doubts. "But by colonizers and invaders, not by anarchist bank robbers, admittedly. It's a stretch."

"You might have to root around for the connection later," Hawker suggested. "After the fireworks."

"Copy that," Jacob agreed, reaching forward to cut the call. "Keep us posted, jarl."

Hawker grunted. "Charlie's going to take over for a few hours. I'm running on near thirty hours without sleep."

"Sweet dreams," Val signed off. Jacob cut the call.

Val turned to Jacob, animated once more. "You know what? There's another connection. Al Hoceima is right next door to the city of Nekur."

"Of course," Jacob agreed, keeping his face straight. "Why didn't I think of that?"

Val laughed, a little giddy once more. Come to think of it, she couldn't remember the last time she'd had a proper night's sleep, either. "Bjorn Ironside's raiders landed in Nekur a few years after they dropped Miguel's ancestor off in Seville. They did their Viking thing, trading when convenient and raiding when it wasn't, dropped off a few more expats, and went home. Over the centuries, Nekur was razed and rebuilt a few times until the Spaniards of 1925 put an end to it for good. So there's another connection."

"Okay?" Jacob scowled through the windshield. "You ever think maybe you have *too much* history crammed in your head, and it's confusing the case?"

"No such thing as too much information."

"Fine. Fine. What does any of this have to do with Cleopatra?"

"No idea!" She struggled to stay serious. "You know you've got a vein popping in your temple?"

"Little shit," Jacob muttered. "I'm still thinking about calling a Lyft and *sending* you home."

Val settled back in her seat. She arranged the fabric of her new tunic over her legs. She was starting to like the way it flowed. You could hide so many holsters beneath that much fabric. "Funny story. Once upon a time, Viking raiders in Nekur captured the king's harem. The emir had to step in and pay their ransom."

"Forcing the Muslim ruler to fund more raids on his own lands." Jacob snorted. "Okay. That is kinda funny."

"I doubt the heist would have worked out so well for the Vikings if the women of the harem hadn't cooperated. Goes to show that even the most powerless people can affect the course of history." Val grew contemplative. "Come to think of it... This whole Cleopatra mess isn't so different, is it?"

"I don't follow."

"The bastards are taking American firms hostage and demanding ransom." Her good humor was slipping away. "Could be planning to use America's own money against it."

"This is all way in the weeds," Jacob speculated. "Our guy Aahil or Salim or whoever might have an ax to grind. Could be payback for Operation Polygamy or a dozen other grievances. Leave the digging to Hawk."

"Sure," she conceded slowly. He had a point. She needed to keep her focus on the here-and-now, at least while she was pursuing armed and dangerous criminals. She let a few seconds of peaceful silence pass before speaking up again.

"By the way... Who are you?"

"Huh?" Jacob glanced over his shoulder and changed lanes.

"You and the company and everything. I don't think standard consultants go out on a job with clown masks and high-tech listening devices in their go-bag."

"We're all-purpose badasses," Jacob clarified crisply. "Marine Corps. Oorah."

"Hawker has been running some pretty extensive searches *really* fast," she went on. "I think it would have taken the techies at Asher and Asher at least a day to get us the connection to al-Hadid. There's some serious intel connections up at the Viking headquarters." She paused and thought, *What the hell, we've been reckless all day. Why stop now?* "Taggert never retired from the military, did he?"

A long silence stretched out as Jacob glared out the windshield.

"Listen," he answered finally. "I'm a field-level operative. What the jarls do back home is above my pay grade. My job is to keep skinny little geeks like you from getting killed."

The GPS beeped their arrival and he let out an audible sigh of relief as they turned off the main road. "So for now, Val Kearie, let's keep our heads in the game."

CHAPTER ELEVEN

Offices of Global Ventures,
Al Hoceima, Morocco
Friday Evening

"Mr. Pinkerton?" A heavyset Moroccan man swept into the front lobby of Global Ventures with his hand outstretched and ready for the most enthusiastic of handshakes. "You must be Miss Kearie," he guessed, clasping Val's hand next. "Thank you so much for coming. I am Makeen Armstrong. You can call me Mak."

He wore a loose, billowy kaftan that flowed and scented the air with cinnamon and cumin where he walked. "Please." He waved for them to follow him past the lobby and into the heart of the building.

Like most buildings in Al Hoceima, the office of Global Ventures was a white-walled villa with sweeping columns and windows that opened to a sea shimmering in the deep blue of twilight. Swirling mosaics of geometric patterns covered the walls and floors, tempting Val to stop and take pictures. Back in the States, a building like this would be found only in the likes of Malibu, screaming opulence and new, showy wealth.

Around the Mediterranean, it was how people built: with an eye for history and design.

"Armstrong," Jacob pondered as they followed Mak down a wide hallway. "American?"

"Do I look American?" Mak chuckled. "I've lived in Morocco my whole life. My father was an exchange student from Chicago. I took his surname after my mother died." He paused to mutter a quick prayer in Arabic. "It's better for business, you know? Especially this business." He pushed open a wide red door and led them into a private office where a wide desk sat in front of an open window overlooking the sea.

"Especially this business," Mak repeated. "You Americans. You're a suspicious lot. Much more likely to contract your financial strategies initiatives to Mak Armstrong than Makeen al-Ashry."

Val winced, but Mak didn't seem to mean the comment as an insult. He bustled into the office, where a slender man in a dark tunic sat in front of the desk nursing a delicate cup of tea.

"Mr. Pinkerton, Miss Kearie, this is Talid. He is another consultant I brought in for the job."

The slender man set his cup down and stood, turning to shake formally with both of them as Mak fiddled with the electric kettle on his desk. Talid's face was gaunt and hard, almost expressionless. His motions were stiff, and Val couldn't help but notice an unusual bunching around the waist of his tunic, about where one might wear a gun holster.

"Mister…" Val asked slowly.

"Talid," Talid answered without a flicker of expression. "I represent local interests."

Val didn't have to ask what he meant by local interests. Talid could not have screamed "police" or "military" louder if he'd had a bullhorn.

Jacob gave Mak a curious look. "No offense, Mak, but the hackers' first demand was to not involve the authorities, so why…" He nodded at Talid.

"I don't see any authorities in this room," Talid asserted indifferently.

Mak snorted and spooned loose scented tea leaves into the cups. "Yes, yes, they demand no involvement from the authorities. I'll be damned if I sit around and watch these whoresons steal from my company and the Moroccan people. You got here fast, yes, and thank you—but Talid got here faster."

"I'm only here as a friend," Talid agreed. "In an unofficial capacity. But I will call in the authorities if it becomes necessary."

"You said they're stealing from the Moroccan people?" This put up alarm bells in Val's head. Gallagher Solutions worked for the Spanish banking system but didn't actually handle any of those monetary transactions. If Global Ventures was more directly tied to the local financial markets, these hackers might be after one hell of a payday.

"We do a lot of investing in small businesses and local startups," Mak dismissed. He offered her a cup of steaming tea, which she took with grace. "Bringing them into compliance with the MCC requirements as a form of community service. I believe in charity, Miss Kearie." Mak offered another cup to Jacob, who took it with polite disinterest. "These people are undermining my work."

"I understand you have been tracking this hacking operation for a few days already," Talid remarked.

Val nodded. "They hit a firm in Spain. They—"

Jacob cleared his throat and broke in. "The good news is that we already have the coding to kick Cleo out of your systems. I've had someone at HQ adding some neat features to my debugging code. We can free your system from this bug, Mak, but if you allow Viking Inc. access to your system to run a full diagnostic, we might be able to track the perpetrator in real time."

"You do?" Val started, then bit her tongue at the strange look the two Moroccan men cast her way. She wondered why Jacob had stopped her from further briefing the men and decided he might suspect one or both of them to be involved. Following his lead, she decided to button up the details.

"Yep." Jacob brought his tea to his nose, sniffed, and tried a tiny sip. "We're doing a postmortem, but if we can run the updated program during an active attack, we've got a better shot at catching him in the act and pinning his location."

"Why would these hackers use the same virus against us if you already have the antidote for it?" Talid wondered.

Val felt a brief sense of vertigo as she stifled the urge to provide a timeframe. Had it really been only half a day? Felt more like a week since she had set foot in Seville. "They might have updated their security protocols already and are hoping that our countermand will no longer be effective."

"Doubt it." Jacob grunted. "They haven't had enough time to analyze what we did *and* build in protections *and* infect Global Ventures. It's probably a time bomb."

"Time bomb?" Mak sounded mildly alarmed.

"It means they had a copy of the original Cleo virus uploaded into your system days or weeks or even months ago," Val explained. "It was coded to remain inactive until today, when it turned itself on. Like a robocall. It's a good thing. It means she'll be easy to take down."

"I bet they didn't expect us to stop the Seville attack so quickly," Jacob theorized. "I bet they were casting a wide net, hoping to catch *many* firms with their pants down all around the same time."

"And make it impossible for people like us to help all of the victims in time," Val agreed. She caught his meaning quickly with no small measure of dismay. "Meaning *someone* was going to have to pay the ransom. I'll let HQ know." She reached for her phone. "We should be on the lookout for more Cleopatra attacks coming, and soon."

"Good thinking." Jacob grunted as Val texted Charlie. "I hate to ask, Mak, but do you think any of your employees might be capable of turning on you like this?"

"What?" Mak's face lost a little of its color. "No, no... most of my people work out in the field. I only have a few employees with access to this office and... I thought I hired good men and women."

After a moment of contemplative silence, he went on. "The only incident I can think of. Early last month, I had a tech working overnight to get some files ready for a deadline. It was after hours and he had a couple of his friends come by. They said they were only there to drop off McDonald's because Kalib was missing supper, but they hung around a while until the security guard found them and kicked them out."

"McDonald's?" Val repeated.

Mak shrugged. "Is very popular. I like the fries."

"Any chance you have the IDs of the guys who did this late-night delivery?" Jacob inquired.

"Ah, yes. Rashim wrote up an incident report. I have it here—" Mak bustled to a filing cabinet in the corner of the office, fished in the top drawer for a moment, and brandished a sheet of paper.

Talib reached for it. Val reached for it faster.

"This will only take a second," she promised Talib's disapproving frown. She snapped a picture of the report with her phone, saw that the back side was empty, and passed the original back to Talib. He looked none too pleased to be taking it secondhand.

"The names are listed on the report." Val attached the image to her text and hit send. "Hopefully HQ can track these guys down quick."

"Fingers crossed," Jacob agreed.

"You can fix this?" Mak asked anxiously.

"No problemo." Jacob smiled. "Do we have your permission to run the diagnostics I talked about?"

Mak nodded.

Jacob met Val's eyes. "Great. We already took her off her throne, so let's not reuse that metaphor."

Val considered for a moment. "Let's rip the wheels off her chariot?"

Jacob nodded his approval. "Auto vandalism, coming right up. Take us to the server room, Mak."

Mak led them into a small room that smelled like plastic and ozone and hummed with electricity. The building may have been classic Mediterranean in style, but apparently, all server rooms looked and smelled about the same, no matter where in the world you were.

"Good evening, Kaberi," Mak greeted the young man sitting behind the computer bank.

Kaberi, who couldn't have been older than nineteen, jumped when the door swung open and stuffed something into one of his pockets.

"Stop that," Talid ordered sharply, pushing between Val and Jacob to get to the tech. "What have you got in your hands? What are you doing?"

Kaberi stared up at Talid, terrified. Slowly, he drew his hand from his pocket. He was holding an old iPhone.

Talid snatched it from his hand and stared daggers at the screen as Kaberi stammered something in Arabic. Talid grunted and dropped the phone back in the kid's lap. Val caught a flash of bright colors and shining candy. He had been playing Candy Crush.

"I'm sorry, Mr. Armstrong," the kid stammered, turning to Mak. "But with the network down, I didn't have anything else to do—"

Talid muttered something under his breath. Val didn't have to speak Arabic to know a curse when she heard one. Grumbling, Talid brushed past her out of the room. "I have to make a call," he told Mak.

"I'm sorry," Kaberi continued babbling. He would likely

continue until someone absolved him of the sin of wasting company time.

"Water under the bridge," Jacob assured Kaberi and slid into the chair beside him. Kaberi did not look the least bit reassured at the sight of this massive pale-skinned American suddenly looming over him. "Kaberi? Can I call you Kaberi? I'm Jacob." He held out his hand. Kaberi took it, looking more than a little dazed.

"You the network admin in these parts?" Jacob asked.

"Sort of." Kaberi was uneasy as he glanced at Mak. "Mr. Armstrong told me to stay off the system until the experts got here."

"Here we are." Jacob cracked his knuckles. "I'm gonna need your help, Kaberi. You ever swept a system before?"

No tech expert herself, Val paced the hall outside the server room and brooded as the hour slipped by. Mak checked in on them every twenty minutes or so, offering her coffee or a refill on her tea, which she politely declined. She was still hoping to get a good night's rest, and the caffeine would do her no favors.

"It's this Cleopatra connection," she burst out the third time Mak came to check on them. "More and more, everything about this is pointing to Islamist terrorism. I don't understand why they named their weapon Cleopatra."

"Must the name have some deep meaning?" Mak inquired politely.

"It's more than a name. Whoever made this thing included an entire animated sequence of Cleopatra." She shuddered. "Not a *good* one, but it did take added work. It was deliberate. It means something to the creator."

Mak nodded wisely but said nothing. He reminded Val

a little of the fat grinning icon you found in Chinese restaurants, but with better hair.

She smiled tiredly. "I'm sorry. I'm sure you've got enough to worry about without me using you to bounce ideas."

Mak shrugged. "You and me, we're not the computer people. We're the ideas people, aren't we?"

Val was about to answer when a faint, tinny tune came from the open server room door behind her.

"Hey!" Jacob barked, sounding a tad irritated. "Val Kearie. Can you grab that call? I kinda got my hands full."

With a hasty apology to Mak, Val darted into the room and snatched Jacob's phone from the desk where he was working. His eyes were glued to lines and lines of code.

The ringtone was *Barbie Girl,* and the caller was Charlie Evans.

"You've got to be kidding," Val mumbled under her breath as she picked up the phone. "Hey," she told Charlie. "Jacob can't come to the phone. He's in the middle of a game and can't pause."

"Got it," Charlie confirmed cheerfully. "Then you'll have to pass the update along to him."

Val glanced over her shoulders and slipped into the most secluded corner of the room. "What have you got?"

"One dead runner. Seville police tracked the black SUV to the docks. Driver dead in the front seat, single bullet to the head, no gun at the scene. Looks like a professional hit."

Val's stomach sank. "ID?"

"They're still working on it. I'll let you know when I find out."

"What about the gear he had in the trunk? They were clearing hardware and computers out of that warehouse."

"Hmm. Nothing about that in the report so far. I'll chase that down, too, but I'm guessing whoever took out the driver looted the car, too."

Charlie sounded terribly cheerful for a woman reporting on a violent death and the possible formation of a new terrorist cyberwarfare campaign. Val checked the time and gritted her teeth. It was about three a.m. back in Virginia.

"The three the cleaners took?" she asked.

"In police custody, and they've upped the security. We can't count on getting much useful information from them. These sorts of cells operate on a very need-to-know basis. I've looked over Hawk's notes, and I think he's right. Aahil al-Hadid probably recruited and managed these men directly, but a man like him is the money behind the operation, not the mastermind."

"Have they said anything?" Val was growing frustrated.

"Only that they do what they're told, and they have no idea who wrote the virus or who decides when and how to deploy it."

"So we're still in the dark about who's actually calling the shots here."

"So far," Charlie agreed. "I'll keep at it. You take care."

Val huffed uncharitably and hung up. Still no leads on the mastermind. Only his mysterious signature in the form of a creepy Cleopatra animation. *What have I missed?*

Val set her jaw and started pacing again.

CHAPTER TWELVE

Offices of Global Ventures,
Al Hoceima, Morocco
Friday Evening

When Jacob and Kaberi trudged out of the server room a little while later, they both looked exhausted.

"I got a secure connection set up," Jacob shared with Val as Kaberi headed for the exit. "HQ is now in control of the Global Ventures network. Hopefully, they don't need me holding their hands to get our countercode and the tracer running."

Val checked the time and sighed. "It's late. But Mak's still in his office."

Jacob nodded. "Let's touch base with him and then see if we can't steal a nap somewhere."

Mak was alone when the two of them returned to his office. He lifted his eyes from the report he was reading. His eyes were heavy and red-rimmed with fatigue.

"No Talid?" Val tried not to sound relieved.

Mak shook his head and set the report aside. "He's gone back to his office. Following up on the young men from the delivery incident."

"He's got leads on them already?" Jacob sounded surprised. Viking Inc. had been unable to dig up anything on the names listed in that report yet. Talid was most definitely tapping into some extensive local resources. *Police*, Val guessed.

Jacob brought the conversation back to Cleopatra. "The good news is that we've got people cleaning up your systems right now. If all goes right, they'll have this thing licked by morning."

"Excellent. Thank you." Mak stared down at his broad palms, a little shamefaced. He sipped cold tea. "This cannot happen again," he murmured. "I will not *let* it happen. This virus got in somehow. Your people—can they do anything for my network to keep out future attacks?"

"The biggest point of failure for network security usually isn't within the hardware or the network itself." Val stepped in as Jacob stifled a yawn. "Cleo almost certainly got in through a human vector."

Jacob nodded. "My guys will look at your system, Mak, but your best bet is to implement some better IT security measures here in the real world. No more unauthorized McDonald's deliveries, stuff like that."

"Good. Good. You can help with that, then. Help me develop better security."

"Sure. Someone from Viking can consult with you on that, no problem. But Val and I have our hands full, trying to figure out who's behind this mess. Can't afford to dally, or the perp will update this virus faster than we can keep up."

Mak rose to his feet. "Of course, I'm so sorry. I have been a bad host. You have had a busy day, and you are exhausted. I had my secretary reserve two rooms for you at the inn across the street."

"You're a gentleman and a scholar, Makeen." Jacob clasped his hands in front of him and gave a small bow. "Come on, Val Kearie. Let's crash."

Manzil Ealaa Alma
Al Hoceima, Morocco
Friday Night

Manzil Ealaa Alma was an old inn, small but well-appointed. Most importantly to Val at that moment, it was a two-minute walk from Global Ventures. Jacob left their car parked in Global Ventures' private lot, and by the time they rang the bell at the inn's front desk, it was well past ten p.m. The tired-looking woman behind the counter handed each of them a separate physical key and gestured at the stairway before slumping back in her chair.

Val followed Jacob up the stairs in moody silence, ticking down the seconds until she could fall into a real bed and close her eyes and not open them again for a good eight hours.

Jacob stopped abruptly before they reached the end of the second-floor hallway. When he lowered his duffel bag to the floor and reached for his hip, Val's fatigue turned into something sharp and alarming. She glanced around

Jacob's bulk to see that the door at the end of the hallway was hanging slightly ajar. Pale wooden splinters littered the faded carpet. Someone had forced the lock.

It should have alarmed Val. It should have made her afraid, or cautious, or wary.

Instead, it made her mad. She reached for her gun and loosened it in the holster. Jacob did the same and, moving with surprising stealth for such a big guy, he sidled up to the door and peered through the crack. He gestured for Val to stay behind him, then pushed the door open with one hand while his other hand held the gun steady. He entered the room with Val on his heels.

She was checking the darkened bathroom for any sign of life when movement in the side of the room caught her attention. A long-haired young man, barely more than a kid, sprang out from behind the wardrobe and threw himself at Jacob's gun hand. Another guy, nearly as big as Jacob himself, came from around the corner, lifting his fist for a swing.

The little guy tackled Jacob like a rabid animal and wrapped around his forearm, biting viciously at his wrist as the big guy attacked Jacob in a headlock. Jacob yelped and dropped the gun, which went skittering under the bed.

Val coiled both fists around the butt of her gun and slammed the barrel into the bigger thug's ribs. He groaned and released his headlock on Jacob, doubling over with a curse. She kicked him again, sinking her heel into the kidney. He hit the floor with a gurgling *whoosh*.

A third guy, skinny and small like the first, had materialized and was hanging around Jacob's neck, trying to choke the wind out of him as Jacob grappled with the first kid.

"How many goddamned thugs are hiding in this room?" Val snarled, snatching up a freestanding coat rack in the corner and whirling to bring it crashing into the side of the kid trying to wrestle Jacob down. There was a crack of wood, and the boy bellowed and staggered to the side. Jacob released him to reach for the little fucker glommed onto his windpipe.

The first kid came staggering toward Val. She tried dancing out of his reach but stumbled over the arm of the guy she had already dropped. She went wheeling forward as the kid lifted his fists.

He punched her in the face. Her vision turned gray and hazy, and she staggered and collapsed against the side of the bed. Thinking she needed a moment of stillness to make the world stop swimming, she slid to the floor with a *thunk*. For a moment, her world became a place of confused shouting and moving shapes, then scrambling, fading footfalls.

The next thing Val knew, she was alone in the room, slumped beside a shattered coat rack, and people were shouting in the hallway.

Guess I better see what that's about.

She dragged herself to her feet and went to the doorway, swaying a little.

Jacob stood blocking the hallway, exchanging some heated words with the innkeeper, who waved a phone like she was threatening to call the cops. The men who had attacked them were nowhere. As Jacob argued with the innkeeper in gruff Arabic, a few other doors opened and people peered out into the hallway.

Jacob and the innkeeper seemed to come to some accord, because he turned and blinked, surprised to see Val standing behind him.

"You okay?"

"Are we going after them?" Val leaned on the frame, still dizzy.

"No." Jacob stepped into the room and shut the door behind him. "They were cheap hired thugs sent to intimidate us. They won't know shit." He frowned down at her. "It's too late in the day to get a different hotel. Besides, we're not in any shape for another hoedown. Follow my finger."

He tracked the motion of her pupils and must have decided she didn't have a concussion. He ran a washcloth under the tap and handed it to her.

She sat on the bed and pressed it to her face. Her cheekbone throbbed. "I'm going to have a black eye," she marveled. "God. Haven't had one of those since…eighth grade? Oh god. It was Tommy Griswold. He was so obnoxious." Yawning, not quite knowing what she was doing, she laid her head on the pillow. Jacob knelt and picked the broken coat rack off the floor. At a loss for what to do with it, he turned and stuffed it into the wardrobe. "I hit him first, though," she added.

Something stiff brushed her cheek. It was a business card. She picked it up and squinted. It took her a second to make sense of the mess of symbols and numbers forming an ASCII image of Queen Cleopatra in her serpent tiara.

A message beneath the image read:

You Have Been Sentenced

"Son of a bitch." She sighed.

"What?" Jacob looked around sharply. Val held the card out to him. "They were kind enough to leave a calling card, and I just got my fingerprints all over it."

Jacob frowned and studied the card before taking it carefully by the edges and setting it on the wardrobe. "I'll send a picture to Hawker. You get some rest."

Sure thing, she thought, dozing off. *Another fight, now I've got a black eye and a target painted on my back.*

Dad's going to love this.

Manzil Ealaa Alma
Al Hoceima, Morocco
Saturday Morning

Val woke up with a nasty headache, but she could see straight, count backward from a hundred, and swallow a fistful of painkillers, so her injuries couldn't have been that bad. Things looked up even more when Jacob arrived carrying a tray of fried eggs, fresh bread, and absurdly strong coffee.

"I was a little worried about you," he admitted as they sat down to eat.

Val smiled. She'd grabbed a quick shower and changed, but she hadn't brought nearly enough concealer to cover up the shiner on her left eye. "Honestly, it's not as bad as it looks. I think I was just so tired last night that it made everything seem worse." She spooned honey from a small pot into her coffee and drizzled some on her bread. "What about you? How are you holding up?"

"Much better after a good night's sleep," he admitted. He had a faint bruise on the side of his cheek and a welt on his arm where the smallest guy had bitten him, but at least it hadn't broken skin.

"Me too," Val agreed cheerfully. "Let's get back to work. Where did we leave off?"

Jacob eyed her for a moment before swallowing a bite of egg. "Hawk called me with an update before I went down to get breakfast. The three guys in Seville lockup still aren't talking. We finally got an ID on the dead man in the SUV."

"Al-Habib?" she pressed hopefully.

"Oh hell no. I think we'd have known a lot sooner if it was the son of a Saudi oil magnate."

"Stepson," Val corrected him.

Jacob waved this off. "Whatever. No, al-Habib is in the wind. The dead guy in the SUV is Luis Moreno."

Val shrugged. "Doesn't ring any bells."

"It shouldn't. Just some guy from Seville. A pencil pusher working for a medical supply company in *La Empresa*."

She scowled. "No connection to al-Habib? Or a recent religious experience or political extremism or *anything*? The guy died for his shady mission. Something motivated him."

"Hawk is still looking into it."

Val swallowed the last of her bread and sat back, folding her arms and glaring through her window to the narrow, brick-lined streets of Al Hoceima. "So that calling card is the only new information we have," she muttered. "And I got my fingerprints all over it."

Jacob chuckled. "I'm pretty sure that thing has been passed through so many hands that it's no good for prints anyway."

Someone had taken the time to re-create Cleopatra's iconic face in hashtags, ampersands, and rogue punctuation marks. "That woman *means something*," she insisted, wiping a crumb from the corner of her mouth. "Cleo…the name means 'glory of her father.' The story is that her father favored her over the other kids because she was so clever."

"Yeah?" Jacob sipped coffee from a tiny white cup as he waited for her to finish her thought. "We've been over that."

Val continued to spitball. "Originally, she ruled in triumvirate with her two brothers. Then she had them both killed."

"So what? Nasty bitch, but aren't most kings and queens of Ye Olden Days right bastards?"

Slowly, Val felt herself smile. "I think we're looking at this all wrong."

"By all means!" Jacob declared, setting down his empty cup with an emphatic *tink*. "Grace us with your insight!"

Val's grin broadened as she focused on her partner. The blow to the head, the good night's sleep, or the combination of both had done her a world of good. "We've been assuming there's some guy or male-dominated group using Cleo's face. All things being equal, it's a fair guess. Most cyberattacks and extremist operations are undertaken by men. But this isn't a common job or a common cyberattack. What if it's a woman behind this?"

Jacob frowned. "That's really far off the profile. Everything else about this job reeks of Islamism. Not a lot of women masterminds in that little sphere of the world.

"Look... Humor me." She reached forward and patted his hand, then tossed back the last of her coffee. She set the cup down with a satisfying click and rose to her feet. "Just ask Hawk if Luis Moreno has any siblings."

CHAPTER THIRTEEN

Holiday Inn
Al Hoceima, Morocco
Saturday Morning

After breakfast, Jacob insisted on moving their operation to the Holiday Inn up the road, which Val found a terrible pity. Questionable security measures aside, she quite liked *Manzil Ealaa Alma*.

"We'll keep paying for the rooms at *Manzil*, though," Jacob assured her. "Our guy apparently knows we're there. We'll keep the light on in case he decides to send any more messages."

By the time they got set up in their new rooms, Hawker had sent along a full dossier on Talid, which Val devoured eagerly while she slurped hotel-lobby coffee. She was working at the desk in Jacob's room while he sat on the bed with his computer.

"Holy smokes." She turned, moving her laptop to her

knees so she wouldn't have to take her gaze off the screen. "Talid al-Abbas, deputy vice-chief of the *Qism al-Amn.* Basically, Moroccan Homeland Security. This guy has a crazy track record. Over three hundred arrests in the last four years, all for charges like sedition and terrorism and conspiracy."

"A bona fide professional hard ass," Jacob observed.

"At least he's on our side. Nine commendations. He's the Arabic James Bond." Val shook her head with a whistle.

"Don't get ahead of yourself. He's on the side of *Morocco*. If he decides we're working against his country's interests, he'll try to put us down just as fast as any of those unfortunates he's arrested."

"Duly noted." Val scratched her cheek. "He's got a ton of local resources at his disposal, though. We should probably brief him on everything. We'll work better with full cooperation on both sides."

Jacob reached for his phone. "Sure. I'll have Mak set up a meeting."

She was a little surprised at how readily Jacob followed her lead, and it must have shown on her face.

"What?" He gave her a smirk. "You're supposed to be the nerdy girl with the ideas. I'm just the computer guy."

"And the clown with a gun."

"*Bodyguard.*" He snapped his computer shut and tossed it across the bed to her. "I'll set up a meeting. You start your homework."

"Homework?" She reached for the second computer, puzzled.

"HQ put together that security protocol package Mak

wanted. Since we're here for the day, you're going to need to present it to his people."

"Already?" She had assumed it would take at least a few days for Viking Inc. to assemble the package, and she'd figured she and Jacob would be long gone by then.

Jacob shrugged and walked to the door. "This is what we do. Some bright spark has written software. Enter the different variables, strengths, and weaknesses, and let it run. It automatically pulls together the optimum package."

"How can they be sure it's right?" Val was stunned. "Every business and firm is unique. They have unique vulnerabilities and risk needs. You can't just plug Global Ventures' HR files into some program and expect it to spit out a worthwhile security protocol."

Something told Val that network security was not something you wanted to leave *entirely* to automated software.

"Viking Inc. has been running this operation for years. There's a whole team dedicated to doing it right." He opened the door and smiled at her over his shoulder. "Trust me. It's how we make our money."

"Well, shit." She could think of little else to say. "Why do they need me then?"

His smile broadened into a grin. "Someone's got to explain all the mumbo-jumbo to the clients."

Offices of Global Ventures,
Al Hoceima, Morocco
Saturday Morning

It was surprisingly difficult to find high-quality makeup on short notice, not to mention concealer pale enough to match Val's skin tone. She didn't consider herself vain, but she felt terribly vulnerable walking into the office of Global Ventures, looking like a victim of domestic abuse. Mak's secretary glanced over her like she was a piece of furniture when they stopped to check in at his desk.

Val didn't know whether to be grateful or concerned about the man's apparent blindness to a fist-size bruise right out in the open. She might have thought he showed the tiniest glimmer of satisfaction, but she knew Jacob had already checked the secretary. He had reserved the rooms for them at *Manzil* the night before, but he had done it via a compromised computer network. It wouldn't have been hard for the hackers to find out where Val and Jacob were staying.

Mak, on the other hand, cared quite a bit about the bruises. He and Talid were waiting for Val and Jacob in the conference room.

"Why didn't you call me? Or the police?" Mak demanded when Jacob gave them a quick summary of the attack.

Talid folded his arms and regarded Val and Jacob with the same blank-faced indifference she had seen last night. She suspected that particular poker face was hiding some severe disappointment.

Jacob showed them Cleopatra's latest calling card. "Because it's personal. And law enforcement will slow us down. Besides." He gestured at Talid. "I'm telling the police right now."

Mak glanced nervously at Talid, whose lips twitched in

the barest indication of a scowl. "I received a report from the Seville police regarding three men in custody and another one executed in the streets," he explained. "Apparently this job has involved a lot of violence already, and for some reason you didn't feel the need to share that information with me."

Val used her best professional-polite tone as she set up her laptop. "Mr. al-Abbas, please understand... You didn't even give us your full name last night. We had no idea who you were. It would have been downright irresponsible to share sensitive information with you before checking you out."

Talid's face remained carefully blank, but she thought she felt the heat radiating from him. "What did you find, Miss Kearie?"

She opened her mouth but was cut off by a guitar riff. "*I wanna feel what love is... I want you to show me...*"

"I gotta take this." Jacob had the grace to look somewhat embarrassed as he left the room. "But we found out that you're on the level," he called to Talid over his shoulder before the door clicked shut.

Val was determined to defy the awkward silence. "Besides... We're putting everything on the table now, Mr. al-Abbas. We think we could get this job done faster working in full cooperation with—"

The conference room door swung open and Jacob burst into the room, brandishing his phone. "You were right! We found our lead."

Val barely had time to recover from the whiplash before Jacob thrust his phone in front of her face. She saw a picture of a gorgeous sandy-skinned woman with straight jet hair and heavy kohl lines around her eyes.

"I was?" Baffled, Val took the phone.

"Claudia Moreno." Jacob sounded unduly self-satisfied, as if the sibling connection had been his hunch. He sat at the table and started typing into Val's computer. "Two brothers. One of whom was found dead at the harbor in Seville yesterday morning. You wanna know the real kicker?"

Val showed the picture to Talid, who took the phone with a faint frown. Jacob was grinning. He didn't wait for Val to guess what the real kicker might be.

"She's a computer programmer."

"Not just any programmer," Talid murmured. "I know this woman. She's a top expert in the field of systems programming. Moves in some powerful circles. We have long suspected that she has ties to some black-market dealers but have never been able to prove it. No strong religious affiliation that we're aware of."

"That background means she's perfectly capable of whipping up a bug like Cleopatra." Val considered adding a few other observations but decided to hold her tongue. At this point, Claudia's dark-eyed aesthetic and the similarity of her name and Cleopatra's were superficial connections.

Mak was frowning at the image on Jacob's phone. "Why would such an educated, independent woman ally herself with terrorists?"

Val stuffed her hands in her pocket and started pacing around the conference table. It was a damned good question. The connections to Islamic extremists were too big to ignore.

"Maybe it's not about ideology for her," she theorized. "Maybe she's working with the likes of al-Hadid because it's a means to an end, not because she's down for the jihad."

Out of the corner of her eye, she saw a satisfied look flicker over Jacob's face as he studied the screen. Emboldened, she kept talking. "There are three big reasons someone would engage in this kind of attack: Money, vengeance, and ideology." She ticked down one finger. "We've already decided it's almost certainly not money. You could target a hundred different firms that could pay bigger ransoms than Gallagher or Global Ventures. Ideology?" She made a so-so gesture. "It's not *impossible* that a brilliant woman would fall in with the jihadi types, but it's pretty rare. When it does happen, those women all tend to be very outspoken about their religious motivations. That flies in the face of the Cleopatra imagery, anyway."

Val stopped her pacing and leaned over the wide glass conference table. "That leaves vengeance. This woman has a bone to pick. She feels insulted, scorned. She's been hurt. The people who hurt her are the same ones the terrorists want to hurt. So they've formed an uneasy alliance."

She saw that Jacob's bright look had not wavered, and she gave him a hard stare. "I'm right, aren't I?"

"About five years ago, there was a little incident in a village outside of Seville," Jacob informed her, turning the computer around to show her a field report. "Word got out some al-Qaeda operatives were trying to drum up recruitment in Spain. Spanish enforcement cracked down on the village with a little under-the-table help from some US operatives." He held up a hand to fend off Val's interruption. "Not us. I don't know who it was, but that wasn't a Viking gig. Anyway, there were a couple of civilian casualties. One of them was Javier Moreno. Father of Claudia, Luis, and Renaldo."

Val let out a long, low whistle. "Sorry we're starting late on your protocol presentation, Mr. Armstrong," she told Mak as an afterthought.

The big man waved both hands animatedly, like a soccer fan watching the last half of a close championship game. "No, please. Continue."

"So we've got a coherent theory, but so far, all of the evidence is circumstantial," Val pointed out.

Talid surprised her by chuckling. It was a dry, raspy noise, as if Talid weren't much in the habit of laughing. "In my experience, circumstantial evidence is often all there is to work with. When enough bits line up, possibilities become probabilities. You either sit back and wait for proof to come to you, or you act on what you have." He slipped his hands into his pockets and nodded at them. "Mr. Pinkerton. Miss Kearie. Mr. Armstrong. Thank you for your assistance. I'm going to take this back to my office."

"And do what?" Val demanded, a little louder than was probably appropriate in a professional setting. She moved toward Talid, who glanced over his shoulder and gave her a silent, appraising look.

"You're going to act on my theories?" she pushed. "We want in. We'll come with you."

"We have the matter well in hand. This is what we do, Miss Kearie," Talid retorted in his cold, utterly professional voice.

Val leaned forward and turned her head to give Talid an unobstructed view of the massive bruise purpling around her eye. "This matter is decidedly *out* of hand," she suggested softly. "This bitch has attacked and threatened to kill us. This time, we're going to go knock on *her* door."

CHAPTER FOURTEEN

Holiday Inn
Al Hoceima, Morocco
Early Saturday Afternoon

"We're gonna get a bill from the hotel to install new carpet in this room," Jacob snapped.

Val stopped pacing and stared at him, her frustration momentarily waylaid by pure confusion. He pointed at the cheap hexagon-patterned carpet running from the room door, past the television and down to the windows. "You are wearing holes with your pacing."

Val squinted down at the red and gold hexagons. She looked up at Jacob with narrow eyes. "Am not."

He took this opportunity to throw a ball at her head. She reached up and caught it and gave a casual squeeze. It was soft gator skin, a surprisingly banal toy he'd pulled from his magic bag. She wondered if a bomb detonator was hidden inside it or something. "Do you have, like, any *clothes* in there?"

"You don't ask a gentleman what he has in his bag."

Val huffed and started tossing the ball from one hand to another. "This is stupid. We're holed up in here doing fuck-all while Cleopatra is still out there somewhere."

"Talid's not going to box us out of the operation," Jacob assured her. "Taggert talked to him. Don't worry. We're still on this case."

"Really? What did Taggert tell him?"

Jacob shrugged. He folded his arms across his chest, leaned back on the pillow, and shut his eyes. Val had seen this before, and noticed a lot of military people had an ability to fall asleep at the first sign of a lull in action. "I don't know, Kearie. It's above my pay grade."

Val began to pace again.

"Okay, fine!" Jacob sat up straight, covering his eyes with a glower. "Sit your ass down."

Startled, Val plunked into the desk chair. It swiveled, rotating her away from Jacob as she felt herself flush. She'd pissed off her evaluating partner. Not a good look.

"A group of hired goons have taken Elon Musk's baby daughter hostage and are holding her for ransom," Jacob snapped. "Intel says they're hiding her at one of their bases in a warehouse in the port of Los Angeles. You're on a team of four agents tasked with rescuing the baby. What's your plan?"

"*What?*"

Jacob gave her a hard stare. "I hear DnD is making a comeback with the youths. *Roleplay*, bitch."

"Oh." She bounced the ball against the ceiling and frowned. "What do we know about the enemy's numbers and resources?"

"You think it's between five and ten gangsters, with the kind of firepower you can buy off the streets. They style themselves as techno-anarchists, and while they've got a little bit of tech savvy, their security systems are something you could put together from parts you salvaged from a run-down Radio Shack."

"I…redirect a giant tunnel-boring drill to run beneath the warehouse and open a hole right beneath the baby."

"You're funny," Jacob noted flatly. "The warehouse is built on docks. Over water."

Val resisted the temptation to suggest building an implausible submarine device to sneak into the air ducts and extract the trapped child. "These aren't professionals with much kidnapping experience," she suggested. Jacob gave a permissive nod.

"I send two of my team to create a distraction of some kind. Stages of disruption, if necessary, but they have to come fast so nobody has time to regroup or realize they're being fucked with. Draw as many of the enemy away from the nursery as possible. At peak chaos, get the remaining two operatives in there. One to grab and carry the baby, the other as backup and cover. They regroup with the distraction team at a predetermined location and vamoose."

Jacob considered the plan. "All right," he granted. "But the plan only works if it's truly a bunch of rookies doing the dirty."

"Sure," she conceded.

"What if they're pros? Go ahead and assume they're working with roughly the same level of equipment you are." He held up his hands. "Before you say the obvious, let's assume that paying the ransom is out of the question. I don't know why. It just is. We're pretty confident these guys will, in fact, shoot the baby if they don't get their dough by the deadline."

"Rough crowd," she muttered, squeezing the ball at intervals like a heartbeat. "They'll be expecting some kind of gambit. Honestly, Pinky, you can't just throw a vague hypothetical out there if lives are, hypothetically, on the line. It would be flat-out irresponsible for me to give you a plan of action right now, because I don't have nearly enough information."

"Clock's ticking," he pushed, merciless. "Twenty-four hours to baby mincemeat."

"Dick. You know what Lincoln said? If he had an hour to chop down a tree, he'd spend the first fifty minutes sharpening the ax. The world is complicated and that's what you've got to do: prepare. Gather information.

"I'm not gonna spend ninety percent of that twenty-four hours running intel, but you better believe my first priority is getting a clear and complete understanding of the situation. You gotta know what makes the enemy tick."

Jacob retorted in irritation, "Fine. Smartass. You have *one* hour to rescue the baby."

Val chewed her lip. "Trying to take a guarded facility with an inferior force is stupid, but if you gotta do it, I guess your best bet is to try for stealth. Take the least-guarded route into the nursery and try to neutralize anyone you come across without raising an alarm." She gave him a dirty look. "Unless you're gonna tell me that all my people are wearing wooden-soled shoes that for some reason we can't take off."

Jacob rolled his eyes, but she thought the twitch in his shoulders indicated a suppressed chuckle. He moved on. "That's fine for now. Next scenario: You're part of a security team hired to escort a minor head-of-state through unstable territory. You've gotten word that—"

He broke off, interrupted by a sound Val almost didn't recognize: a plain, classic telephone ring. "Crap." He patted his pockets until he found his cellphone. "Crap, it's Taggert. I've got to take this."

He surged to his feet and vanished into the bathroom.

Val spun in her chair, irritated. He could have at least finished describing the scenario before he ran off, so she had something to think about while she counted the seconds.

Jacob came out of the bathroom and dropped his phone onto the mattress. "That's our cue. Pack your bags. We're moving out."

"Relocating again?" Val sat up. "Where to?" *And why?*

"Casablanca. Cleopatra's taken over *Mustashfaa Lil'amrad Alnafsia*. It's the country's only high-security psychiatric prison."

Val wasn't sure if she was supposed to laugh or not. As far as jokes went, it wasn't all that funny. "So far she's been going after business firms. This doesn't sound like Cleo. It makes no sense."

Jacob threw his jacket and socks into his magic duffel bag. "Sure it does. This ain't any old American prison. It's extremely well-funded, almost like a private hospital or rehab center. One with bars on the windows."

Realizing Jacob was serious, Val climbed to her feet and put her computer away. If Cleo had indeed popped up in

Casablanca, they had to move before she slipped away again. Val was beginning to think of this whole job as a game of high-stakes whack-a-mole. Something about that bothered her.

"What's the American connection?" she asked.

Jacob shrugged. "Structurally, not much. There's a couple of inmates at the facility we should be concerned about, though. You ever heard of *Ahriq al-Nasr?*"

Val was not too keen to admit that she had not.

He snorted as he checked his pistol and loaded a fresh magazine. "*Real* crazy fuckers. Death cult shit. Translates to something like 'Burn the eagle.' The group started as an *al-Qaeda* splinter but was disavowed for their indiscriminate targeting of non-combatants."

Val gasped, wondering how she had never heard of a terrorist cell so nasty that even The Base had turned them out.

"The Moroccan security forces managed to capture most of these cultists," Jacob shared, grabbing his tooth-brush from the bathroom. "I'm sure Talid could tell you all about it. But it looks like a couple of the ringleaders wound up in front of a sympathetic judge, who sentenced them to *Alnafsia* instead of a more traditional hellhole. So there's the American connection—that place is home to some crazy bastards with a real hate-boner for the US and all things Western."

He tossed the last of his toiletries in his bag and zipped it shut. "Are you gonna pack or what?"

She shouldered her messenger bag. "I'm already good to go. I do a full pack out every morning if I'm not sure where I'll be sleeping that night. My suitcase is just inside."

"Not bad," Jacob approved, pulling open the door to his room. He followed Val to her room and waited as she swiped her card and grabbed her bag.

"This is bothering me," she admitted as they trudged toward the lobby. "Attacking a mental facility feels desperate. Are we sure it's not a distraction to get us out of Al Hoceima?"

"If it is, it's a damned good one. They've given *Alnafsia* forty-eight hours to pay a ransom."

"They haven't put deadlines on the ransom before." Deep discomfort trickled down Val's spine. "What happens after forty-eight hours?"

Jacob met her eye, and he wasn't smiling. "Some threats you don't need to spell out in words. Especially not when you control the door locks in the prison housing all of North Africa's worst psychopaths and serial killers."

Mustashfaa Lil'amrad Alnafsia
Casablanca, Morocco
Saturday Afternoon

If Val hadn't known that *Alnafsia* was a prison for the criminally insane, she would have loved the building and architecture even more than she had liked Global Ventures or *Manzil*. Bright white walls, wonderfully elaborate chipped-tile mosaics on the floors, and high, arched ceilings. The atmosphere in the lobby was borderline religious.

Unfortunately, armed guards at every doorway and the lack of windows ruined the effect. The potted plants were fake, too. That struck Val as particularly egregious, like the whole operation was a cheap front masquerading at some noble purpose.

The guards looked around disapprovingly at every sound, as if the heels of Val's sneakers broke some obscure rule with every faint squeak. They wore uniform vests with circular emblems on the shoulders, the logo of the company that provided security for the prison.

Val and Jacob were subjected to a thorough security pat down, which was fair enough, considering the situation. When the guards tried to put them in separate rooms for the checks, though, Jacob put his foot down.

He growled some decidedly unfriendly-sounding Arabic to the guard when he tried to guide Val through a closed door. It was a tense moment, not at all helped by the deadly silence of the entire facility. The quiet was shattered when the chief security officer returned from the back room and told his man to stand down.

"Your boss has talked to my boss," the chief told Jacob. "Mr. al-Abbas vouched for you. Come on. He's waiting." He waved for them both to follow him through the reinforced doors into the heart of the facility.

"This could be a blood bath," Val murmured. She tasted the tension, heavy and sour, in the air.

Beside her, Jacob nodded grimly. "Perfect chance for a couple of enterprising young fanatics to spring an escape if this goes FUBAR."

She studied him out of the corner of her eye as the guard led them through hallways lined with offices and conference rooms.

Jacob strode with his shoulders out. His swinging fists

clenched and never strayed far from his holster. It was the walk of a man who had been here before. Maybe not in *Alnafsia* specifically, but in dozens of places like it. As she had back in *La Empresa*, Val felt a twinge of unease regarding her partner. Despite Dad saying that Jasper Taggert had a reputation for running clean operations, contractors like Viking Inc. tended to be landing pads for bad eggs that had washed out of the military for one reason or other.

Val wasn't sure Pinkerton was Jacob's real name. She wasn't entirely sure she wanted to know his real name.

The security chief waved a keycard in front of a sealed door and stood aside to let Val and Jacob step into the server room. It was a soulless office—all steel benches, uncomfortable chairs, and no-nonsense filing cabinets. A box fan in one corner circulated the hot, stale air pushed out by all the electronic equipment.

A tall, lanky man with midnight-dark skin and a shaved scalp sat at a central computer.

"This is Ekon Musa." The security chief grunted. "Our head of IT."

Val noted at once that Musa's uniform vest bore the same emblem as the security guards. "Head of IT," she observed, careful to avoid offense. "But not *Alnafsia's* IT, is that correct?"

Musa grunted and tore his eyes from the screen for the first time. "Yes. The prison director asked me to take a look at the problem. I assure you, I have never seen this system before in my life." He had a thick Nigerian accent. He nodded at the security chief, who left the room and shut the door with an unnecessarily loud *click*.

Ekon Musa stood, looming noticeably above even Jacob's frame. He shook Jacob's hand but only nodded politely at Val.

"You are the Vikings," he verified. "Mr. al-Abbas and the warden said you would be here to handle this virus."

"Which we've already beaten twice," Jacob explained warily. "So no offense, Mr. Musa, but I'm afraid you might have wasted your time coming here."

With a sigh, Musa agreed. "Probably. But *Alnafsia* is our biggest client. We do not specialize in cyber security, but it seemed prudent to come and assure our client that we are nonetheless invested in *Alnafsia's* continued security on all fronts. We can afford no more mistakes. I will be very happy if you can fix the problem quickly and we can all go home."

"Ditto," Val chimed in. Musa glanced down at her and seemed vaguely surprised, as if he had forgotten she existed. She flushed, not from the puzzled stare of this tall fellow, but simply because *ditto* was not professional parlance.

"But there is something we have to warn you about, Mr. Musa," she went on as Jacob set down his bag and started pulling out his own computer equipment.

"It's been over forty-eight hours since we first encountered and defeated this Cleopatra program. There's a chance that her code has been altered or has evolved in response to our counterattacks."

"You are saying it may not be so easy." Musa regarded her calmly. She was struck by how prominently his eyes stood out from his dark face.

"I'm saying we have to be ready for anything."

Musa nodded his understanding. "Let's hope your company lives up to its reputation."

Jacob concurred. "Amen to that. I've got network access. So far, it looks like the same bitch we've been chasing. I'm about to initiate the countercode. Hold on to your butts."

Val and Musa stood quietly behind Jacob, watching the screen as he input commands to the prompt window. New lines of code started to scroll down a black background.

"We're off to a good start." Jacob leaned back in a self-satisfied stretch. "Now we just—"

The screen flickered and turned a flat, shocking shade of crimson, like freshly-spilled blood. A gasp escaped Val. She didn't think she had ever seen such a color on a computer screen before. It wasn't eye-searing like a glowing stoplight, but solid and ominous, as if someone had coated the entire monitor in thick paint.

A blinking cursor appeared in that sea of red. Slowly, letters appeared.

You have sent your armies against me and failed. Your lives are now forfeit.

CHAPTER FIFTEEN

Mustashfaa Lil'amrad Alnafsia
Casablanca, Morocco
Saturday Afternoon

Klaxons began to wail. The server room door slammed open. Val whirled, her hands lifted and ready for a fight, but it was only the security chief—Adil, according to his name tag. He pulled the door shut behind him as he babbled a long, incomprehensible stream of Arabic into his radio.

Behind Val, Musa and Jacob scrambled from monitor to monitor, frantically trying to regain control of the system.

"What the hell happened?" Adil forced his words out quickly, stumbling over his thick accent.

Val spat out the only answer that made sense. "The virus has evolved."

Jacob was digging through his duffel and called over his shoulder, "That's right... The bitch was hiding all kinds of new code up her skirt." He pulled an external drive from the bag and plugged it into the nearest computer. "Musa, can I get a hard reset?"

Musa ran to the side of the room, where he punched a large power button on a stack. The monitors went black and half the electronics in the room hissed and died, but the klaxons wailed on. Adil babbled into his radio, exchanging bursts of animated arguing with his colleague.

"Can we shut that damned siren up?" Jacob hollered, but if anyone knew which lever to press for the klaxon, they weren't listening to him.

"System coming back online now." Musa jammed the power button once more. "Hopefully, you can—" Whatever he had hoped for didn't matter, because as the monitors powered up, they were all the same shade of hellion red.

"Can you get the security systems back online or not?" Adil demanded.

Jacob shook his head, typing away at the laptop hooked to his external drive. "I'm looking into the source code now but it's not responding to the same commands we used in Seville."

"My people say they've lost control of the automatic door locks in the prisoner housing sector," Adil snapped.

Val's heart skipped a beat. "The cells are open?"

Adil hesitated, listening to all the radio chatter. "No. Everything is still locked down, but we are locked *out* of the system."

"That means someone else has her finger on the button," Val murmured and sucked in a breath. *And she's probably itching to press it.*

Adil glanced at her, surprised. "I'm going to inform the

local police. We've got to alert the authorities. They'll want to lock down the block."

Val wasn't going to argue the point. There was something to be said for not involving the authorities, but if the inmates were about to break out of Arkham Asylum, someone ought to make sure the locals had plenty of warning.

"Jacob?" Val asked nervously. "You got a Batman cowl in that bag?"

He didn't seem to hear. He gave his keyboard a frustrated slap. "Fucking hell. She's not responding to *any* Greek now." He combed his fingers roughly through his hair. For the first time since Val had met him, he seemed on the edge of real stress. "What other languages, Val?"

"What?"

"What other languages did Cleopatra speak?"

Val's mind raced. Jacob must think the programmer had switched away from using Greek. A fair guess.

"Um. Okay. She spoke the languages of the Medes, Parthians—" Val closed her eyes, scrabbling at the file cabinets of her brain. "The troglodytae, Syrians, the Ethiopians—"

"Did she speak anything we have a snowball's chance in hell of guessing?" Jacob barked.

"The Arabs, the Hebrews—"

"Arabs." Jacob spun to Musa. "That's it." He spoke to Musa in rapid Arabic, but Val cut in. "No! No, you're wasting your time. She wouldn't have switched to Arab. Anyone in this neck of the world could cut in."

"Then what the hell, Val?" Jacob glowered.

A lightbulb went off in her head. "Hebrew! Do any of you know any Hebrew?"

"Why the fuck would she be using Hebrew?" Jacob demanded. He seemed more frustrated with his own confusion than with the loss of network control.

"Because Arabic is too obvious and nobody speaks those other languages anymore," Val explained, equally exasperated.

"I have reports of security personnel locked in the break room and outer corridors," Adil warned, keeping his ear pressed to the radio. "I have four men in the housing ward with nothing between them and the inmates but electronic door locks that we no longer control."

"I know Hebrew." Musa grunted and reached for Jacob's computer.

Jacob could only stare, startled. "Uh. You do?"

Musa muttered something under his breath. Val had had several Jewish professors and could recognize a Yiddish curse when she heard one.

Well, thank God we have the country's only Black Hebrew Israelite in the room with us.

Val heard an ugly beeping sound and saw Adil forcing the electronic door lock free of its casing. He crimped a few wires together and hissed as a few sparks danced off the circuit board. The door lock clicked as the bolt fell out of place.

"I'm not staying locked in this room during an emergency," he told her.

She held up her hands. "Hey. You don't have to explain that to me."

Adil put his shoulder against the heavy door and

shoved, pushing it open about a foot. "I've got to organize my men. I'll send a few guards back to cover you."

"Don't worry about us," Val assured him. "We can bar the door and protect ourselves. Your guards can be of more help elsewhere."

"You don't understand," Adil explained grimly. "I'm not sending them to protect *you*. All of our network and security systems run through this room. If anyone in this facility wishes to ensure the success of their escape, this is the first place they will come. If they can take control of everything and destroy the equipment, we'll have very little hope of regaining control of the situation."

"Well...fuck," she muttered, watching Adil retreat down the corridor. The emergency light system had switched on, bathing the white walls in an orange glow that pulsed to the beat of the sirens. It was almost surreal, and all the scene needed now was some heavy dubstep.

Black eye, target on my back, and now sitting duck in a goddamned hot spot. Val watched Jacob and Musa exchange frantic commands in a mush of English and Arabic. Musa threw his hands up in frustration and leaned over to type frantically in the command prompt.

Jacob met Val's stare. "Apparently he's a Jew."

"Is she answering to Hebrew?" Val asked.

"Better than she did to Greek," Musa mumbled.

"Good." Val pointed at Jacob's duffel. "Pinky, I hope you have some extra tricks in your magic bag."

Mustashfaa Lil'amrad Alnafsia
Casablanca, Morocco

Saturday Evening

The evening's stew had gone cold, filling the room with a vaguely unpleasant smell of overused cooking oil and peas from a tin.

In the distance: sirens.

Brahim lay on his cot, his hands folded across his chest in the repose of some old deathless saint on display, some preserved corpse beneath museum glass.

Not Brahim *al*, not Brahim *family name.* He was Brahim, son of Terah, father of Ismael, father of nations, chosen of God, returned to Earth as the Last Prophet. He had come to return all the lost children to the shining path of God. For that, he had been betrayed and unjustly imprisoned by weak men who couldn't understand what courage and fortitude it took to send your beloved followers to wage spiritual warfare in bomb-filled vests.

At least that was what he assured the doctor every time the monthly visit came around and it was time to fill out a new psych evaluation and get a new prescription bottle.

That was the interesting thing about anti-psychotics, he had discovered: they only seemed to *do* anything if you bought your own story.

Three years was a painfully long time to lay in this cell, staring at the same four walls, muttering the same Koran verses forward and backward every few minutes, whether an armed orderly was nearby or not. If those pathetic men weren't watching him, the cameras were. The cameras were always watching.

In the last few months, Brahim had begun to wonder if his darling pen pal, the demon seductress, the uppity bitch, actually *was* a figment of his imagination. But if that was the case, shouldn't the pills have dissolved his dear bene- factor and all the coded messages she had hidden in the margins of those lovely handwritten letters?

The last letter had been a lengthy recounting of some petty neighborhood drama, pure drivel save for the one beautiful, breathtaking phrase hidden in the letters: *stand by*.

In the three years Brahim had spent in the hellhole *Mustashfaa Lil'amrad Alnafsia*, the sirens had only rung for drills and to summon guards to break up the occasional fight between prisoners. But it was the wrong time for a drill, and Brahim heard no distant sounds of fighting. Just the beautiful trill of a bell.

He waited, eyes closed, and listened to the distant wailing go on and on. A few other inmates down the cell block were shouting, demanding silence, demanding answers, but interestingly, no guards or orderlies came to answer questions or beat dissenters into silence.

Brahim smiled. He lifted a shriveled hand and fished beneath the foot of his cot, pulling out a long linen *djellaba*. It was cheap and flimsy, but good enough for street wear.

Moving with a lion's quiet confidence, he stripped out of his prison jumpsuit and donned the tunic. Even if the cameras were working right now, the guards surely had bigger problems.

Brahim slipped back into the baggy prison garb and regarded himself with satisfaction. He'd lost a good deal of weight these last three years, both fat and muscle. That was perfectly fine. A thin man was a holy man, and besides, it helped hide the tunic.

The shouting up and down the hallway grew louder and more insistent as Brahim's unworthy neighbors grew restive, pounding on their cell walls and demanding answers.

Humming softly, he laid back down in his cot and resumed his leisurely repose. Twenty seconds later, the speakers lining this cell block roared to life, echoing the wail of the distant klaxons, loud enough to make the other inmates scream and howl with rage. Beneath all that angry clamor came another sound. He would have missed it if he didn't know to look for it: the electric buzz of the cell locks deactivating, followed by a fatal, dramatic *click*.

Brahim fought to keep his face straight. It was true. His beloved pen pal had been right all along, and had the skills to do what she had promised.

Maybe he *wouldn't* kill her the first time they met face-to-face.

He listened to the music of a dozen fools shouting and beating at the walls of their cages until suddenly, someone put a fist against his cell door and discovered that the locks had been deactivated.

A cry ran up and down the cell block. Anger turned to confusion, then elation. The sound of doors slamming open drowned out the wail of klaxons.

"Return to your cells!"

Ah, there it was. The bray of one frightened, frantic guard screaming into a bullhorn at the end of the cell block. The guards must have managed a manual override of the exterior door and sent in thugs for reinforcement. *"Return to your cells, now! This is your only warning!"*

There came the sound of cheering, of angry men set

free on their captors, of screaming metal—had Michael finally ripped a leg off his cot, as he had been threatening to do for months? Feet and fists thudded into flesh, then the unmistakable *zaaaaap* of cattle prods and taser fire filled the air with the crackling smell of ozone and screams of pain instead of triumph.

The music of battle made a glorious hymn. Brahim listened, analyzing every sound. He heard the thump of bodies falling to the floor as a few prisoners were violently subdued, the slap of feet on cement, and the bellowing of ecstatic, free men rushing past his cell. Some prisoners, cleverer than the first bunch, retreated from the guards and took the secondary exit from the cell block. Silently, Brahim wished them luck.

He trusted that his co-conspirators had resisted the lure of immediate freedom and remained in their cells like him. He had trained them well. They understood the plan.

Angry guards broke into groups. One stayed behind to corral the escaped and subdued prisoners—as if they could do anything, having given up all physical locks and bars in favor of electronic prisons they no longer controlled. Another rallied and ran up the cell block in hot pursuit of the escaping prisoners.

"Brahim!"

His eyes fluttered open and he was genuinely surprised to see Rabban, one of the night guards, standing in front of his cell door. The little guard stared, dumbstruck, at the defunct lock and the crack in the door frame where it hung open and useless.

More than the surprise of the sirens and the uprising,

Rabban seemed shocked to find Brahim still lying patiently in the corner of his cell.

"You stay?" He sounded almost disappointed that his favorite crazy inmate hadn't jumped on the chance for a prison break. No, perhaps that was not disappointment, but suspicion. "You *stay* in your cell? Why?"

Brahim thought quickly and gave Rabban a small, scornful smile. "My hour has not come. A lion does not stampede with wild pigs. God put me in this cell and here I will remain until the appointed time." He lifted one skinny hand and made a dismissive gesture. "Go tend to your pigs, small man, and leave the lions to rest."

Rabban shook his head and lifted his truncheon to follow the beckoning call of his comrades down the hall. "Crazy bastard," Brahim heard him mutter.

"You will thank God," Brahim called after him for good measure. "When the hour comes for the lion to burn the eagle and set our people free, *you will thank God!*"

He could not resist. He sat up in his cot and leaned forward, peering down the hallway to watch Rabban vanish around a corner. In the other direction, more guards argued about how best to subdue prisoners when, to use their own eloquent phrasing, none of the fucking locks worked.

Brahim chuckled and laid back down.

His hour would come.

CHAPTER SIXTEEN

Mustashfaa Lil'amrad Alnafsia
Casablanca, Morocco
Saturday Evening

"How's that Hebrew going?" Val stood behind the server room door with her face plastered to the small bulletproof glass window. She caught occasional glimpses of movement down the hallway as shadowy shapes and clusters darted down cross-halls, but thankfully nobody had yet turned up in the direction of the server room. Val, Jacob, and Musa had received word on the radio: the prisoner cell locks had been deactivated.

Behind her, Musa groaned something in Arabic. The man's skin had turned waxy. For an IT person in a security company, he did not manage pressure all that well.

"Not so hot," Jacob translated. There was no mistaking it now. The edge to his voice was pure steel and fraying nerves, and that worried Val more than anything else. The clack of fingers on keyboards was louder than ever.

When Val had asked Jacob for another trick from the bag, he'd reached in and handed her the sort of Crocodile Dundee knife she had dreaded back in Seville. She had taken it without hesitation and was practicing a quick draw to keep her hands busy.

Adil's guards flanked the door on either side of Val, exchanging nervous glances as they gripped their weapons. One of the men fiddled with his radio.

Down the corridor, a giant shadow of a man in a prison jumpsuit rushed down a cross-hallway, followed by half a dozen fellow escapees. Val ducked and listened for the sound of approaching footsteps as some crazy bastard came to investigate the little blonde woman snooping around his new kingdom.

"There's fighting in the corridors," one of the guards reported. The other muttered something in Arabic. Probably a prayer.

"Pinky, we got any luck on those door locks?" Val risked another glance into the hallway, where the bloody orange emergency lights flickered and swayed. "The velociraptors are gonna be here any damn minute."

Musa cursed again.

"No good," Jacob gritted. "It sure looks like Cleo's speaking in Hebrew, but she's not actually responding to any code."

"What about a direct uplink to HQ?" Val thought back to the job in Al Hoceima. "Can we get support from someone back home?"

"Already trying that. Keep getting booted—"

He was interrupted by the sharp crack of nearby gunfire. Everyone in the server room reflexively ducked.

When her heart resumed beating, Val checked the hallway. No shooter in sight, and another burst of distant gunfire told her that the fighting was happening somewhere far away, maybe outside the prison walls.

One of the guards started speaking rapid Arabic into his radio.

"We've sent a request for reinforcements," the other translated. Val could smell the sweat and fear spilling off him. "They're on their way."

"Let's hope they get here before anyone else," Val muttered.

A blurt of radio feedback, sharp and ear-splitting, was followed by a chorus of staticky screams and shouting.

"What the hell is that now?" Jacob bent over and dug around in his duffel bag again. He pulled out what looked like a submachine gun to Val. The guard next to her saw it too, and his eyes bulged to the size of ping-pong balls.

No idea how you got that past security, Pinky, or why you brought it, but I sure as hell hope we don't need it.

"We just got a message from the facility perimeter," the guard with the radio whispered. "There's fighting out on the streets outside the prison. All guards redirected to protect the facility."

Val was about to ask what the hell he meant, but Jacob was way ahead of her.

"Cleo must be coordinating with an outside strike team," he clarified. "Insurgents moving in from the outside just as the inmates are trying for a prison break. It's a three-pronged attack: virus, inmates, insurgents."

As if to underline his point, they heard another distant but unmistakable round of gunfire, followed by screaming.

"We're not getting those reinforcements, are we?" Val put her knife away. It probably wouldn't do her much good in a gunfight.

The radio squalled with chatter again.

"I can't focus with all that noise!" Musa screamed, gripping his temples in white knuckles.

"The door opens into the hall," Jacob told the guards calmly. "We can't bar it from this side. You need to get out there and keep anyone from getting a line into this room." When they hesitated, his tone turned sharp. "Our best hope for regaining control of the situation is *right here*. We need to focus, and we need you to cover us."

They exchanged glances and nodded. Val pushed the door open for them to dart through and pulled it shut behind them. She glanced through the tiny window and saw both men draw their weapons. Not tasers or batons, but real pistols.

A mass of bodies appeared at the end of the hallway.

"Hey Pinky." Val pulled back and drew her pistol in a smooth motion. She braced herself and trained her eyes on the tiny window into the outside world, where men in prison garb were coming in fast. "Now might be a really good time to wave around the gun you're cuddling there. We've got company coming in fast."

Fast was an understatement. The corridor erupted in screams, and the window showed a flurry of motion and wrestling bodies. She watched, transfixed, as one of the guards lifted his weapon, screaming warnings and commands. Then someone swung a crude metal club, possibly the leg of a prison cot, into his throat.

Blood sprayed across the tiny window, turning it red.

Val moved back, brushing up against Jacob's warm bulk. He stood beside her now, and together they lifted their guns.

The door swung open. A man in a prison uniform stood on the threshold. His shoulders hunched and his face twisted into a mask of terror at the muzzle of the gun pressed to his temple.

The man holding the gun was tall and lean with long salt-and-pepper hair and the beginnings of a downright epic wizard beard. Val only had to look into his eyes for the span of a heartbeat to know this man was the absolute epitome of everything the prison had been built to confine.

The captor pushed his hostage into the server room. Through the door behind them, Val could see a sliver of the hallway. Two more prisoners had taken the guards' guns and used them on the rest of the inmates.

Wolf in sheepskin, was the first thing that came to Val's mind. The inmates might have banded together, thinking they were all of one accord, but these three men had turned on the others. Or, more likely, they had been planning a hostage situation all along.

This is the inmate prong of the attack. Not a wild card of crazies, but coordinated.

"Well." Val licked her lips. Every muscle in her body was wound tighter than a rubber band about to snap, and the awful silence was about the worst thing she had ever heard. "Welcome to the party, boys."

It was all she could think to say. She didn't know if these men understood English.

To her surprise, the mad-eyed man hiding behind his human shield gave the tiniest of nods. "Thank you."

He spoke softly, with a distinct British accent. He prodded his hostage with the pistol's muzzle to force the man forward another step. "I brought some entertainment. I hope you don't mind."

Whatever Val had expected, it wasn't this man running with the improv. She opened her mouth—to say what, she didn't know, and why start thinking too hard about it now? She closed it again when Musa stood from where he'd been hunkered behind a server stack.

He lifted his hands, palms out. His face had gone pallid, his eyes bulging in their sockets. "Please, don't do anything. Please, whatever you want." He babbled and gestured manically toward the computers. "It's yours—"

Calm as spring rain, Jacob turned and punched Musa in the chin. The tall Nigerian collapsed into a pile of bones on the dirty carpet, unconscious. Val and the inmates stared at Jacob, flabbergasted. The ringleader opened his mouth, ready to say or do something undoubtedly nasty, but Jacob was already talking.

"Sorry." He shook out his hand with what might have been a wince. "But he was just going to make things complicated. Let's—"

Nearby, a radio came to life with a blurt of nasty static and feedback. Val made out a babble of mishmashed English and Arabic.

"Server room! This is Adil. Check in. What is your status?"

Silence followed, broken only by the tiny, terrified gasps of the meat-shield captive. Val stared at the ringleader.

"Brahim," one of the armed inmates called from the

hallway. "We're running out of time. We need to destroy those computers."

Brahim, the ringleader, snapped, "Shut up." He only took his eyes off Val for a fraction of a second, but in that instant, she experienced the profound, bone-deep desire to pull the trigger and watch a hole open up in the side of Brahim's head. Her lungs burned, her hands itched, and she became aware of the strangest sensation in her upper back, like her muscles were about to crawl off her skeleton and strangle this motherfucker if she didn't pull the goddamned trigger *right now.*

"You two," Brahim commanded Jacob and Val. "Drop the guns. Get away from the computers."

"Nope," Jacob refused.

I want to make him die. Val's anxiety and anger had looped back upon themselves, becoming cold, righteous fury. *I can do it. I can kill that man right now.*

But could she do it without hurting the hostage?

"Issac," Brahim called behind him.

A gunshot rang out from the hallway, deafeningly loud and close enough to rattle the air. One of the hallway captives fell onto the tiled floor in a pool of blood, dead. The remaining guard screamed.

A crazy little voice spoke in the back of Val's mind. *No. This isn't a job for guns.*

"Surrender or more of them die," Brahim insisted.

Jacob opened his mouth, and somehow Val knew what he was going to say. He was going to tell Brahim and Issac and the other to go thoroughly fuck themselves.

But that wouldn't do anyone any good.

"All right!" Val held out her hands, fingers spread.

Brahim's head snapped around. He stared at her. Beside Val, Jacob went stiff as she turned, slowly, to set her pistol on the desk. "All right," she repeated. "It's your party, after all." She gave Jacob a smile that was half apologetic, half coy. *You better fucking have a moment of telepathic insight*, she thought fiercely.

If he understood her gambit, he hid it well. His face became a blank mask.

"Sorry," she told her partner as she turned to Brahim and his captive. She let her smile crawl up to the corners of her eyes. "But honestly, hon, the inmates have taken over the asylum. It'd be downright *crazy* to get in their way now."

Something flickered at the corner of Jacob's mouth. If Val had a million years to think on it, she could not have decided whether it was a smirk, a scowl, a sneer of disgust, or something else. At this point, it didn't matter. She was all-in.

She swung around to face Brahim. Her sudden movement made him tense and press the muzzle of his gun tighter into his captive's flesh. She gasped a little, holding up her hands to show they were empty as she crept closer to the two men. She could smell the sweat of fear pouring off the captive, and the sour musk of years of confinement and prison food caked up on his skin. "Oh, no, sorry. I didn't mean to scare you. I didn't mean to scare anybody. It's okay. We're all friends here."

"Stay back, whore," Brahim snarled.

Val froze and tried to look genuinely hurt. "Come on. Why you gotta be like that? I put the gun down." She glanced at the hallway, where Brahim's two co-conspirators stood grim-faced, their weapons trained on three inmates who seemed to deeply regret leaving their cells. The guard lay on the tiles between them with a red hole in the center of his forehead.

She looked over her shoulder at Jacob. "You too, Jake. Come on. You're scaring Brahim and his two friends in the hallway. We don't need anybody else getting hurt."

She stared a dagger into Jake's forehead before plastering on the nervous smile and facing Brahim. She felt the seconds drag past like the wail of a distant siren, somehow impossibly slow and inevitable.

More distant gunshots from somewhere at the far end of the facility, or perhaps outside. Another blurt of static from the downed guard's radio.

"Brahim—" one of the lackeys begged nervously.

"Fine!" Jacob snapped, commanding all attention once more. Moving with careful, deliberate motions, he lifted his hands, then reached over to set down his gun. "Guess I've been outvoted." His glare at Val looked genuine. "Fucking turncoat *skank*."

"Don't be jealous," she teased. She glanced back at Brahim in time to see something very interesting, and very welcome.

Brahim's captive had been watching the entire drama unfold through wide, watering eyes, flinching with every loud noise. He was a bundle of strained nerves, in other words.

Watching Jacob relinquish his gun broke the last of the poor man's fraying psyche. He exhaled an almost comical little sigh of relief as he slumped forward and fainted.

Nobody expected this development, least of all Brahim.

He didn't release his arm from around the man's neck quite fast enough, and was pulled by the big man's weight. Brahim stumbled forward, off-balance.

As if there had been some unseen force sitting in the driver's seat of Val's brain, waiting for exactly this moment to stomp on the gas, she surged into motion.

She lunged, flicking the blade from the long sleeve of her tunic and planting it somewhere between Brahim's ribs and his kidneys.

Jacob was waiting for such an opening and drew his side pistol with a speed that would have made John Wayne proud. Val's left eardrum exploded and for the next several seconds, she heard no sound at all, although she *felt* a bullet whiz over her head. She tackled Brahim, wrestling him for control of his gun. She saw one of Brahim's men go down, clasping a bloody graze across his stomach.

The hallway exploded into chaos as the captive inmates decided they'd had enough crazy for one day, and took this opportunity to run for the hills.

Brahim stumbled away from the fainted inmate, clutching the deep gouge in his side. He rounded on Val, his eyes wide and crazy and his beard flecked with spit. His face was red, and his mouth was moving as he cursed her and her mother and every woman back to Eve, but all she heard was the hypersonic whine of budding tinnitus.

He swung at her, bringing his free fist around with a wiry old-man strength you only found in alcoholics and longtime residents of prisons and psych wards. Pain made him clumsy, and she ducked beneath his flying arm, stepping inside his reach, so close she could smell his dank sweat. She heaved and drove her elbow into the side of his face with a satisfying *crack.*

He stumbled and she pivoted to bury her knee in his ribs. Dark smears of his blood appeared across her tunic.

She sensed a big shape moving behind her, and didn't care. She could tell by the heat and the shape that it was only Jacob running for the hallway after Brahim's lackeys. She could hear nothing but that high tinny whine, but every other sense felt like it had been cranked to eleven. Her situational awareness climbed to new heights as she blocked Brahim's pathetic final attempt to grab her.

She snatched his arm in both hands and heaved him over her shoulder in a bodyslam onto the carpet beside the fainted inmate.

Brahim's bloodshot eyes fluttered shut. He did not move again.

The obnoxious whine faded, resolving into distant shouting and radio chatter. Val peered down the hallway. Jacob had disarmed the second lackey and now had both of Brahim's goons at gunpoint. He was facing Val's direction. He didn't see a new group of men appear at the end of the hallway, running in their direction like they had somewhere important to be.

Val lifted her knife and pointed, about to scream a warning to Jacob, when she saw that all these new men wore tactical vests with the security company logo.

She let her shoulder slump.

The reinforcements had arrived.

CHAPTER SEVENTEEN

En route to the airstrip
Casablanca, Morocco
Early Hours, Sunday

Val did not wait for the rear SUV door to slam shut before letting Jacob have a piece of her mind.

"This is bullshit!"

Jacob settled into the seat beside her and buckled his seatbelt. Talid's special forces unit had pulled out the fancy ride for their guests. The SUV still had that new-car smell, and Val could barely sense the hum of the electric motor as the driver pulled them away from the front gates of *Alnafsia*. A screen of fogged plexiglass divided the front and back seats, giving Val and Jacob privacy.

Jacob reached into the small cooler built into the center console and pressed a cold water bottle against his temple. He eyed her blearily. "Aren't you tired?"

"Why would I be tired?" At least two hours had passed since the guards and Moroccan police had regained control of the facility, but she still felt like a squirrel on a sugar high. She checked her phone. "It's only two a.m. local time."

Jacob groaned. "What time is it back home?"

"I don't know." She put her phone away. "I'm not going to do that math right now. Time has lost all sense of meaning. It doesn't matter. It's *time* to go back there and pry that cold dead bug out of the prison network!"

Jacob heaved a sigh. He'd spent the last two hours arguing with the likes of Adil and Musa in a mesh of English and Arabic while Val helped the remaining guards and city police regain control of the prison. Six prisoners and three guards had been killed in the attempted prison break, and there were dozens of casualties on both sides, but at least everyone was accounted for.

Everyone in the system, at least. The insurgents that had attacked the prison facility from the outside had bled away into the night. Local police were conducting a city-wide manhunt as the driver carted Jacob and Val through the darkened streets of Casablanca.

"Cleopatra is *gone*," Jacob told her. "I looked everywhere for her. She deleted herself entirely from the system around the time the city police showed up."

"What did Brahim and his goons want in there, anyway?"

Jacob shook his head. "Best guess? To destroy as much of the network as they could before security could regain control of the facility. Cleo brings the defenses down long enough for her guys on the inside to get the drop on the guards. While everyone's distracted, they get to the server room and fuck the security for good. Half the inmates in that prison would be in the wind right now if they'd had their way."

I should have stabbed Brahim again. The thought came to her calmly, almost like an afterthought. She shook herself to chase the casual bloodlust away. It made her uneasy. "But they couldn't get their half of the job done before the police arrived," she murmured.

"Hey." Jacob poked her. It was meant to be a friendly gesture, but he was tired and unaware of his strength, and she was covered in a mosaic of bruises. She winced, and he winced in sympathy.

"*We* slowed them down," he assured her. "You saw how Musa cracked. He was about to hand them the network on a silver platter."

"The guards said Brahim had been locked up for three years," Val mused. "He must have been planning this a long time."

"Did you get any leads on how?" Jacob asked.

She shook her head. "He's been getting letters from a few family members and pen pals all this time. Prison archives have them all on file, and copies of the letters he sent in reply. Adil thinks there must be some kind of code hidden in them, something security missed."

"They'll figure it out." Jacob leaned back and let his eyes fall shut. "I had a moment to talk to Talid before they bundled us off. He's working with another security team at Viking. Between them, they should be able to figure out how all this happened."

"I don't like it," she protested. "The way he just showed up after the fireworks and bustled us out the door."

"He's not double-crossing us," Jacob replied dryly. "I

checked with the boss. Taggert confirms he wants us back on the plane to Manassas."

That didn't sit right with Val. "Job's not done," she grumbled. "This cyber attack was different. Seville and Al Hoceima were just practice runs for the ransomware phase of the plan. Taking control of a general network is one thing. Taking control of an entire prison's internal security systems is very different. She didn't whip this idea up on the fly. I think breaking someone out of that prison might have been her plan all along." Val let her eyes flutter shut. The battle high was finally starting to fade as she was lulled into a deep lethargy by the monotonous hum of the engine. She was suddenly tired like the dead. "Probably Brahim, but maybe not. We need to look into all of those inmates. Find out how they're connected to Claudia Moreno."

She heard Jacob snort softly. "Sure thing. Right after a quick nap."

Val forced her eyes open. "Fine. I'll stay awake until we reach the airstrip."

"You can *relax*." Jacob pointed at the dark screen separating the front and back of the SUV, indicating the driver. "Amina's clear. Viking's worked with her before."

"I'm just saying. This seems like the point at which a seemingly innocuous bystander turns traitor and drives the pesky agents straight to the bad guy's secret hideout," Val argued. "Or off a cliff."

Jacob closed his eyes and rolled his shoulders. The interior of the SUV was roomy, but he still had to hunch to nap through the hour drive back to the airstrip. "Well, if that happens, you'll have the perfect chance to say, 'I told you so.'"

Viking Inc., Business Division
Manassas, VA
Monday Morning

Five people sat at the long table in the Manassas office conference room. Val and Jacob sat on one side, the jarls on the other. It was early, and the smell of coffee was strong. Staring at those three solemn faces, Val couldn't help but feel like she should have had a damned lawyer at her side.

The interrogation that followed didn't make her feel any less on the defensive. Taggert, Hawker, and Evans grilled each of them, firing off a rapid series of questions like they were reading from a pre-arranged murder mystery script, and Val and Jacob were the prime suspects.

Why did they decide to flag Velasquez and De Leon as suspects in Seville? Why was Val wandering around the building by herself at night? How did they guess that Cleopatra was speaking Greek? Were they sure no uninvolved civilians could connect the two clowns from the *La Empresa* business park to Viking Inc.? Why didn't they immediately switch hotels when they were attacked in Morocco? Why was Val initially reluctant to follow the *Alnafsia* lead? Once they had reached the prison, why didn't they realize right away that the Cleopatra virus had evolved, and why did it take so long to attempt to speak to her in Hebrew?

At several points, Val glanced nervously at Jacob for reassurance or to poke him into fighting back, but he only took the interrogation in stride, answering each question they fired at him with a calmness that might have come from experience, or might have been pure fatigue.

After what felt like an endless gauntlet of questions, the jarls finally fell silent. Taggert noted something on his legal pad, Hawker frowned as he flipped through the Gallagher Solutions file, and Charlie scrolled through something on her phone.

"Can I ask a question now?" Val tried not to sound sarcastic—and she wasn't, honestly. She didn't begrudge the bosses for wanting a full play-by-play of the football game, but for fuck's sake—wasn't anyone interested in how the game actually *ended*?

"Sure," Taggert agreed amiably.

"What about our Cleopatra?" Val inquired. "Claudia Moreno? Talid took over that end—what's the status of the investigation on her?"

The three jarls exchanged glances.

"There isn't one," Hawker disclosed finally.

Val shot upright. "What? You're not following up? We just spent the last week getting shot at and jerked around by this bitch, and—"

Taggert held up a hand for silence. Val was sorely tempted to not give it to him. Somehow, she managed to bite her tongue.

"Talid got us in touch with one of his contacts in Rabat," Taggert explained. "We had a nearby operative meet up with him and ah… perform a wellness check on our *Señora* Moreno. She's a fairly high-profile businesswoman in that corner of the world, Val. Talid couldn't even rustle up a warrant for a raid and arrest."

"So then…" Val held her hands open, helpless, afraid

that Taggert was about to declare their mission, her *first mission*, a total failure for reasons utterly beyond her control.

"Moroccan police conducted an interview with her last night." Hawker glanced down at his phone. "All of her alibis check out. She hasn't left the country at all recently. She hasn't even left the city of Rabat in the last three months."

"How can you confirm a perfect alibi for three whole months that quickly?" Val demanded. "Have there been security cameras with eyes on her every minute of every day for the last three months? It's barely an hour's private plane ride to Seville. If she has access to a private plane, she could have been there and back in the course of one night. Besides! Why are we assuming she ever had to leave Rabat at all? She could have been working Seville and Al Hoceima through a proxy."

"That's all true," Hawker conceded calmly. "But here's the thing. *We've fulfilled our end of the job.* We handled the Seville attack and the Al Hoceima attack, and now we've got all the data we need to build a good protocol to prevent and counter any future attacks. At this point, the criminal nature of the investigation becomes Talid's problem. Not ours."

Val felt like she'd been punched in the gut. "So what? You're saying we drop her as a lead suspect?"

Charlie folded her arms, studying Val closely over the rims of her spectacles. "You're awfully invested in the assignment, Val. It's just business."

"Business my ass. A masked dickhole cornered me in a bathroom and tried to strangle me." Val looked Charlie dead in the eye. "On day one of the assignment. Claudia

Moreno painted a target on our backs and sent criminally insane felons after us. This is *personal*. If I can't be the one to bring this woman down, then I would like to at least see someone else do it. Because I'm warning you: First chance she gets, she'll come after me and Jacob and Viking Inc. for vengeance."

After a moment of contemplative silence, Hawker leaned forward and tapped the table with his fingertips. "We're not naive, Miss Kearie. Just because we're not actively pursuing Moreno doesn't mean we're not doing our research. I assure you, we'll be watching her very closely. If this goes down how I think it will go down, there's a very good chance you'll get your wish."

Val stared at Hawker, trying to read his obscure expression, but the man had a stoic poker face. She was about to ask for more information when Charlie interrupted.

She slapped a new folder on the table with unnecessary force, and Val, Jacob, and Taggert all jumped. "Now that's out of the way, are you ready to hear about the next assignment?"

It took Val a moment to process this abrupt change of subject, but once she did, she sat bolt upright. "I get another assignment?"

"I'll take that as a yes," Charlie stated dryly.

"So I got the job? For good?"

"We're interested in discussing your future at Viking Inc.," Taggert allowed. "For now, the fact that you're jumping for another job while you still have the bruises from the last one is good enough for me."

Charlie spoke as Val reached forward and picked up the new file. "We've been contacted by a pharmaceutical company based out of Waterford, Ireland, about a case of potential industrial espionage. They believe they're on the brink of a major medical breakthrough, but leaks of past products and formulas have them on edge. They want us to conduct an independent investigation to determine the threat level, evaluate their staff for potential motive and means, and analyze their security systems for potential flaws and exploitable weak points."

"What's the breakthrough?" Val asked. Medicine had never been a terribly keen interest of hers—she had no brain for organic chemistry—but if this group thought they had an upcoming breakthrough worth the protection of some hired guns, she wanted to know why.

"Interesting stuff." Hawker settled back into his chair with the self-satisfied air of a nerd about to expound on his favorite topic. "It's a broad-spectrum antidote for nerve agents. Originally intended as a counter to chemical warfare, but it's showing good promise as an antidote for a few classes of naturally-occurring toxins and venoms. The reported effect on neurotoxins is—"

"*Not* pertinent to the assignment," Taggert finished. Hawker looked wounded.

"The company vets their employees and security personnel carefully, and from what I can see of their operations reports, they run a tight ship," Taggert went on. "But *someone* is leaking some lesser industry secrets, and they're worried that top-level staff might be involved."

That would mean a lot of interviews with scientists who would rather be back in the lab. Here she was with a black eye the size of a dinner plate, which was likely to cause some distraction.

Still…

"Waterford," she muttered, reading the location off the top sheet of the report. She typed something into her phone, keenly aware of her employers' amused stares.

"You've…heard of it?" Taggert ventured.

The first Google page loaded, and Val glanced down at the top results of her search. She grinned and slipped the phone back into her pocket. "Sounds fantastic. I'm on it." She collected the folder and turned to Jacob. "When do we leave?"

Jacob sighed and scrubbed his fingers through his hair. "I'm guessing there's another meadery in Waterford?"

Val and Jacob made arrangements to meet at the airstrip Tuesday morning, and Val scurried off into the humid Virginia morning, saying she was late to meet her family for brunch.

"I am reminded of a candle with a wick on both ends," Taggert remarked after the door clicked shut behind her.

"Is it excitement or pure nerves?" Charlie probed, turning a hard stare on Jacob.

"Or off-the-books Adderall?" Hawker put in. His tone suggested it wouldn't be the first time he'd seen agents— especially young ones with something to prove—lean on some chemical assistance to give them a little extra edge.

Jacob shook his head. "If she's popping pills or smoking meth, she's *really* good at keeping it hidden." He stared through the office window, a faraway look on his face. The jarls weren't wrong to wonder where that woman got the energy and reckless courage generally reserved for four-teen-year-old boys experiencing their first hits of natural testosterone. The bruises on his shoulders and the faint but persistent whine of chronic tinnitus in his ear didn't make Jacob Pinkerton feel old. *Val Kearie* made him feel old.

"She's got real teeth." He turned to give the jarls the report they were really waiting for. This job had turned out to be more than the cakewalk anyone had anticipated, but it was still the evaluating assignment for a new recruit. "She's got a decent head for systems analysis."

"We already gathered that much from her résumé," Hawk reminded him impatiently.

"Sure. She's confident and effective in hand-to-hand combat, defaulting to what looks like a combination of discipline jujitsu and good old-fashioned bar fighting. Doesn't like knife fighting, but then nobody with a functioning brain stem likes knife fighting. But she'll wade in when necessary." He remembered her viper strike at Brahim's side in the server room at *Alnafsia*.

"Firearms?" Taggert asked.

"She's clearly familiar," Jacob conceded. "Good etiquette and habits, but also not keen on pointing a gun at another human being and pulling the trigger." He chuckled. "She's perfectly fine pistol whipping someone into a light coma though, so I suppose that shows a degree of innovation."

"What about her attitude?" Charlie wondered. She had been staring at the door since Val had left. Deep concern creased her brow. "She took Cleopatra's taunts very personally."

Jacob guessed that Charlie had a lot riding on Val. She didn't put a lot of candidates forth for consideration, so she was likely more alert to potential red flags in their new recruit.

Jacob shrugged. "It was her first assignment. I think most people take it personally the first time they get shot at. None of us expected the Seville job to turn so hot. I get the sense she even surprised herself with how easily she took it in stride."

"Or she's simply compartmentalized, and the shock will set in shortly," Hawker suggested

"Then I guess it's a good thing we've got a few hours to spare before I head off to Waterford. We'll see if the tea turns bitter."

"The what?" Taggert asked, baffled.

Jacob's ears felt hot. "It's an analogy my grannie used to make. You never really know what kind of tea you have until it's had some time to steep in hot water. Maybe it brings out the strength and good flavor, or maybe the tea turns bitter.

"She looks pretty innocuous, right? A little chatty, almost careless with her words. Kinda like the girl in high school who had good grades, even though she was always a little bit ditzy? But when confronted by danger or aggression, she morphed into...maybe something bigger than herself. Very focused."

He stopped himself short of saying "a little scary." Hawker wouldn't say anything, but Charlie would never let him hear the end of it.

"Elaborate," Taggert prodded.

Jacob sighed. He'd had almost twelve straight hours of sleep since returning from Morocco, but the jet lag was still nagging at him. *I'm only thirty-three. Am I already old?*

"That's the thing." He let his voice fall. All the professional affectation slipped away as he met Taggert's curious stare. "I can't. Back in the Marines I would hear stories about guys who would change in combat, like someone had flipped a switch and turned Clark Kent into Superman.

"I never met anyone like that. I figured it was all wishful thinking. Guys wanted to believe that when the chips were down, they had more to fall back on than training and the same old nerves and guts they always had. They wanted to believe there could be some inner caveman or god of war buried inside, ready to pull their asses out of the fire."

He shook his head, took a long drink of his coffee, and let the silence settle. "I still think it's bullshit," he concluded, setting the cup down with a soft *click*. "But I think it's the kind of bullshit guys come up with after watching people like *her* get into a fight."

"Adrenaline," Hawker suggested.

"Maybe. I don't know. I'd have to see more."

"Do you think she's ops material?" Charlie demanded. This additional unknown clearly made her uneasy. "If not, we need to pull the plug now."

Jacob chewed his lip and wondered if there was any more pie in the fridge. "Yes. Maybe? I'm not sure. But I can say that Val Kearie is far more than she appears to be. If we *can* harness that other side of her, I think she'll surprise us all."

Hawker pointed out, "It's that 'if' we're all afraid of."

CHAPTER EIGHTEEN

Black Sheep Restaurant
Manassas, VA
Late Monday Morning

The Black Sheep was one of Val's favorite places, a cozy, reliable brunch stop sitting on the corner of Main and Forty-Fourth. They'd hosted the monthly Kearie-Pearson brunches since before Mom left. It had good food, great specials, fair prices, and friendly staff who remembered their orders. As Val slid into her customary chair across from Hank and Grams, she realized one terrible thing about it: it had *great* lighting.

"What the *hell* happened to you?" Hank set his coffee mug down with a thunk and gaped at Val.

She flushed and self-consciously brushed her fingers over her bruised eye. Apparently, even the heavy-duty concealer she'd brought out of reserve hadn't been enough to hide this shiner. Especially not from the eagle eyes of protective older brothers.

She was the last of the family to arrive at their corner table, and she avoided Hank's question as the waitress confirmed their usual orders. A cheeseburger with a fried egg and coffee for Hank, a short stack of pancakes with a side of sausage and orange juice for both Dad and Puck, a three-egg and cheese omelet for Val, and corned beef hash with a mimosa for Gram. As was traditional, the waitress requested Grams' ID. Also per tradition, Grams grinned and cursed her out.

Val hoped the ritual would take her family's mind off the bruise, but no luck. As soon as the waitress was out of earshot, everyone stared at her again.

"So I got into a fight with some unfriendly locals," Val dismissed. "Don't worry about it."

Dad and the boys leaned in closer.

She sighed and set her napkin across her lap. "I can't go into the details," she explained quietly. She trusted her family to understand the nature of secrets, but this did not soothe any of the concern on their faces.

"What happened to these unfriendly locals?" Grams probed.

Val smiled. "*They* got into a massacre."

Grams nodded her satisfaction. Hank leaned back with a chuckle that was only a little uncomfortable.

"But never mind all that." Val waved the air between them clean and reached into her messenger bag. She pulled out the bottle of *Sabor Del Cielo* mead and set it on the table with a heavy thunk. A man busing the next table paused to give her the stink-eye, but Val only smiled back. He must have been new. The Kearie-Pearson family brought their own bottles into the Black Sheep on the regular.

"I will never understand your passion for that stuff." Dad sighed as Val pulled the cork and reached for the empty water glasses around the table. "You sure as hell didn't get it from me."

"Because you're a Neanderthal, Dad." Val took Grams' empty glass and poured a slosh. She offered the same sample to her father and brothers, who each took it with grace, if not enthusiasm. "You never could appreciate a good mead."

"Neither do mead drinkers," Dad complained. Still, he lifted the glass and sniffed, then tossed it back. "After the first mug, you're stone-cold drunk!"

Val smiled and kept pouring her own glass. "Lightweight."

"Honey-tasting goat swill," Dad countered with a decisive nod.

Val set down the almost-empty bottle and sipped her drink. She let out a long, delicious sigh and let her eyes roll back. "Oh *god*, that's good."

"I'll have what she's having," Grams quipped into her own drink, making Val chuckle. Her brothers, who still hadn't seen *When Harry Met Sally*, shifted uncomfortably in their seats.

Val sat down her glass. "Now that I'm properly fortified, we can talk about how you boys are going to train me."

"Training?" Puck sat up, instantly alert. "In what?"

"In dirty tricks beyond what I already learned growing up with you two. I realized last week that a lot of my jujitsu training was in form, theory, and technique. Not in, you know…" She punched her open palm. "Actually putting a real human being on the ground so that he *stays* there.

207

"Clean matches are for the competition ring. I want to get comfortable fighting *dirty*." She paused to sip her drink and added, under her breath, "Also some knife fighting."

If she'd hoped this would slip under the radar, she was disappointed. Hank and Puck both froze, their faces going blank. Grams and Dad leaned forward. Dad wore his Serious Helicopter Face, and Grams looked downright *hungry*.

"You think you need this why?" Dad inquired softly.

Val pointed at her black eye. "Because this isn't a good look, and I don't intend to try it out again. I'd rather know the best ways to...uh, neutralize someone when I need them to go down and stay down for a while. I'm not looking to kill anyone—although I suppose you should teach me that too, so I also know what *not* to do."

"That's all fair," Hank interjected. "But Jesus, Val—knife fighting?"

"As a last resort," she promised cheerfully. "Better to have that tool and not need it than to need it and… Well, you know. I have the basics. Stick 'em with the pointy end. I'd like to know the best ways to do it without getting myself gutted."

"Sensible," Gram agreed.

Seeing that Val was serious, Dad and the boys stared at one another and leaned in for a manly huddle while the waitress set plates of food in front of them. Val allowed them their moment as she buttered her toast and asked Grams after her cat.

Puck finally addressed Val. "My CO has me flying all around the hemisphere for the next six months. But you come up to Dad's place when I'm between ops and I'll show you what I know about defensive knife fighting."

"Will do," Val accepted brightly. "I'll likely be doing a bunch of traveling myself, but I'm sure we'll find some time to overlap."

"Hank and I are going to be in town for the foreseeable future," Dad put in. "Evenings and weekends mostly free. You come down home and we'll work with what we have."

"You guys are the best."

"Seriously, though, Val." Hank lowered his voice, forcing Val to lean in close to hear him. "Whatever Viking has you doing, if it involves knife fighting and hand-to-hand, then you need to be careful. *Very* careful. We don't know if those guys will look out for you."

"I know." She let her smile fade. Hank had that distraught look on his face, the one he'd inherited from Mom, the one that made Val feel like she needed to reassure him that she took it seriously. "I have my concerns too, Hank. I'm not going in blind. But a part of me *loved* the job I just did. I owe it to myself to explore that a little more before deciding if it's truly right for me."

Dad groaned and pushed his empty glass toward her. "Maybe I'll have a little more of that mead after all."

On the Viking plane
Manassas, VA
Tuesday Morning

"You sure about this job?" Jacob sat in the seat facing Val, blowing steam from his cup of airplane coffee. She was slightly disappointed to note he had shaved. Through the little round windows of the Gulf IV, the morning sky was light gray. It was early, but at least not *cripplingly* early.

"After the last one?" Val gave a laugh that turned into a yawn. She leaned back, stretching her arms and glancing into the cockpit where the pilot was running through his pre-flight checklist. "This should be easy, right?" She smiled at Jacob. "I figure you guys still owe me that cakewalk we talked about."

"There's always a chance that a job can go hot," Jacob grumbled. He sipped his coffee tentatively and winced. "But usually not *that* hot."

"I'm fine," Val assured him. "My family is from Ireland, and I've never had the chance to visit the motherland. It'll be like going home. Besides." She waggled her phone in her fingers. "MeadFeed loves the place. Can't throw a dead chicken without hitting a meadery."

"You do know we're going on business, don't you?"

"Wake up on the wrong side of the bed, Pinky?"

"We're not tourists," he snapped and took a large gulp of coffee. Judging by the grimace that passed over his face, it was still too hot.

"I'll take that as a yes." She brushed some nonexistent wrinkles from her blouse and picked up her own paper cup. It was blisteringly hot. Someone needed to adjust the thermal settings on the plane's coffee machine.

"I don't get what you Neanderthal types have against it. The drink of the gods dates back thousands of years. Many people believe it even predates beer and wine, so—newsflash—even those hunky warriors of old swigged it. Many people associate the word 'mead' with medieval times and all those upper crust lords and ladies swanning around in their finery, but there is evidence that it was around in China as far back as 7000 BC."

"You sound like a tour guide," Jacob groused.

"I'll take that as a compliment."

He sighed. "It is seven a.m. on a Tuesday morning. Can you drag your focus off your concerning alcohol hobby for a few minutes to review our assignment?"

"Philistine."

Jacob adjusted his seat. This was no commercial airliner, and the chair reclined at least ten inches before hitting the bulkhead behind him. "It's a step up from Neanderthal," he reasoned.

"Nah. It's much worse. Neanderthals were Proto-European cave hobos doing their thing. Philistines, on the other hand, were actively responsible for plunging the Middle East into one of the darkest ages in their history." She tapped her forehead. "It's all about choices, Pinky."

CHAPTER NINETEEN

Offices of Vanguard Pharmaceuticals
Waterford, Ireland
Tuesday Night

Vanguard Pharmaceuticals loomed on the outskirts of
Waterford. It was a classic 1830s stone-and-mortar
country estate, refurbished and re-designed for the
modern world.

A town car passed through the wrought iron front gates
and left Valerie and Jacob on the wide paved steps before
turning in the circle drive and rumbling off again. As its
tail lights vanished down the darkened country road, Val
turned and tilted her head up to peer at the building. It was
almost nine p.m. local time, and most of the windows were
dark save for a small cluster on the east side of the second
floor. If not for the *Vanguard Pharmaceuticals* sign hanging
above the wide double doors, Val might have assumed the
place was an art museum.

Val was about to pull out her phone and call their

contact when the front door swung open. A woman in her early forties leaned out, smiling warmly at them. She wore a long white lab coat, and her auburn hair was pulled into a bun that was somehow both elegant and messy.

"Good evening." She waved them in. "The staff has gone home for the night. Please come in, Mr. Pinkerton. Miss Kearie. I'm Muirne Donnehy."

"The founder's daughter," Val noted. They stepped into a grand entryway that was lit only by a few scattered Tiffany glass lamps that added surprising warmth to the high stone walls.

"That's right." Muirne pulled the door shut behind Jacob. She jiggled the handle, double-checking it was locked, and gestured for the two of them to follow her past the empty receptionist's desk and up the sweeping double-wide staircase. "Lugh and I run the day-to-day operations. Dad's mostly retired, but when this nastiness started with Pharmaguard, he wanted to be involved. Come on up, and we'll go over the basics."

She led them to a set of heavy wooden doors on the second floor and pressed her thumb to the pad on the access panel. The doors swung open on automatic hinges.

Handprints and retinal scans in a manor styled after a medieval castle, Val marveled. *Bio-chem research in the dungeons. What's next, bodyguard knights wearing suits of armor made of nanotech and carrying laser swords? Forget SteamPunk—welcome to Castle CyberPunk.*

Muirne led them down the hallway and into a large wood-paneled office. A fire crackled in the fireplace along the outside wall, where two men cradled glasses of amber liquor in velvet-padded armchairs. The younger of the two men, a fellow in his late forties with flecks of silver in his short auburn hair, rose to greet them. "I'm Lugh. Thank you for flying out here to meet us."

The older gentleman apologized, "I'd stand, but my knees are killing me. The weather must be about to turn."

"No trouble." Val held her hand down to the old man. "Aiden Donnehy, I presume. I'm Val Kearie. This is my partner, Jacob Pinkerton."

Aiden had cold liver-spotted hands, but he gazed up at her with the bright interest of a much younger man. "Kearie. That's an Irish name."

Val smiled. "Guilty. My grandparents were immigrants."

"Can I offer either of you a drink?" Lugh gestured at a set of expensive-looking crystal on the sideboard.

Jacob shook his head and Val gave a truly regretful smile. "Between the jet lag and the job, Mr. Donnehy, I don't think either of us really knows which way is up. I like to save a celebratory drink for a job well done."

Lugh shrugged and drained his last finger of what was likely a good Irish whiskey.

"Make yourselves comfortable." Muirne pulled three more padded chairs from around the office and set them around the little coffee table.

"Don't mind if I do." Jacob set his bag on the floor and reached in for his computer. "I'd like to start by going over some details in our case files. Would you mind giving me an overview of the problem in your own words?"

The air in the room had already been fairly somber, but when the glow of the laptop screen blossomed over Jacob's face, the office grew as quiet as a church before the first hymn at Mass. A log popped in the fireplace.

"We became aware of it eighteen months ago," Lugh finally began. "When a rival company released a stem cell therapy drug while we were in the final testing phase of a near identical product. Pharmaguard pulled the product after a few weeks on the market due to undesirable side effects."

"Did your own product ever go to market?" Val asked.

Lugh shook his head. "Our late-stage testing revealed the exact same side effects that tanked the Pharmaguard product, and we pulled the plug on the project."

"That's why we're sure Pharmaguard stole our research and that it wasn't an unfortunate case of parallel evolution." Muirne's face had turned stony. "They were trying to beat us to market, so they took shortcuts in the last phase of testing. If they'd done their due diligence, as we did, they'd have known the drug would fail."

"Stem-cell therapies are all the rage," Val pointed out. "You had no indication that Pharmaguard was already working on something like this?"

Muirne smiled tightly. "I can show you their patent application if you want. It's publicly available. You'll see how it matches up to our formula. Pharmaguard didn't bother to tweak it for plausible deniability."

Jacob typed something into his computer and nodded. "Fairly clear-cut. What's next?"

Lugh went on, "Eight weeks after we first became aware of the stem cell leak, we got an interesting job application from a man looking for work in clinical research. He'd recently quit Pharmaguard for personal reasons, and he gave us a top-level overview of a few products Pharmaguard was testing at the time."

He held up his hands as if to ward off an expected attack. "Don't worry. I'm very familiar with the laws around trade secrets and non-compete contracts. He didn't tell us anything that could get either him or us into legal trouble."

"But it was enough to make us worry," Muirne added. "We've been working on a specific niche product for quite a while and are in the active trial phases of two different versions of a biochemical weapon prophylactic."

"Would this be the broad-spectrum antidote Hawker told us about?" Val asked.

Muirne shook her head. "It draws on the same body of research, but no. A prophylactic is something you give someone *before* exposure to minimize the effects of exposure. Sort of like a vaccine. Yes, we are also working on an antidote, which is a treatment meant to mitigate the effects of a toxin *after* exposure."

"My grandfather lost sight in both his eyes to mustard gas in the trenches of World War I," Aiden explained. "I started this company when I was young and foolish and believed I was a good enough scientist to restore what had been taken from him. I've dedicated my life to fighting the brutality people call 'chemical warfare.'"

"Amen to that." Jacob tipped an imaginary hat with genuine sincerity.

Val nudged the conversation back on topic. "So you learned that Pharmaguard was working on some chemical warfare prophylactics at the same time you were."

Lugh nodded, looking wistfully into his empty glass.

"How did you learn about it if neither you nor the applicant violated trade secrets and non-compete clauses?"

Lugh cleared his throat. "I'm sure you both know how easy it can be to gather information from what people do or don't say. This industry has terms that allude to things without saying them outright. We coined a few strictly for internal documentation on these projects. We heard enough to know what they're doing."

"I'm very sure those prophylactics were developed from *my* research," Muirne insisted. "The similarities are too obvious. Somehow they keep getting hold of my work, and they're trying to beat us to market with the breakthrough."

"Ripping off three products in such a short period of time," Jacob observed. "That sounds personal."

Val nodded. She hadn't wanted to say anything, but to her it sounded downright *stupid* that one company would be so brazen about stealing trade secrets from another. This seemed like more than cutthroat patent competitions. A personal angle might explain the recklessness.

Aiden gently swirled the centimeter of liquor in his glass. "Connor Gilgan is a greedy man. And reckless, and unethical. But he is far from stupid."

Jacob stared at Aiden over the top of his computer. "I sense a personal story coming."

Aiden nodded and finished his glass, then set it down with a soft *clink*. "I brought Connor into the company in 1972. He was a refugee from the Troubles up north. Brilliant young man but had a real chip on his shoulder. Not that I blamed him. I thought he just needed the right kind of support to grow into himself, and he would settle down.

"I helped him obtain his doctorate, and a few years later, I made him a full partner in Vanguard. He got married and had a family, and I thought all was well until I found out he'd been corresponding with a former CIA contractor by the name of Sarkis Soghanalian."

"Holy shit." The words slipped out of Val like a burp during supper prayer. Muirne and Lugh looked at her, eyebrows arched. She flushed. "I'm sorry. The...uh...the Merchant of Death?"

Aiden nodded. "That's about what I said too when I found out. 'Holy shit, here's my longtime partner Connor, chatting about chemical agents to the man who sold arms to Saddam Hussein.'" He laughed harshly. "He told me he was trying to get a beat on what the bad guys were doing, that he never intended to give those bastards anything, but I..." He shook his head. "I'd had enough. I fired him and dissolved the partnership."

"Why didn't you take what you knew to the police?" Jacob asked. Val glanced at him and didn't hide her worry. She wondered the same thing but didn't see how scratching a fifty-year-old scab could help them.

"Because I wasn't *sure*." Aiden sighed. "If I was sure he intended to deal with those bastards, I would have. But he swore up and down that he was only doing research. I thought I was doing him a favor by not turning him over to the police. I thought he'd take the hint, start fresh, keep his nose clean. Not get involved with anything shady. He was like a little brother to me, and I was trying to protect him."

The old man fell silent for a long time, staring at the dwindling fire with his thin, papery hands folded across his lap.

"Connor didn't see it that way," Aiden concluded. "He felt I'd betrayed him. He had a reputation in the industry for hotheadedness and couldn't find work in the country.

Not work that would keep him and his pretty new wife in the lifestyle they expected, anyway. So he found some investors and formed Pharmaguard. He's been trying to smear my name and undermine my company ever since."

"Ever since their success with a few gene therapy treatments, Pharmaguard has had the budget to outbid us for every new talent that comes onto the market," Lugh offered.

"It's more than that," Muirne insisted. "They've started poaching away our old guard. Whittling down our *existing* talent pool."

"Connor is an old man now." Aiden chuckled dryly. "I've met his son Ethan a few times over the last decade, to my great regret. He may have been a promising boy once, but drugs and avarice have killed whatever chance he might have had at taking over Pharmaguard once his father retires for good."

"I know the type," Val sympathized.

"So I think Connor is looking for a payday." Aiden rubbed his bony knuckles. "He's trying to push up the value of his company before selling it and retiring with a golden parachute."

"And along the way, looking to see if he can line his pockets with the fruit of *my* research," Muirne commented darkly.

Jacob leaned back to roll some kinks out of his shoulders. "So you have a few examples of Pharmaguard *probably* stealing your secrets over a year ago. No proof—" He held up his hands before anyone could object. "—but I'll grant you that the circumstantial evidence is certainly enough to look into."

"We can't afford to lose out again," Lugh divulged. "We run a small operation with very little turnover. Thank God, we've managed to hold on to the same senior leadership team since the leaks first started."

"That means you have good people working for you," Val reassured him. "Unless one of them is, as you suspect, a double agent."

Lugh nodded. "This antidote... It's a breakthrough. It's big for us.. We've got interested buyers within the US and UK armed forces already lined up, when it passes final testing."

"It's about more than possibly losing out on massive contracts," Muirne fumed. "My antidote works against ninety-eight percent of all known chemical warfare compounds. If someone unscrupulous gets hold of the formula, my biggest fear is that they'll turn around and sell it to a monster like Hussein."

"Which will give them a jumpstart on developing new weapons to circumvent the antidote," Val concluded. "Starting a chemical warfare arms race. Fantastic." She met Jacob's eye over his computer screen and mouthed, *"cakewalk."*

"Well, you've effectively underlined the stakes of the job," Jacob told Muirne. "When you put it that way, how could we *not* want to help you keep this operation under lock and key?"

Lugh appeared relieved. "Where do we begin?"

Jacob began to type again. "We start by running some deep background checks on everyone involved. Muirne, if you could get me a list of all personnel, I'll send it along to the intel team and they'll start digging, see if they find dirt on anyone. Conflicts of interest, motives, money problems."

Val reached into her bag for her computer. "I'll begin an initial basic security analysis." Hawker had sent along a shiny new Viking model with the company's proprietary security software already preloaded. Jacob had given her a primer on how to use it on the plane.

"I'll need the specs for the current security systems you're already using, and a description of your organizational structure. The computer will automatically comb our databases for known liabilities." She placed the computer on the table and stood to stretch. "In the meantime, I'd like a tour of your labs. Let's get a feel for the place while it's empty before we start the interviews tomorrow."

White Lion Inn and Tavern
Waterford, Ireland
Tuesday Night

It may have been well past ten p.m. local time, but Val's internal clock insisted it was dinner time. The tavern's dining room was closed for the night, but after some haggling Jacob convinced the cook to throw together a couple of sandwiches they could take up to their rooms.

Like most buildings in this neck of the world, the White Lion Inn and Tavern was built to a scale about twenty percent smaller than what red-blooded Americans like Val and Jacob were accustomed to. Each room had a full-sized bed, an old-fashioned wardrobe, and space for not much else.

Jacob and Val sat cross-legged on his bed, their knees almost touching as they chewed through a couple of BLTs.

"Well, the *hardware* of Muirne's security systems seems all in order." Val thumbed a smear of mayonnaise from the corner of her mouth and checked her notes. "The automated systems require that everyone entering or leaving the active lab areas undergo a complete decontamination procedure that includes a change of clothes and body scan. They're not slipping memory cards or USBs in or out. Project data exists only on a secured network inside that zone."

She tapped the side of her head. "*Assuming* the automated systems have no glitches. Still waiting for the Viking software to tell me if there are any known gaps. *Assuming* one of the employees hasn't found a way past the scanners, either unintentionally or on purpose. Security failures usually stem from software vulnerabilities."

"The human element," Jacob supplied.

"Right. With everybody gone home for the night, I can't speak to how well her staff is adhering to the protocols."

"We'll get a more comprehensive view of their security system and how it stands up to human error in the morning," Jacob agreed.

"What's most interesting to me is how little evidence there is of an active, current leak." Val frowned, remembering the timeline Lugh had laid out for them. "Vanguard invested heavily in new security equipment after the last leaks, over a year ago. Since then, nothing. Unless there's something they're not telling us, I don't see any immediate reason to think project AFI is in danger of being compromised the way the last ones were."

"We may just be dealing with some very cagey clients," Jacob agreed. "It sounds like AFI is the biggest development since those last leaks, and they *really* cannot afford for it to be compromised at this stage." He swallowed the last bite of his sandwich and wiped his hands absently on his jeans.

"They're hyperfocused on Connor Gilgan," Val muttered. She eyed the untouched spear of pickle on Jacob's plate. "You gonna…"

He pushed it toward her. "Should have told them to hold the pickle," he complained. "It got pickle juice all over my chips."

"*Crisps,*" she corrected. "You're not going to eat those, either? How can a guy like you be a picky eater?"

The corners of his mouth tugged down into something approaching a pout. "I'm going to add Ethan Gilgan's name to the list of people for Hawk to sniff out," he decided. "*Aiden* might be sure this is all Connor, but if Pharmaguard is actively spying on Vanguard, I really doubt their team is limited to one seventy-year-old retiree." He started to type.

"Ethan has almost as much on the line as his father," Val agreed. "Put the Donnehy's near the top of the priority list, too."

"Really?" He lifted an eyebrow.

"Yeah. They have better access to the company secrets than anyone else in that organization. If there is an active leak, we need to rule them out first and foremost."

Jacob nodded. "Good thinking. We'll start combing the company server tomorrow. Read through old emails, see if anything raises flags." He noticed her pushing a soggy potato chip around her plate listlessly. "What?"

"Digging through a year of emails fishing for something that may or may not even be there..." She shrugged and ate the last scrap of pickle. "Thrilling."

"Hey. That's the job. It can't all be car chases and gunfights." He finished typing his email and pressed the send button. He settled back onto his pillows. "All right. Until we hear back from Hawker or get access to the Vanguard server, that's all we can do tonight." He opened the drawer of the tiny bedside table. "Did you see a TV remote anywhere?"

Val snapped her computer shut and slipped it into her bag. She glanced at the far wall and the older model television on top of the wardrobe. "Are you sure that thing even *has* a remote?"

Jacob didn't answer.

She collected the empty plates. "I'll take these back downstairs. I noticed the bar was still open. You wanna grab a drink?" As an afterthought, she promised, "Nothing heavy. We're on the clock."

Jacob hung over the edge of his bed, using his cell phone as a flashlight and scanning the floor for a possible television remote. "Yeah, I saw the bar is open," he grunted. "I saw all those fancy heavy bottles right on the center shelf, too."

Val smiled, a little rueful. "You're keeping an eye out for mead for me? That's sweet."

He snorted. "Get some sleep, party girl. I know it's only dinner time our time, but in this job you gotta catch the Z's when you can."

"Yep. Gotta be in top form to read all those emails tomorrow."

"Ah-hah!" He fished a remote out from beneath the bedside table, sat up triumphantly, and punched the power button. Nothing happened. Crestfallen, he turned the remote over to see it was missing batteries. He tossed it aside in despair. "Enjoy your drink," he groused.

"Goodnight, Pinky." *I'll convert you yet,* she thought as she pulled the door shut behind her with a heavy *thud*.

CHAPTER TWENTY

Offices of Vanguard Pharmaceuticals
Waterford, Ireland
Wednesday Morning

Val stared at her computer screen and waited for the words on it to resolve into something sensible. They did not.

"Hit the bar a little hard last night?" Jacob swung into the conference room chair beside Val. He held a large mug of steaming coffee, black and sweet. He sounded annoyingly chipper.

Lugh Donnehy had cleared out a private meeting room for them to work in and instructed his staff to cooperate fully. Aside from the secretary popping in to deliver coffee and take a donut order, the employees had given Val and Jacob a wide berth. Nobody wanted anything to do with this audit if they could help it.

Val sighed and scrubbed her temples. "No. The barkeeper was cleaning up for the night and I didn't have the heart to ask her to dirty another glass."

"Uh-huh." Jacob eyed her over the lip of his mug. She must have looked even worse than she felt.

"It's the jet lag," she insisted. "It's killing me."

"There's a cure for that," Jacob shared amiably. He reached across the table and picked up the pot of coffee Lugh's secretary had brought for them. He poured a mug and pushed it in front of Val. "It's called 'drink your coffee and quit your bitching.'"

Val took the cup with a smile. After the luxury of real Turkish coffee, this brew was a bitter disappointment, but she closed her eyes and chugged her medicine.

"I'm not looking forward to this," she muttered, setting the empty cup aside. At least the words on the screen had started to make sense. She checked the notes Lugh had left for them and logged into the Vanguard network, then into the backup server. "Okay. Time to read some goddamned emails."

From the corner of her eye she saw Jacob reach into his bag and fish out a small USB. He leaned forward and slotted it into the side of Val's computer. A new window prompt appeared on her screen. *Run scanning program?*

"What the hell?"

Jacob grinned. "Chill, Val Kearie." He turned the computer and typed in a few commands.

"What the hell?" Val repeated.

"Hawk put together a little search tool for us and sent it through early this morning. It'll sift through the backup email files using specific keywords and highlight any possible matches."

"So all we need to do is sit and watch it work?" The thought made her cranky.

"You forget to take your Adderall this morning?"

"Even if it's boring, I'd rather have *something* to do than nothing to do."

There was a knock on the door. It was the secretary, pushing a trolley loaded high with brown banker's boxes. "Oh, don't you worry about that." Jacob took the first box off the stack and plopped it on the table between them.

"That program is only looking at emails. We've got plenty of hard copy to go through! These are the disciplinary files. HR was kind enough to pack current and past employees separately, so we hopefully don't need to go through them all."

"Oh. Right." Val grabbed one of the boxes and pulled it closer to her. "*Yaaaaaay.*"

Still, she had to tell herself that it was better than being shot at.

Wasn't it?

The secretary returned with lunch a few hours later, and Jacob paused to nosh on a cold corned beef sandwich while Val jogged a few laps around the building to clear her head. She returned feeling somewhat refreshed, until she saw that Jacob had eaten both rice cereal treats on the lunch platter.

"But I saved the pickles for you." Jacob pointed out.

"How gracious."

They had finished reviewing the disciplinary files for all current employees and found nothing to raise a red flag. A few write-ups for time mismanagement and one official warning for drinking on the job—in his defense, the lab tech insisted, it was his birthday, and he *had* brought the whiskey to share. All in all, Vanguard had reported far fewer disciplinary incidents over the last year than Val would have expected for a company this size.

Hawker's program was still combing the backlog of saved emails, so once Val had finished her sandwich and third cup of unappealing coffee, she reached for the first box of ex-employee files.

"You sure about that?" Jacob watched her doubtfully. "Kind of hard for any of those people to leak out Vanguard secrets if they no longer work here."

Val shrugged. "Unless they still have connections with current employees. Friends. Family. Illicit workplace lovers."

It had been hard to get the brain engine running this morning, but now she was on a roll, and as long as they were stuck here, they might as well be thorough. As she spoke, the idea sprouted and took root in her brain. There was something to it. She knew, without knowing how she knew.

Jacob turned and shuffled through a box of files they'd already cleared. "Hang on," he muttered. His fingers flicked through the rows of manila envelopes. "Hang on, hang *on*…"

He made a triumphant, or maybe just surprised, grunt and pulled a file free of the box.

"Wait here." He pushed out of his chair and left the conference room in a rush of what must have been Old Spice body spray. He returned a moment later and hastily wiped the crumbs of their lunch off the table. "Lugh's on his way down with the HR manager."

"Why?"

Jacob waved her into silence and cleared space at the

table as Lugh Donnehy led in a small, nervous-looking man with a pink nose and an unflattering tonsure. The ID clipped to his pocket protector named him Harold Burke.

"We didn't find much of interest in the current employee files," Jacob told the room, "but Val suggested someone might be connected to a troubled past employee, and it rang a few bells. Since there are a *hell* of a lot of past employees, I thought Mr. Burke here might be able to tell us where to start looking."

Harold adjusted his glasses nervously and looked at Lugh for direction. The eldest Donnehy offspring frowned into the middle distance. The bags under his eyes suggested he hadn't been sleeping well.

"In the past couple of years, have you had any employees leave Vanguard on bad terms?" Val inquired, unsure if she should be directing the question to Lugh or Burke.

"Oh, sure." Burke fiddled with a pen. "Same as any company. Some people fired, some resigning before they can *be* fired, some just aren't a good fit…"

"Eoin McCay was right pissed when we told him to clear out," Lugh mused. "That was what, six months ago?"

"Eight," Burke corrected. "He was a lab tech. Had four write-ups for incorrectly entered data. We tried to put him on a performance improvement plan but he wouldn't have it. Threw a fit. Said it wasn't his fault we hadn't trained him properly. Had to have him escorted out of the building."

"He still have any friends in the organization?"

"He didn't get on well with much of anyone," Burke

admitted. "But he was past flatmates with one of the lads in accounting. That reference was how he got the job."

"McCay…" Jacob shuffled through one of the boxes and pulled out a file. He slapped it on the table. "Who else should we look at?"

"Rory Phillips, one of the lab managers, got a better job offer from some Swedish firm." Burke twirled his pen through his fingers. It was a cheap pen, and as he fiddled with it, Val saw the point starting to unscrew from the casing. "She was upset when we couldn't match the pay. She said she deserved better from us after ten years of good work."

Something about his tone troubled Val. "Did she?"

Burke glanced nervously at Lugh, who sighed. "Probably, but after we lost those projects last year, we had to slash budgets in every department. There simply wasn't enough wiggle room to give Rory what she was asking for. She was well-liked, though. I'm sure she still swaps Christmas cards with more than a few of our people."

Burke released a startled squawk that made him sound a bit like a high-strung chicken. "Doyle!" He sat up straight and shoved his pen into his pocket, where it fell to pieces. "Nancy Doyle. She's still here. Her sister Shauna was a lab tech until about thirteen months ago. Mr. Donnehy fired Shauna when we found out she was selling…" Color swirled in his chubby cheeks and his words dissolved into incoherent mumbles.

"Favors," Lugh clarified dryly.

"Favors?" Val lifted an eyebrow.

"Oh, aye." Lugh straightened his jacket. "Normally, I wouldn't give a damn, what with this being the twenty-first century and all. I don't care what my people are doing on OnlyFans or the Craigslist back page or whatever, as long as it's off the clock and they're not leaking company secrets."

"So what was Nancy doing, exactly?" Jacob pressed.

Lugh gave him a tight, uncomfortable smile. "She broke that first rule. She was doing it on the clock."

"She wasn't just doing it on the *clock*," Burke fretted, eyeing the corners of this little conference room nervously. "She was doing it *on the table*—"

"She was fired for misuse of company resources," Lugh broke in crisply.

There was a moment of contemplative silence. Then Jacob pushed away from the conference table like a terrible thought had occurred to him. "Burke, you don't mean *this* table?"

"We sold *that* table," Lugh assured him. "At auction. And took a loss. The employees insisted. But aye, turns out she'd been having her own sort of conference in this room for quite a while."

"We found boxes of 'supplies' in her desk," Burke elaborated darkly. "Once Shauna was terminated, she wasn't allowed back in the building. I had to ship her *supplies* back to her flat—a*nd* have her sign for them to cover legalities."

Val leaned forward and rested her face in her cupped hands. Next to her, she saw Jacob's shoulders twitch. "How long was this going on for?" He struggled to remain professional.

"About a year, best we can figure," Burke admitted unhappily. "The postage alone was outrageous. Plus I had to explain to the accountant why I was shipping out boxes of dil—"

Val clapped a hand over her mouth.

"Oh, laugh it up," Lugh snapped. "We used this room for informal meetings and staff gatherings. Other than that it stored cleaning supplies. There was no earthly reason we should have had a camera in here."

"Would it have stopped her?" Jacob wondered.

"Absolutely not," Burke maintained.

The dam broke, and Val and Jacob both fell into a fit of giggling, which Burke and Lugh endured with tired patience.

"So how many employees got fired for joining in that, um, naked circus?" Val followed up once she'd finally caught her breath.

"Seven," Burke reported. "I remember it well. It was my first month on the job."

"That's one hell of a probationary period," Val noted.

"It's gotten easier since then," Burke allowed graciously.

"All right." Jacob sighed and turned back to the stack of bankers' boxes. The giggles were gone and it was time to get back to work. "That's seven more files to dig up. What are their names?"

While the four of them combed the boxes, there was another knock on the door and Muirne entered the room. Between the boxes and five people, it was growing quite cozy.

"Mornin' sis," Lugh told her tiredly. "What brings you down to the love dungeon this fine day?"

Muirne skipped past the niceties. "We're there. Final

test analysis came in an hour ago. AFI is ready to move to final trial phases."

Val paused her initial perusal of the McCay file. Muirne's news sounded good, but the look on the scientist's face was stone sober.

"I've told them to re-run one of the tests," Muirne explained. "There was a minor irregularity in one of the results that I could use to justify it."

Lugh set his current box aside and reached for another. "How much time does that buy us?"

"About a day and a half," Muirne replied quietly.

Lugh's shoulders slumped.

"You're trying to delay moving forward with AFI," Val concluded, looking from brother to sister.

Muirne nodded. "Moving AFI out of the lab and into the trial phase means more people know about it. More chances for a secret to slip out. I want to buy us a little more time to be sure we won't lose control of this project, too. Technically we can decide when, but we can't delay too long. You already know why."

"We're on it, Miss Donnehy," Jacob assured her. He picked up a file, checked the name, and tossed it onto the growing stack on the table. "What can you tell us about Nancy Doyle?"

"Nancy?" Muirne sounded surprised. "She does data entry. Sweet lass. Couldn't tell a chromosome from a caterpillar. You don't think she's got anything to do with the leaks, do you?"

"We're not looking at Nancy exactly, Miss Donnehy." Burke's chronic low-level flush deepened.

"We're looking into Shauna," Lugh clarified.

A complex mixture of emotions warred across Muirne's face. Understanding, frustration, disgust, and even some amusement. "Oh. That little trollop. She was up to no good, I'll give you that.

"Nancy had nothing to do with it. Poor girl was so embarrassed by the whole affair. Came crying to me the night we sacked Shauna, so worried I would blame her for her sister. She took out a protection order against Shauna. I don't think the sisters have said a word to each other since all the nastiness went down."

"That's good to hear," Val agreed. "I'd still like to look into the Nancy-Shauna connection. I'm sure it's nothing, but we're not here to leave any stones unturned." She smiled, trying to mollify Muirne, who seemed downright protective of the "sweet lass."

That feeling had returned to Val's gut, the deep and unaccountable sense of *knowing* there was something there beneath the surface.

Muirne sighed and nodded. "I'll send Nancy in for an interview if you like."

"We'd like that," Jacob agreed. "Our initial analysis of your security hardware is complete. Val was correct. You have a very good system in place. That makes it all the more likely that if there *is* a vulnerability, it's going to be human weakness or error. Probably not from within your company, but we'll see."

"Lugh said you'd be combing through the emails. Find anything there?" Muirne asked.

Val glanced at her computer. "That program is still running. We'll let you know if anything turns up."

Lugh checked his phone. "The three of us have a senior

staff meeting in ten minutes." He stood, gesturing for Burke and Muirne to follow him out of the room.

Muirne lingered in the doorway and turned back to Val and Jacob with a thoughtful look. "I'll bring Nancy down for a chat after the meeting. Then I think I could use a stiff drink. Have you ever been down to the Viking Triangle? They've just opened up a new—"

"Meadery," Val finished. "We haven't been. But we'll go. We'd love to go."

Muirne blinked.

"She has this hobby," Jacob explained as Val busied herself in the files to hide her embarrassment.

"A drinking hobby?" Muirne lifted an eyebrow, and her mouth quirked. "How very Irish. It's a date, then. I'm off, but let the secretary know if you need anything else."

"You really think there's something to this?" Jacob questioned Val once the three Vanguard employees had gone. He waved at the pile of flagged files sitting on the table between them.

Val exhaled, relieved he wasn't going to give her shit for the way she had pounced on Muirne. She reached out to see what Harold Burke had written about Nancy Doyle. "Kinda," she replied.

"Got a toe twitch?"

"Huh?"

Jacob snorted softly. "It's Charlie's thing. Any time she gets a strong feeling about something, she says it makes her big toe twitch."

Val smiled. She didn't know Jarl Evans well, but that struck her as apropos. "Sure. I got a toe twitch."

"I've seen a lot of files today," Jacob observed. "None of

them point us back to Connor Gilgan. So far, we have no evidence against him except Aiden's word. I know revenge can be a powerful motivator—very Irish—but there's nothing here." He gestured at the stacks.

"If Connor is actively facilitating corporate espionage against Vanguard, this isn't about revenge."

"It's not?" Jacob lifted an eyebrow. "You think it's all money or ideology, then?"

"A little of each." Val opened up a browser tab on her computer. "Are you familiar with the Brehon laws?"

"Let's…assume I am not."

"Right. It's Irish legal code from back before the English started seriously sniffing around the Isle. It put a lot of emphasis on not only justice but *restitution*." The first Google result gave her a primer on a legal code she hadn't read about in at least three years. She skimmed the page as she spoke.

"When you had a lot of warring clans, you needed very clearly defined laws to make sure that at the end of the day, everyone felt like justice has been served and the people who had been wronged were properly compensated. If Connor truly believes he was wronged when Aiden dissolved their partnership, he may be trying to take what he feels he's entitled to."

"If he was entitled to it, he'd have legal avenues to pursue."

"Ancient laws and modern laws aren't the same," Val asserted. "There were a lot of English laws inserted into the Irish legal system over the last few centuries. If Connor is a nationalist, he might not accept the current legal code. He might think the Brehon laws are more legitimate."

"That's a lot of *if*," Jacob noted doubtfully.

"Sure. But hey. You said that's the job." Val snapped the file shut with a sigh. She needed more coffee. "Even if there's nothing here, it won't hurt to be sure. Muirne had a good point last night. This is *not* the kind of project we'd want leaking out to unscrupulous agents."

"No argument there," Jacob agreed. "If there is still an active leak at Vanguard, the big question now is, *how* would they get any classified data through the security systems?"

"And what extremes they're willing to go to, to do it."

CHAPTER TWENTY-ONE

Viking Triangle
Waterford, Ireland
Wednesday Evening

"I hope we didn't push Nancy into a nervous breakdown or anything." Val glanced at Muirne in the rearview, searching for reassurance. Muirne caught her eye and smiled. The biochemist had swapped her white coat for a silk blouse, jeans, and a pair of knee-high boots that, despite their low heel, could only be described as *sexy*.

"Nancy's always been high-strung," Muirne shared. "She'll be right as rain in the morning, you'll see."

That was good to hear. They'd had a short interview with Nancy before leaving Vanguard, and the woman got only as far as confirming she hadn't spoken to her sister in over a year before tears began to collect at the corners of her eyes. Jacob thought that indicated guilt, but Val thought it was the tragic result of growing up in a sea of emotional abuse, a theory Muirne quietly confirmed.

That was behind them now. Jacob had insisted on driving the two of them out to the Viking Triangle. Val suspected it was so he could have the pleasure of grumbling about how much he hated chaperone duties.

"You don't have to chaperone shit," Val had told him. "I'll drive back."

He shut her down. "You will not. Not until you're cleared for foreign country driving."

The Viking Triangle was a district of Waterford renowned for its signature blend of historical pride and old-world kitsch. Muirne was surprised but pleased when Val asked for the whole tour.

"She's a history nerd," Jacob explained. "We'll be here all night touring museums and getting drunk on mead if she has her way."

Muirne's face split into a grin. "That sounds fantastic! You'll have to come back on the weekend sometime," she told Val. "We'll have a right palooza on the Triangle on a day when I don't have to work the next morning."

"It's a party!" Val agreed, and the two women fist-bumped.

"I'm not gonna be getting back in time to watch the Cardinals game, am I?" Jacob complained as they stood in line for a tour of a longhouse built inside a thirteenth-century friary.

"This is the chance of a lifetime!" Val was aghast.

"Oldest city in Ireland," Muirne claimed with a touch of pride. "Founded by Vikings in 914."

"We'll skip the last museum if you insist." Val relented when she saw the intense ache that spread over Jacob's face. "I'll buy you dinner. Okay?"

Jacob grumbled but nodded. Muirne insisted on paying for the tours. Val agreed on the condition that she be allowed to buy a round of drinks before the night was over.

Then it was their turn to take the virtual tour. Jacob fiddled with his headset in sullen silence, but ten minutes later he was standing in the center of the longhouse replica, swinging a virtual longsword at the virtual Viking tour guide lecturing on the unique carpentry style of the ancient Northmen. Val and Muirne took turns egging him on and hanging off the AI tour guide's every word. By the time the thirty-minute tour was over, Jacob was sweating and breathing hard.

"Where can I buy one of these?" he asked the lady at the ticket counter as he returned his VR headset. "With all of the virtual gear and stuff. Do you guys have a program on Oculus?"

Val and Muirne fell against each other, laughing. Jacob turned pink at the ears. It was an almost endearing flush on such a brick of a man. "What? It's a good workout."

"Not sure the designers meant for the tour to be quite that interactive," Muirne teased.

Jacob pointed at a woman walking past in a cotton skirt and bodice. "Gimme a break. These guys dressed up for the occasion. I saw a guy back there wearing a vest made out of deer skin."

Sunset found them strolling through the cool stone hallways of the Reginald Tower museum. Muirne acted as translator, smugly pointing out all the places where the English and Irish info placards on the artifacts didn't match up. Val lost track of time listening to Muirne's musical recitations. She regretted that she didn't have all the time in the world to learn Irish, Celtic, and a dozen other languages.

Jacob beat them to the last room before the exit, and when they stepped through the arched stone doorway out of the longboat exhibit, they found him sitting on a bench with his arms folded across his chest, staring at a painting hung on the wall. He waved them over.

Val checked the time on her phone with a flush. "Sorry. I totally lost track of time. You ready to get dinner?"

Jacob didn't answer her. He pointed at an empty spot in front of the painting. "Go stand over there."

"Huh?" Val followed his finger. The painting was a large wooden panel at least four feet wide and six feet tall, curling at the edges and faded with age.

It depicted a woman wearing a blood-stained cuirass beneath a flapping crimson cloak. Blonde hair spilled across her shoulders in a torrent. Her feet were planted firmly on a pile of corpses, men slain in battle with their faces twisted into expressions of agony and dismay. She held a spear aloft, the tip pointed directly at the viewer as if to say, *"You're next."*

"That's new," Muirne observed. She wandered to the side of the painting to read the info placard. Val hardly heard her. She stepped forward, unconsciously going where Jacob had pointed.

"'Untitled Painting,'" Muirne recited. *"'Discovered in a storage room in Waterford last year. Artist unknown, likely one of the monks that lived in friary.'"*

Mirror, Val thought. That should have been the painting's title. *Valerie's Mirror.*

She stopped when she reached the velvet rope

protecting the painting. She stared up into the woman's face and had an absurd thought: *She made it through that scuffle without a black eye.*

"'*The female figure wears a style of armor commonly found in Viking clans of the time,*'" Muirne went on. "'*She might represent an actual woman who participated in the tenth-century raids, or she is perhaps a representation of Valkyrie, the old Norse spirit of battle and war.*' Huh." Muirne moved away from the plaque and cocked her head, regarding Val in front of the painting. "Small world, isn't it? Didn't think you'd find a picture of your great-great-gran in Waterford, did you?"

Val bit her tongue, resisting the bizarre temptation to correct the older woman. *That's not some distant ancestor. Can't you see? That's me.*

Nostalgia as profound as despair washed over Val. She wanted to reach up and touch her doppelgänger, take the offered spear, and stride off into that world behind the painting. She wanted to open a door that didn't exist and sink into a world that wasn't real, a world of howling winds and light as sweet as honey. She wanted to grow wings and fly home.

Val looked over her shoulder. Muirne smiled, but Jacob only watched her with that flat, unreadable expression.

"I had my hair that long for a while." Val tried to sound lighthearted, but her mouth had gone dry. "I couldn't imagine taking that mane into battle. It'd get all over the damn place."

Muirne chuckled. "You want me to take a picture? It's not every day some thirteenth-century friar paints you into a masterwork."

"No thanks." Val forced herself to walk away from the painting. The hair on the back of her neck was standing upright. "Come on," she told Jacob in a low voice. "I need to get the fuck out of here."

Offices of Vanguard Pharmaceuticals
Waterford, Ireland
Thursday Morning

"Hey, Lugh!" Val smiled as the elder Donnehy sibling entered the conference room at eight o'clock the following day. "You've got a great little attraction district in Waterford. Muirne says you haven't been back there in years. What—" Her smile vanished as Lugh turned and she got a good look at his face. "What's wrong?"

Lugh was a pale fellow, but this morning his skin was downright waxy, and the bags under his eyes sagged all the way to the corner of his smile lines. He shoved his phone into Val's hands. "I just got this."

Jacob rolled his chair closer to look over Val's shoulder. At first, she wasn't sure what she was looking at. A drab room, badly lit and devoid of furniture. Then she recognized the figure tied to the chair at the center of the screen.

Muirne was barefoot, and her velvet pajamas were wrinkled and bunched oddly at her middle, as if her elbows were bound together behind the back of the chair. Her hair stuck to her face in great sweaty clumps. Her eyes bulged as she stared into the camera with a dazed expression and dilated pupils.

She was gagged with a nylon stocking.

"Jesus Christ," Jacob hissed. "When was this taken?"

"I got the text a few minutes ago." Lugh took his phone back and stared at the screen, his face haunted. "It's from an unknown number. They're demanding the AFI files within forty-eight hours, drop details to follow."

Jacob reached forward and took the phone from Lugh. Lugh looked offended, then relieved, as if Jacob had relieved him of a terrible burden.

"You went down to the Triangle last night," Lugh stated as Jacob scanned the text conversation.

Val's hackles rose. "We dropped Muirne off at her flat before midnight. Jacob waited for her to get inside her door before driving off."

It was the gentlemanly thing to do, ensuring the lone woman wouldn't be locked out of her home. Home, which should have been *safe*.

"God," Val murmured. "They must have snatched her before she laid down to sleep. Look, she's still got a few hairpins in."

"Metadata checks out." Jacob's tone was as cold and flat as stone. "The picture was taken at five-forty-three this morning. It doesn't appear to have been edited. I can send this to HQ. They might be able to pull some details out of the image to help us pinpoint the location."

"Do it. For God's sake, do it. Find my sister." Lugh's voice wavered.

"Who else knows about this?" Val probed as Jacob busied himself at the computer.

Lugh licked his papery lips. "I haven't told anyone else yet. It says not to involve the authorities—God, I can't tell Dad. He'd have a heart attack."

"There's no need to panic," Jacob assured him. "They haven't sent drop details yet. As long as we have what they want, they're not going to hurt Muirne."

"Should I call the police?" Lugh tugged his necktie. "I feel like I'm supposed to call the police. That's what you do when some bastards have stolen your family."

"You have to do what you think is best," Jacob responded evenly. Too evenly, Val thought. As if he'd had this conversation before, and more than once. "At this juncture, I advise against involving the authorities.

"This confirms there's a spy in Vanguard. The kidnappers found out about project AFI somehow. If we can find the leak, we may be able to trace it backward. It could give us a hint about where they're holding your sister. The kidnappers have an idea about AFI, but none of the details. If we involve the authorities, the details might come out before you're ready."

Lugh looked like he'd bitten into something sour. "Muirne would murder me. She'd curse me from beyond the grave. Aye." He nodded. "What...what do we do? What should I do?"

Val and Jacob exchanged thoughtful looks. "We have to figure out how they found out about AFI," Val maintained. "It all comes down to that. They've got a fly on the wall or *something*."

Jacob's mouth opened, but no sound came out right away. "Fuck," he remarked matter-of-factly. He spun and bent over, digging through his duffel bag.

"Uh... Fuck?" Val repeated. She glanced at Lugh, but if there was anything unprofessional about swearing in the workplace, those rules must go out the window once the kidnapping started. "Fuck what now?"

"Fucking *fuck*," Jacob blurted. "Fucking *fuck me* for not *fucking* thinking of it sooner because it's so fucking simple, is what."

He yanked a handheld device from the bag. It reminded Val of a portable bar scanner at a supermarket checkout line, one with an entire keypad embedded into the handle.

Jacob pushed to his feet and bustled out of the room, waving the scanner out ahead of him. Lugh and Val followed him into the hallway.

"What are we doing?" Val hated being as in the dark as the client.

"Hunting flies." Jacob moved down the hallway at a lazy saunter, brandishing his scanner slowly in front of him. "It's a modified wireless signal detector. It should show us every router, phone, Fitbit, Nintendo Switch, computer— every device within range that transmits data via wireless signal."

"You mean we're going on a bug hunt," Val translated.

"Yep. Lugh, I'm going to need you to give us another tour of the building. All of it, top to bottom. Every nook and cranny. We'll leave no toilet seat unturned." His voice dropped into a growl. "Because I'm just about sick of these bastards."

Pharmaguard Laboratories
Connor Gilgan's office
Thursday Morning

"Mr. Gilgan?"

Connor set down his teacup and pressed his fingers into the bridge of his nose. He missed his old secretary. The new boy, Rick, insisted the proper modern term was "administrative assistant." Connor didn't want an *administrative assistant*. He wanted Mauve back. Mauve, and her pencil skirts and her ridiculously long legs. *Hold on a little longer,* he thought. *A few more months and you can retire to an island where the girls wear grass skirts and are perfectly happy being called secretary.*

"I asked not to be disturbed, Rick." Connor tapped the desk phone patiently. "That's what the orange light on the switchboard means."

Rick's head sunk between the padded shoulders of his badly-fitting corduroy jacket. "Yessir, but you also said to notify you when the call came through…"

Connor grunted and made a sharp *shooing* motion. Rick seemed to understand at least that much and made himself scarce.

Connor leaned forward and picked up the blinking red phone line.

"Shauna, darlin'. How's my wee little boy?"

"I got your package, Gilgan." The voice that came through the speaker was screechy and nasal. Connor winced. "You didn't tell me it was a live one."

Connor sighed and picked up his tea. One of these days, someone would have to teach Shauna some manners. He had hoped Ethan would be the one to do that, but for reasons utterly beyond Connor's comprehension, Ethan had a mushy spot for the girl who had conveniently mothered his child.

What the Americans would call a shotgun wedding might have saved some face with the Gilgan extended family and high society in general, but no. Ethan had a taste for wild oats and couldn't be bothered to make the trollop an honest woman. Connor was left keeping his son's mistake in house and home as the man-child trotted the isle, dropping in to play the role of involved father for Christmas and Easter. Connor was left mollifying this brat who was neither friend nor family but simply the kazoo-voiced mother of his only grandson.

"They came without calling ahead, too," Shauna complained. "I had to send Niall's nanny packing when your goons burst through my door waving guns. I wouldn't be surprised if the poor lass refuses to come back, and it's been *so* hard to find someone Niall likes."

God curse the faithless children, Connor prayed. "My package won't cause you any trouble, my dear," he assured Shauna. "My lads will handle our guest for the next day, two at the most. Muirne's a bright woman. She understands the stakes. She won't make any trouble for you. Send the nanny's name to my secretary. We'll make sure she's comfortable coming back to work once this is over."

"What happens after two days?" Shauna's tone turned from fussy to suspicious.

Connor turned his chair to look out over the harbor at Waterford. It was a perfect foggy Irish morning, beautiful and calming. Boats cut silent lines over the moody sea. "Don't you worry about what happens to our guest," he repeated. *"My lads will take care of it."*

"You go ahead and use my home as a halfway house for

your little side deals, Gilgan. God knows why I put up with it—"

Your *home? Without me, you'd be whoring yourself on the street for China White.*

"But you're family, so I look the other way."

How gracious of you, my lady. Connor supposed that if Shauna were forced to guess at the value of the farmhouse she lived in with her son—the house Connor Gilgan had paid for—she'd miss the mark by an entire order of magnitude.

"But whatever you plan on doing with the Donnehys, I want it done *out* of my house. I won't have my son mixed up in your dirty deals. It's bad for his development."

Connor's patience was beginning to wear thin. He would put up with a lot of nonsense for his grandson, but this malarkey about the boy's development was a bridge too far. "Profound" was the word the doctors used when describing Niall's condition. Back in Connor's day, they would have called it "drooling idiocy."

Shauna was already making herself a right thorn in Connor's side, leveraging that boy for her own security and comfort. If she was going to try leveraging him for a say in Connor's business affairs as well, she'd be getting that manners lesson sooner rather than later.

Connor soothed her. "Don't you worry. I've thought of everything, and the deal is almost complete. I've put a lot of effort into this Vanguard project, my dear."

"Thanks to me," she retorted.

"Oh, aye, thanks to you. It's about to pay out very handsomely for all of us, so long as we all keep our heads. Have

I led you wrong yet? Would I let anything happen to my wee boy?"

There was silence on the other end of the line. Connor imagined he heard the gears in Shauna's brain grinding against the rust and opiates she'd been shoving into the cracks for years.

"This better be worth it," Shauna relented finally, with the air of a mafia don handing down an ultimatum to a man late on his protection payments. "If anything happens to my boy, I'll cut your balls off and feed them to that wolfhound of yours."

CHAPTER TWENTY-TWO

Vanguard Pharmaceuticals
Waterford, Ireland
Thursday Early Afternoon

Jacob upended a coffee mug, dumping the contents onto the conference table. Val gaped at the half-dozen dime-sized devices that rattled out of the cup. They were black and round and reminded Val of AirPods without the stems. She picked one up and turned it over in her hand, examining the tiny listening device.

"You've got to be kidding me."

Jacob scrubbed his cheeks. "I wish I was. Lugh's chewing on the walls. He needed to feel useful, so I showed him how to use the scanner and asked him to sweep the place again."

"Do you think he'll find more?"

"Who knows?" Jacob slumped into his chair. "These were bad enough. One each in Lugh and Muirne's office. The other four were spread across the labs."

"The secured lab?"

Jacob nodded.

"How did anyone slip that past the security system? Nobody gets in the secured labs without stripping naked!" Val had gone through the procedure when Muirne gave her a tour that first night. She knew it was thorough.

Jacob stared at her like this was the stupidest question he had ever heard. Val looked down at the device in her hand. It was small. It could easily fit—

"Ew." She dropped the bug and looked around for somewhere to wipe her hands.

"This explains how the kidnappers knew about AFI but don't have any of the juicy details," Jacob suggested. "Unfortunately, it's kind of hard to pump a microphone for information. We still don't have a solid lead, and we still don't have proof this is Gilgan's work."

Thoughts churned slowly in Val's head. "No... It's not proof, but it still fits. And it fits *better*."

"What do you mean?"

"Look." Val pointed Jacob at the timeline she'd compiled while he'd been playing exterminator. "Eighteen months ago, the first leaks started. The Donnehys get confirmation that Pharmaguard is working on projects too similar to theirs to be pure coincidence.

"The leaks continued until early last year when Shauna got fired. Things quieted down. No more evidence of leaked research. Nothing at all until yesterday, a few hours after Muirne announced they're ready to move forward with AFI.

"The people on the other end of these bugs overhear that the Donnehys are really excited about something.

They want a piece of it, so they abduct Muirne right out of her flat." Val's teeth snapped together. "Right out from under our damn noses."

Jacob gave Val a long side-eye. "That's not our fault."

"I know that. I know. It still fucking sucks." She fell quiet for a moment, waiting for her heart rate to return to normal. "Shauna's our leak." Val had never been more certain of anything in her life. "She gave Gilgan the previous projects on a silver platter, and she planted those bugs around Vanguard before she got fired."

Jacob nodded and reached for his computer. "It's a good theory. I'll ask Hawk to run a search for any properties owned by the Gilgans or any known shell companies. Something within an hour's drive of Waterford where they could stash a hostage. I'm betting they didn't take Muirne very far."

Val had been combing keyword search results for nearly three hours when Hawker's program finally coughed up an interesting note on real estate deals. "Here's something. Why would Connor pay half the rental on a farm leased to one Bryan Moore?"

Jacob flipped through a stack of files he had set aside. "Bryan Moore... I saw that name somewhere in the write-up on Pharmaguard. Oh. Yep. Right here." He slapped the file onto the only remaining empty spot on the table and flipped it open. "He's known Connor from childhood. Working for the man as muscle, as far as I can tell. Some kind of valet and bodyguard for Ethan. He retired about a year ago."

"Which fits the time frame, more or less." Val frowned. "But how does it fit with Shauna?"

Jacob eyed her over his computer. "You're really convinced this is about her."

"Yes. Like you were convinced about the terrorists."

"And I was kind of wrong about the terrorists."

Val ignored him. Something in Moore's file caught her eye, and she opened another Google search. "*Abhaile,*" she mouthed. "The farm has a name. It's Irish for *home*. We need information about this place. We also need to have a real talk with Nancy."

"That woman has the constitution of a wet paper towel. She could barely talk to us without falling to bits. She's got nothing."

"Maybe," Val admitted. "According to Muirne and a few others, Nancy and Shauna were pretty chummy before they had their falling out. We need to find out *why* there was a falling out. You don't take out a protection order on your sister because she hurt your feelings." Val hopped onto the Vanguard server and checked the employee schedule.

"The Donnehys won't be happy if we send Nancy into a nervous breakdown," Jacob reminded her.

"The Donnehys won't be happy if they don't get Muirne back. We'll skip the thumbtacks. If Nancy's a halfway decent person, she'll understand and she'll want to help." Val pushed herself away from the table. "Nancy's shift ends in ten minutes. We gotta grab her before she leaves campus. Come on. We're running out of time."

Nancy Doyle was donning her raincoat and chatting with the receptionist when Val and Jacob spilled into the lobby. She must have read their faces because her eyes went wide, and she turned away quickly. "I gotta dash," she called as she made for the door.

"Hang on, Nancy!" Val's shout echoed around the high ceilings and drew the attention of everyone within hearing range. Val flushed, but at least Nancy froze with her hand on the door.

"We only need to ask you a few more questions." Val jogged across the stone floor to catch up. "I'm sorry if we frightened you yesterday. You're not a suspect, I promise. But we need your help. Muirne needs your help."

At the sound of that name, Nancy winced and closed her eyes. She drew in a deep breath and moved away from the door. "All right," she whispered. "For Muirne. Let's talk."

Jacob and Val took her to Lugh's empty office. Val figured Nancy would not take kindly to being cornered in the very room where her sister had been doing the deeds that got her fired. "Like I told you yesterday. I haven't talked to Shauna in months."

"Are you sure?" Val pressed gently. "She hasn't texted you or dropped by for the family Christmas party or anything?"

Anger flashed over Nancy's face, a deep rage that surprised Val. "Certainly not!" the sweet little number-cruncher spat. "I took out a *protection order* on the woman. She can't come within a hundred meters of me.

"The police would take her directly to jail. They'd know. I'd tell them. You may not think so. You may think I'd roll over like I've done my whole life, but I'd tell the police all right."

"A protection order?" Val tried to look surprised. Her eyebrows jumped. "You didn't mention that yesterday."

"Oh, aye," Nancy murmured darkly. She sank into the leather chair, coiling her arms tightly around her as if she were cold—or afraid. She glared into the dead cinders of the fireplace. "I told her she had to quit the needle. I told her it was the needle or it was me. She could have one or the other. Not both." She looked away. "Shauna didn't like that."

"The needle?" Val pressed as she sank into the chair across from Nancy.

"Heroin," Nancy clarified unhappily. "There were other things too, but she was always worst for heroin. Shauna had a hard time in school. Fell in with a bad crowd. She'd go for months, even a few years sober here and there, but always relapse. I got tired of it. I got tired of watching her kill herself and her baby." She gave Val a bitter smile. Val saw a ghost behind her wide blue eyes, the ghost of a frightened little girl. Shauna wouldn't have been the only Doyle sister to have a rough childhood.

Nancy sniffed and wiped her nose with the back of her sleeve. "She said it wasn't my business and that I couldn't turn on my family. Then she broke my nose. I went to the station and applied for my protection order."

"That's really rough," Val sympathized softly. She debated patting Nancy's knee but decided against it. "I'm so sorry."

Nancy shook her head. Val couldn't tell if it was to deny the situation or to reject Val's sympathy.

"You said there was a baby?" Jacob followed up. He was

looming behind Val with his arms folded, clearly uncomfortable with this display of emotion.

"Aye." Nancy gulped. Val reached into her bag and fished
out a tissue, which Nancy took gratefully. "Shauna was
about three months pregnant when Mr. Donnehy found out
about her...side business." A deep flush crept across Nancy's
pale cheeks. "She said she had to do it. She said she needed
the extra money for the baby. But I think she'd have had
plenty of money for the baby if she hadn't been shooting up."

"This is the first we're hearing about Shauna being
pregnant when all that went down," Val commented. "Did
anyone else know?"

Nancy shook her head. She pointed at the water cooler
in the corner. "Could you fetch me a drink, Mr.
Pinkerton?"

When Jacob had shuffled off, Nancy lowered her voice
and leaned in closer. "Shauna didn't have a guy." Her flush
had deepened from secondhand shame. "I'm not even sure
Shauna knew who the father was. She called him *Eamon*. It
means—"

"Wealthy protector," Val supplied. Nancy looked
surprised, so Val confided, "I dated an Irish guy for a while.
His whole family called his dad *Eamon*. It was a sort of
joke... The family was dirt poor."

Nancy nodded. "A few months after I cut contact with
Shauna, I heard through the grapevine that she lost the
baby." With a gracious smile, she reached up and accepted
the little cup of water from Jacob.

"Do you know how she lost the baby?" Val asked.

Nancy shook her head and mumbled something about

drugs and a miscarriage. Val was startled to realize that it was *Jacob* making her so uncomfortable. Because he was a man and Nancy was a good Catholic girl talking about shameful secrets? Or because he was a tall, intimidating, and worst of all, attractive man?

Val changed the subject. "Nancy, any chance you know where Shauna is living these days?"

Nancy winced. "I was on the phone with a cousin last week. He wanted to talk about Shauna. Mentioned something about her moving out to the countryside, but I wasn't having any of it." She nibbled her bottom lip. "Maybe I should have asked more. If you think it would help Miss Donnehy…"

"No, no, that's fine. One last question for you." Val glanced from Jacob to Nancy with an apology written on her face. "Was Shauna working…uh, outside the office, too? Or did she keep this side hustle…" Val made a vague gesture to the building around them. "In the family?"

"Shauna would have taken the Archbishop for a ride if there was a shilling in it for her," Nancy confided darkly. She crossed herself and apologized. "I don't mean that for gossip, God knows…"

Val bit back a chuckle. "No worries. I know what you mean." She stood, offering a hand down to Nancy. "Thank you. You go on home and have yourself a nice bath or something, okay?"

Nancy downed her water and left the room hastily, as if afraid Val would change her mind and call her back.

"So Shauna moved out to the country," Val mused once Nancy had gone.

Jacob checked his phone with a grunt. "There's an

Abhaile Farm a few miles outside of town. We can swing by for a little surveillance." For the first time since they'd started this job, he looked genuinely thoughtful. "Do you think Connor is the father?"

Val shuddered. "That would be quite the age gap. But maybe. Or maybe Ethan. Aiden mentioned he liked to chase skirts. Maybe one of the Gilgans meant to sink hooks into Shauna and use her to pump secrets out of Vanguard. But Shauna couldn't keep her vices in check and lost her position at Vanguard."

"Making her useless to the Gilgans," Jacob pointed out. "They'd have no more reason to keep her around. Which makes her a cold lead."

"Unless..." Val started a slow pace of the room, careful to stay on the stone floor and off the expensive rugs. "Unless they have *other* reasons to keep her around. Like maybe she didn't actually lose the baby. What's a better place to raise a bastard grandson than Abhaile Farm, under the watchful eye of Bryan the Faithful?"

Jacob's thoughtful frown deepened. "It's all very tenuous."

"Talid said it on the Seville job. When enough circumstantial evidence starts to line up, you need to at least look into it." Val paused by the cold fireplace and folded her arms, staring out into the rainy afternoon and the foggy moors. "We need to dig into this," she insisted. "I know it. There's more going on here."

Jacob sighed. "Well, it's the strongest lead we have right now. We'll have to look for ourselves."

"Now?"

He smiled sardonically. "Yeah, that should work. We'll

roll right up to the front door and ask to speak to their hostage." He cracked his knuckles in a way that suggested he wouldn't mind having that conversation. Then better sense took over. "No. Not right now. I don't suppose you brought along an all-black outfit?"

She turned to him, her eyebrows raised high. "Of course not, Pinky. I assumed you always kept a couple of ninja outfits in that bag of yours."

CHAPTER TWENTY-THREE

Suir River Overlook
Waterford, Ireland
Thursday Afternoon

It was late afternoon, and the ever-present mist had pulled back to reveal a rolling landscape that shimmered a thousand different shades of green. Val sat on the hood of their rented Kia, sipping tea from her thermos and staring over the Irish countryside. It was every bit as gorgeous as the tourism commercials promised. She couldn't stop grinning. Her cheeks ached. Then she thought of Muirne, taped to a chair in her pajamas, and her chest ached.

They were parked along a hilly ridge where an ancient stone wall split the landscape—orderly streets and modest suburbs on one side and postcard-perfect Irish hills on the other. Jacob had pulled the car off the road and into the shade of a gnarly old oak tree. He stood beneath the twisted limbs studying the landscape through binoculars.

They had been lounging at this scenic overlook for a

few hours, taking turns watching the old farmhouse and outbuildings about a kilometer to the west.

Jacob consulted his watch. "Looks like they're working in two-hour shifts." Val couldn't remember the last time she'd seen someone wearing a watch, but she had to admit it was a handier way of checking the time than pulling out a phone every few minutes. Maybe she'd buy herself a fancy new Apple watch when she got home. A present to herself for landing the new job. Or better yet, maybe Viking had some proprietary company gear for her.

Jacob went on. "Their shifts are staggered so each man can take a piss and grab a smoke while the others stay at their posts."

"Same three guys?" She ticked them off her fingers. "Herman Munster, Danny DiVito, and Viggo Mortensen?"

Jacob lowered his binoculars and gave her an odd look. Val tossed back the last of her tea. "Herman was strolling around the property perimeter with his border collie. Viggo's going to town on the tractor behind the pole barn. If he's actually changing the oil, he's definitely charging by the hour."

"And Danny DiVito?" Jacob inquired.

"Last I saw, he was having a picnic on the roof. You know, that totally normal and not-at-all weird thing all Irish guys do on a lazy Thursday afternoon."

"Yeah," Jacob confirmed dryly. "He's still there. They're definitely defensive lookouts."

"You tellin' me there's somethin' afoot on Abhaile Farm?" Val tried out a soft Irish accent that made Jacob roll his eyes.

"There *are* a couple of men moving gear between the

outbuildings," he reported. "So I think we have a few standard laborers mixed in with our undercover guards. I'm guessing there are at least six men down there."

"Eyes on Bryan the Faithful?"

"Too hard to tell from this distance. I don't know what he looks like, anyway. If they're holding Muirne down there, he's probably inside with her."

"*If?*" she demanded. "You're not sold on it?"

Jacob sighed and scratched the side of his neck, where stubble was showing. "No, I am. But I want to make one thing clear. You *don't have to come* tonight. This isn't part of your job. You were brought on for analysis and consulting, not..." He made a vague gesture. "Ops."

Val snorted a laugh, as much from amusement as disbelief. "You expect me to sit this out? After Seville and Morocco? After they kidnapped Muirne?" She threw up her hands. "The horse has left the barn, Pinky! I'm in. I'm *all the way* in. Muirne's down there, she needs help, and I'm not gonna let you go it alone."

"I'm kind of a professional at that."

She gave him a hard look. "Sure. I picked up on that much. I'm *not* a professional. But look me in the eye and tell me I'd be more of a hindrance than a help."

When he hesitated, she sprang to her feet and tossed her empty thermos through the open car window. It was time to get moving. "I'm not sitting in a hotel room waiting to hear back from you like some Army wife. Stealing secrets is one thing, but these assholes are stealing *people*. I'm not gonna stand for it. I'm not."

"*Stand for it?*" A deep frown creased his brow. "We're not here to deliver justice, Val Kearie. That's not the job.

The job is to get in, get Muirne, and get out. Fighting and dead bodies tend to attract authorities."

Val struggled to hide the sharp stab of disappointment she felt. She hadn't thought about it in those terms, but now that Jacob had said it so bluntly, it was hard to deny: she did want to fight. She wanted to teach these men that kidnapping had consequences. If a few of them died along the way...

She shrugged and gave Jacob a smile with only a hint of sheepishness. "Who said anything about dead bodies?" She cocked her head. "You know what would be really useful right now? Tranq darts. A few nifty shots of go-to-sleep like they must have used to subdue Muirne. You got any of those in your bag?"

"I told you earlier. You *don't* ask a gentleman what he has in his bag. Come on." He swung the driver's door open and gestured for her to get in the car.

"That's too bad." She plopped into the passenger seat. "Would be nice to send them all to dreamland and leave us free to raid and pillage and rescue the damsel."

Jacob shook his head and threw the car into gear. He bent around her seat, looking out the back window as he backed into the county road. Val got a whiff of complex scents; warm summer breeze, pollen, diesel from the road, the distant stink of cow manure, and Jacob's warm, slightly tangy sweat.

She flushed and sank into her seat as Jacob accelerated onto the highway. *Raid and pillage? Who talks like that?*

LARPers, she thought. LARPers talked like that. She was falling for the fiction.

She blamed it on Viking Inc.

Abhaile Farm
Waterford, Ireland
Late Thursday Night

And yet.

And *yet.*

Val stared down at the latex clown mask, the one with green hair sticking out of its ears, and couldn't help but feel a strange sense of calm confidence that was utterly and absolutely unwarranted.

You are a twenty-something liberal arts major stumbling her way through an eighties action movie. You have never fired a gun at another human being in your life. You have not had one single day of ops training. Sometimes you cry during Hallmark commercials.

A dark shape moved against the night sky and stopped beside her cracked window. "Are you coming?" the red-haired clown whispered.

Val gulped and tugged the clown mask over her head. She caught a glimpse of her reflection in the rearview. Ugly fucker, but she could get used to that.

She was discovering that she could get used to a whole lot, and she could do it fast.

Jacob had parked the Kia behind a ramshackle milking shed a few hundred meters from the front gate of Abhaile Farm. It was the middle of the night, and the country road was a deserted ribbon of pale asphalt rolling over the landscape.

Val and Jacob walked along the ditch to the side of the road, sticking to the long grasses and deep shadows.

From their vantage point earlier that day, they had been

able to peer down into the Abhaile lands and get a good view of the compound. The garden wall surrounding the main farmhouse, seven feet tall and tipped with iron spikes, had appeared much shorter from up in the hills.

"There's got to be a catch, right?" she reasoned nervously as they approached the front gate. A security box with a number pad stood in front of a gate wide enough to permit a car, but the human-sized gate right next to it appeared to operate on an old-fashioned lock and key. "They can't leave their doors open to any asshole with a lockpick."

Jacob pressed his body against the gate and drew two slender metal rods from one of his many vest pockets. "This is a pretty typical security arrangement for houses in the area," he whispered as he jimmied the lock. "Gilgan wouldn't want to invest in a fancy security system. It would draw attention. Make people wonder what he suddenly has to hide."

In the deep shadows beneath the garden wall, Val could barely make out what Jacob was doing. She stared through the fence, watching the scattered lights in and around the farmhouse for any sign of movement. They figured these assholes were stashing Muirne on the second floor, somewhere in the east wing. That was the focal point for most of the light and activity, and they'd want to keep an eye on their payday.

The lock fell open with an alarmingly loud *thunk*. Val froze, holding her breath, but nothing stirred in the darkness.

"That's our cue." Jacob tested the gate, found it was not particularly creaky, and pushed it open. Val slipped past him, keeping her back pressed tight to the garden wall to minimize her profile.

"You remember the plan?" Jacob asked.

"Build a giant dick rocket and start marketing plans to build a techno-utopia on Mars."

"That's very funny. When this goes tits up, I'll tell Aiden Donnehy you took the rescue of his daughter about as seriously as you took our off-the-cuff practice scenarios."

"We go in through the servant's door." Val pointed at the corner of the house. The servant's door was on the west face, and they needed to get to the east wing. But the main entrance was much better lit and probably better guarded. "The route up the back staircase should be the least guarded. We get in quietly, find Muirne, and get out. If things *do* go tits up, you draw as many of the bad guys as you can, and I'll focus on evacuating the hostage."

"I can't believe I'm letting you do this," Jacob groused.

"I don't believe you could *stop* me from doing this."

Jacob turned, and in the moonlight, she saw him eyeing her through the holes of his mask. "I could."

The flat certainty in his tone made Val shiver.

Without another word, they slipped around the outer edge of the yard toward the servant's entrance. An exposed bulb above the door cast a small pool of light across a bare stretch of yard.

Jacob crept to the edge of the shadows and held up a hand, scanning the area for movement. Then he waved Val forward.

Val sprinted across the open space. She was three long strides from the door when it swung open. She skidded to a halt. Her heart thudded in her ears.

The Herman Munster–looking guard shuffled from the farmhouse, an unlit cigarette dangling from his lips. He shoved a doorstop into the threshold to prop it open and glanced up—directly at Val.

He stared.

"Hey!" Val waved and spun her hands in a flourish. "I heard the circus is in town! This is the place, right?"

The cigarette tumbled from Herman's lips as his mouth fell open. He drew in a breath to shout something, but Val would never find out what it was.

Jacob surged out of the hedges beside the house and planted a fist squarely into the back of Herman's skull. Herman's eyes bulged. He swayed for a moment before pitching forward, unconscious. Jacob caught him by the collar and guided him to the ground as Val skipped the last few yards to the house.

Shit shit shit.

A man called a string of Irish from somewhere down the hallway. Judging by his cadence, it was a question, and it was directed at Herman. The asker was coming closer.

That didn't take long.

Jacob, apparently thinking the same thing, sighed heavily. "I'll draw them out and away from the second floor." He pressed his back to the wall beside the cracked door. Val huddled behind him. "You get up the back staircase and go."

The door swung open as the second guard came to check on his smoking buddy. Jacob stunned him with an elbow to the side of the head. Before the guard could fall or shout, Jacob flung his arm around the man's neck and pushed him into the corridor, maneuvering him like a clumsy, stumbling riot shield.

"Quiet, meatbag," he growled into the guard's ear as Val slipped past, darting for the narrow servant's staircase branching out from the corridor. She turned the corner and vanished into narrow darkness. Behind and now below her, puzzled shouts bubbled up from the adjoining rooms.

Too many shouts.

Definitely more than six guys, Val thought grimly as she reached the second-floor landing. The staircase opened into a tiny room lined with shelves, an old servant's bunk converted into storage. The only light came from the wide cracks around the door. Val stumbled over what felt like a vacuum cleaner, and it hit the floor with an unreasonably loud clatter. She wasn't too worried about drawing attention to herself. In the corridor below her, scattered, confused shouts had escalated to alarmed bellows. Meatbag had apparently not stayed quiet, and the party was about to come down on Jacob like a ton of bricks. She hoped he was a good dancer.

Val untangled herself from a power cord, reached the door, and turned the knob. She peered through the narrow crack that appeared. The corridor beyond was warmly lit. A few yards down, the left side opened over the grand entryway. She saw the edge of an old chandelier dangling above the sweeping staircase. Past that was the eastern wing of the house. To get there, Val would have to run past the entryway, exposing herself to the growing riot downstairs.

As she watched, a pair of men wearing nothing but long underwear spilled out of the room at the end of the hall, stuffing pistols into their waistbands as they stumbled down the staircase.

Val prayed that Jacob was hanging on to his meat shield, and that these assholes weren't cold enough to fire on one of their own.

No time to waste. Val pushed the door open and swung into the hallway.

At least, that was the plan. When it was open less than two feet, the door stopped abruptly. There was a startled *oof* from the hallway.

Val grabbed the doorknob and slammed her shoulder into the door. The *oof* turned into a shout of surprise and pain.

Val slammed the door again and knocked her rival clean to the floor in a sprawl of limbs.

She skirted into the hallway and fell to her knees, out of the line of sight of the men below.

Danny DiVito gaped at her like a trout utterly shocked to find itself in a boat instead of a river. He cupped his palm against his cheek, where he was going to have one hell of a bruise. Val sighted a pistol holstered on his hip and snatched it before the little guy could come to his senses. She flipped it in her palm and pointed it down at him. His eyes bulged.

"You stay there," Val hissed.

Danny threw up his hands in a comical spasm of panic, squeezed his eyes shut with a nod, and went still as a corpse.

Good enough.

With a stranger's gun clutched in her fists, Val ducked and ran for the east wing. She was about to pull open the first door in the east wing when it flew open. A man came hurtling out, stumbling to pull his jeans up from around his knees. Val got an unfortunately good look at his hairy ass, then saw that he was also clutching a goddamned pistol. Since when did Europeans start carrying around so many guns?

Stupid question. Probably since they got into kidnapping.

The man was too busy stumbling toward the staircase and trying to put his dick away with one hand to notice Val. She swung her clubbed fists and stunned him with a nasty pistol-whip to the back of the skull. He pitched forward, and Val delivered a roundhouse kick that sent him teetering over the railing before plunging to the entryway below. A short scream ended with a nasty *crunch*. Someone else screamed, reminding Val that her clock was ticking.

She turned down the corridor to continue her search.

A woman in a crown of curlers stood in the first doorway. She wore an open bathrobe that hung to her knees and nothing else.

"Shauna?" Val confirmed.

Shauna folded her arms beneath her breasts and tapped her foot impatiently. "I take it you're here for her?" She nodded at the closed door across the hallway. A key chain dropped from her palm and dangled from the tip of her finger, appearing like magic.

"Oh, don't give me that look." Shauna rolled her eyes. "Raul doesn't keep a good eye on his pockets when he's sneaking a slap and tickle. I was gonna take care of the Donnehy bitch, but since you're already here, you do it."

She leaned forward and tossed the keys across the hall in a lazy underhanded swing. Val snagged them out of the air, still too startled to speak. "I think those are his Ford keys on that ring, too," Shauna added thoughtfully. An evil little smile quirked across her thin lips. "Do a girl a favor and run it into a ditch, would ya?"

Val could see into the room beyond Shauna. Against the far wall, something moved behind the bright white bars of a crib.

"You…have a baby in there?"

Shauna's lazy grin melted into a look of pure spite. "Yeah, and it's none'ya fookin' business. Now get the Donnehy bitch and get out of my house." Shauna grabbed the doorknob. "'Fore I change my fookin' mind."

She slammed the door shut with enough force to blow the fake green hair back from Val's clown mask.

Down below, there was the unmistakable sound of something expensive hitting a stone floor and shattering into a thousand pieces, and then a deep, pained grunting that Val hoped came from Viggo Mortensen, not Jacob Pinkerton.

Val spun to the door Shauna had indicated. An old-fashioned skeleton key on the keychain slotted neatly into the lock. Val pushed open the door to find a room hardly bigger than a closet, with a single window shuttered and covered with newspaper. She'd seen this room before, on Lugh's cell phone screen.

Muirne sat duct-taped to a metal folding chair in the center of the room. A filthy length of old pantyhose doubled as her gag. She looked up, blinking groggily and squinting against the sudden flood of light. Her eyes widened upon seeing the clown in the doorway.

"Shit," Val hissed at the sound of more smashing from below. She rushed to Muirne and fell to her knees, dropping Danny's gun and pulling out her knife. "Shit, shit, *shit*," she muttered while slicing at the duct tape. "Hang on, Muirne. We'll get you out of here."

CHAPTER TWENTY-FOUR

Abhaile Farm
Waterford, Ireland
Late Thursday Night

"They've been shooting me up with something." Muirne spat the filthy, slobbery nylons onto her lap, jerking her arms and legs free as Val sliced at the tape. "Methohexital, I think. It wears off pretty fast. Dummies aren't even using the right drugs. "

No time to ask what the hell methohexital was. Val sliced the last length of duct tape binding Muirne's elbows together behind the chair. "Can you walk?"

Muirne staggered upright. Her knees were trembling, but Val didn't know if it was drugs or the result of having been stuck in an awkward position for hours.

"I think I'll find a way," Muirne rasped dryly. Down below, there was an echoing pop of a gunshot. For half a second, Val's heart stopped beating. She met Muirne's eye and saw that the woman's pupils had contracted to the size of pinheads.

Jacob, Val thought. *Jacob, shout, something, let me know you're okay—*

There was still yelling and screaming down below. Shouts of anger and fear, she thought, but not pain. If Jacob had taken a bullet, surely the fight would suddenly be quieter, not louder. Besides, Val had a job to do.

She took Muirne by the elbow and led the trembling woman back to the hallway. "You stay by me. The plan is we go straight down the main staircase and out the front door while Jacob has everyone else distracted. But you stay by me, understand?"

"Got it, Valkyrie."

Sticking to the walls, Val crept down the hallway. Glass smashed from somewhere deep in the bowels of the house. She peeked over the rail into the first-floor entryway in time to see the Viggo Mortensen lookalike dash across the foyer, following the sound of mayhem coming from the formal dining room out of sight. He was loading a magazine into a handgun, and by the sound of things, Jacob already had his hands full.

Val's heart jumped into her throat. Before she could stop to think, she was charging down the grand staircase. Her prime objective was nearly forgotten beneath the violent need to protect her partner.

Something big and gray flew past Val. A metal folding chair plunged from the upper balcony and smashed into the back of Viggo's head with a sound like a ringing bell. Viggo and the chair dropped to the floor.

Val glanced over her shoulder and saw Muirne leaning

over the balcony with a hard glint in her eye as she rubbed the sore spots on her wrists. "Fuck that chair." Her words were only slightly slurred.

A new figure appeared in the dining room doorway. He was over six feet tall, about half as wide, and wore a maniac grin beneath a tonsure of fiery red hair. Val had her gun in her hands and pointed at the clown before remembering the disguises they had worn tonight.

"We gotta get moving." He was cradling his left shoulder and pointing to the front door, which hung open into the muggy summer night. "Pretty sure that's our Bryan." He nodded at the unconscious Viggo. "I heard him yelling about backup on the phone. If they've got more guys stashed in the cottage over the rise, it won't take them long to get here."

Val took the last five steps at a leap, fumbling in her pockets as she went. "There's a Ford by the pole barn," she revealed. "I've got the key right here. It'll be faster than getting back to the car on foot."

Rather than look a gift horse in the mouth, Jacob snatched the ring and led Val and Muirne into the darkness with his overcoat flapping behind him. Muirne stumbled over the threshold, and Val grabbed her for support.

"Thanks." Muirne sounded more than a little dazed as they limped down the path toward the pole barn. "I think I've still got some methohexital in my system. It's awfully spinny out here, isn't it?"

Something moved in the corner of Val's eye, and she glanced over her shoulder to see a tiny line of lights blossoming in the distant hills.

"Is that the backup you promised?" she called to Jacob.

Jacob reached the little pickup and threw open the driver's door. He turned and reached out to take Muirne by the arms as he ordered Val, "Hop in back." He heaved Muirne into the cab and shoved her over. "Hold on tight."

Val didn't wait to be told twice. As Jacob slammed the door shut and the engine roared to life, she threw herself into the truck bed. She understood instantly why Shauna hated Raul's truck. It was a portable junkyard of unsecured tools, spools of rusty baling wire, and a dozen other things no sensible person would want to dance with in the back of a truck going over a bumpy country road in the middle of the night.

At least I'm up on my tetanus shots!

Val braced herself on the side of the truck as it lurched forward. Another car gate at the back of the property was hanging wide open.

The truck banked into a hard U-turn, throwing Val into the spool of baling wire. She yelped like a kicked dog, more startled than hurt. The back window of the cab slid open, and Muirne leaned out. "Jacob says to hang on tight," she called.

"No shit?"

Val braced herself against the toolbox as Jacob swung the truck out of the backyard and onto the farm road. The unsecured tailgate fell open with a bang, sending a spray of tools and discarded nails across the gravel.

The headlights had grown quite a bit larger. The line of cars, Bryan the Faithful's Faithful Backup, was less than a quarter mile behind them and gaining fast.

The truck roared as they hit a straightaway and Jacob

slammed the gas. Val heard shouting from the cab, but she couldn't make out more than a few scattered words. Most of them were curses and apologies.

They hurled down the farm road. The narrow, unlit, pothole-covered farm road.

Still, somehow, the headlights were growing larger. Val could make out the shadows of the men in the front seats of the lead truck, two burly shadows hunched over the dash like wolves on the prowl. They must have been tearing down the road at sixty miles per hour, at least. Jacob could doubtless get more juice out of the truck, but Val didn't know how well she'd be able to hang on. If they hit a bigger pothole at high speeds, she'd become a skid-mark somewhere a hundred yards off in one of the fields.

Fuck that!

The thought wasn't one of fear or dread but of sheer, howling ferocity. Val crouched in the back of the truck, staring at the pursuers in their growling trucks and thought, *I am not afraid of wolves.*

I have never *been afraid of wolves.*

So come at me, pup.

A beach ball–sized knot of re-purposed baling wire rolled around the truck bed like tumbleweed. She hooked her arm through the tangle, coiled the rusted edge through her fist, and kicked the spool.

Come at me, pup, and die!

The bundle of wire bounced once and went flying into the night, wobbling crazily on its axis as it unwound. It hung in the air, silent and still, for one long moment, then crashed through the windshield of the trailing truck. The truck began to fishtail, spraying screams and broken glass the way water flies off a shaking dog. The line of pursuing vehicles slowed, brought to a bottleneck by the swerving truck.

Val released her grip on the end of the wire and watched it whip against the stars.

"That should buy us a little time!" She swung around and screamed into the cab window. Jacob hollered his agreement.

Through the windshield, Val saw the growing red face of a stop sign. They were approaching the turnoff to the main county road, where the gravel drive terminated in a T.

According to the dash, they were still going fifty kilometers per hour. "Hold on!" Jacob shouted and wrenched the steering wheel.

Val plunged her arms through the window and grabbed Muirne's outstretched arms. The truck tipped on two wheels, sending a spray of truck bed junk flying into the night. For a moment, Val felt weightless, half hanging in the air, anchored to the truck by the uncertain grip of a woman who may or may not still be under the influence of heavy barbiturates.

Time slowed in that weightless moment, and Val saw a dozen optional futures laid out before her. She could let go of Muirne and cover her head, allowing herself to get thrown from the back of the truck. She could hang on tight and break her arms against the window frame as the truck tipped and landed on its side. Muirne could lose her grip and Val would slide out of the back of the truck, falling in a hail of rusty nails and tools and quite possibly breaking every bone in her body. Or she could spread her wings and fly away if only she remembered how.

The moment of eternal weightlessness ended when the truck slammed to the ground, all four wheels rolling over blessedly smooth pavement. Val's forearm hit the frame hard enough to leave a nasty bruise, but not hard enough to break. Val thought she might puke.

"They're not giving up the chase." Jacob sounded unfairly calm as he checked his rearview. "But I think you bought us enough time to split. I'm going to drop you girls off at the rental car. Val, I need you to get Muirne out of here."

"What?" Val tasted blood. Somewhere along the way, she'd bitten a nice gouge in her tongue. Teeth were stupid.

At least the road was smoother now, and they were coming up on the dilapidated shed that hid the rental car. Jacob downshifted to slow instead of using the brakes. "Wait until I've lured the whole convoy past the rental, then turn the other way down the road and get the fuck outta here. Don't turn on the lights or the engine until they're past you, understand?" He dug in his pockets and came up with the rental key.

Val swallowed hard and snatched the key from his fingers. "I never did get that foreign country or defensive driving training you talked about, but sure. Yeah. I can totally drive in a foreign country. In a car with the steering wheel and gear shift on the opposite side. On the wrong side of the road."

"It's easy as fallin' off a log," Muirne called. The truck was still rolling, but she threw open her door and stumbled onto the pavement. "I'll show you!"

"You better book it," Jacob stated, glancing into the mirror again. The line of headlights in the distance was still small, but had it begun to grow again? She thought it had. "You stay on the move until you hear back from me."

Val nodded and swallowed hard. She could think of only one thing to say. "Don't die."

She jumped from the back of the moving truck. Somewhere along the way, her legs had turned to jelly, and it took her longer than she would have liked to find her balance again. She nearly dropped the rental keys but managed to keep her grip as she ducked into the culvert beside Muirne.

There wasn't time to scramble into the car, and Val didn't want to risk the interior lights going on and drawing unwanted attention toward them. On the road, the truck engine roared as Jacob hit the gas. The entire slowdown had cost about twenty seconds, and in that time, the pursuers had done a lot of catching up.

Val and Muirne huddled in the shadows, heads down as they listened to the roar of engines flying past. She tried to imagine what she would do if one of the followers had noticed Jacob's pause and decided to hold back and investigate. She could do nothing but pray that each car and truck would sail past, oblivious to the dark Kia lurking in the shadows behind the old shed and the two exhausted women kneeling in the mud.

Then the roar of engines was fading as they all tore off into the distance.

Val counted to five, and when she didn't hear the growing purr of any more motors, she peered over the side of the ditch. The county road was dark. Almost peaceful. The party had already vanished over a hill.

Val took Muirne by the arm and pulled her toward the Kia. "Let's get out of here before you get into any more trouble."

CHAPTER TWENTY-FIVE

Abhaile Farm
Waterford, Ireland
Late Thursday Night

Val drove randomly along the country roads, keeping her speed well below the posted limits and taking Muirne's coaching like it had been handed down by God. All the while, she told herself over and over again that there was no possible way any passing car belonged to one of the Gilgan henchmen—and even if it did, they had no reason to associate this nondescript little Kia with the madcap escape from Abhaile Farm. Anonymity. They were protected by anonymity.

Yet Val felt not at all anonymous. She felt like a spotlight shone on her and that anyone who glanced her way might suddenly notice that she, Valerie Kearie, contained a hurricane of fury and fire.

It took over twenty minutes for her to relax and believe they were well and truly in the clear and that they wouldn't crest the next hill and come face-to-face with more starving wolves dressed as henchmen.

That freed up mental space for her to worry about Jacob. She kept eyeing her phone, weighing the urge to call him against the danger that she might distract him at some fatal moment.

Muirne had found a first aid kit in the glove box and had cleaned up the bloody cuts on her face and wrists. Val had no idea where she had gotten those.

"We made a right bags of that, eh?" the biochemist asked.

"A what?"

Muirne smiled faintly in the dappled moonlight. "A mess. Though I will say, I'd rather be here than back there tied up in that chair, so thank ye that much." She reached forward and hovered her hand over Val's phone. "Do y'mind? I really ought to get a word out to my brother, and I imagine my phone is still floating in the toilet in my flat. The bastards snatched me right as I was getting out of the shower."

Val hesitated. "Go for it. Keep an ear out if Jacob tries to call in, okay?"

"I'll keep it on speaker." Muirne punched in a number, and Lugh Donnehy picked up on the first ring. He sounded more than a touch wound up.

"Have you found my sister?"

Muirne's lips quirked. "Cool your heels, boyo. I'm a bit bruised, but I'll live. You got Dad there?"

"Thank Christ," Lugh muttered. There was a shuffling sound, and Aiden Donnehy joined the conversation.

"Muirne?" the old man demanded. "Can you believe

Lugh tried to hide the fact you'd been kidnapped from me? Had to pry it out of him with the channel locks. The boy never was a good liar."

"I can't be tying up the line very long," Muirne told her father and brother. "We're waiting to hear back from Mr. Pinkerton. But I wanted to tell you, I've got the patent applications for AFI sitting on my desktop, along with authorization to take the project into final testing. I want you to send those out tonight. This very hour, if you're near a computer."

"Muirne, girl, that can wait till the morning," Aiden protested. "We need to make sure you're safe and sound—"

"I'm perfectly safe now, Dad, don't be an eejit. We've seen how far Gilgan is willing to go to get a finger in our projects. We have to move forward now before that *buail-teoir feola* thinks of some other way to jump on our work."

There was a moment of silence on the other end of the line. "Muirne Donnehy," Aiden chided, sounding both amused and disturbed. "Did you call Connor Gilgan a wanker?"

"I'll do worse than that," Muirne promised. "I'll cuss him out to his face if I ever see him again."

Lugh laughed. Even Aiden let out a dry chuckle. "I haven't had to soap out your mouth since you were a wee girl."

Muirne smiled. "Right, Dad. Where do you think I learned to curse?"

The phone vibrated, and Val saw Jacob on call waiting. She nearly melted with relief.

"I gotta go," Muirne told her family. "There's another call to take. Will find you soon and tell you everything."

She made a kissing sound and cut the call before her family could object. She threw the phone into Val's outstretched hands.

"Jacob!" Val cried.

The voice on the other end of the line was a little breathless, but strong and clear. "I'm not sure whose truck that was, but I hope they had good insurance. They're going to want their suspension looked at." He paused. "And probably both axles replaced."

Val bit back a hysterical laugh. "What did you do?"

"I drove it off a bridge. A small one, though. Into a creek. Really a stream. Good news is I lost the bastards."

"That is good news." Val drew a deep breath and pulled the car to the side of the road. "Tell me where you are and I'll come pick you up. Then we gotta get Muirne back to her family."

Vanguard offices
Waterford, Ireland
Early Hours Friday

Val's internal clock had given up and died. She sat in the foyer outside of the high-security lab on the first floor of Vanguard Pharmaceuticals, watching the first inkling of pre-dawn light set fire to the mist outside the narrow window. Jacob sat at a desk nearby, quietly working on his computer and drinking from a mug that was half coffee, half sugar.

"I sent out a company-wide alert." Lugh Donnehy swung his leg over a stool beside a workbench and spun to face Jacob and Val. The man's eyes still carried huge bags, and his shoulders hunched with fatigue and burnout, but a hint of satisfaction laced his tone. "I told them there was a minor fire in one of the labs last night and we're suspending operations for the first half of the day while the department cleans up the mess. We won't be disturbed."

Val glanced at the airlock door, which hid the decontamination chamber, which hid the high-security lab. "Is Muirne okay alone in there?"

"According to her blood oxygen level and her heart rate, yes. She insists she's fine." Lugh shook his head, marveling. "She never knew when to quit."

"We're not sure what drugs are in her system—"

"The lass knows her business." Aiden strode into the room, cradling a smartphone in one hand and a polished mahogany walking cane in the other. He waved the screen at them, showing a live video feed from within the high-security lab. "I've got eyes on her."

He settled into the chair directly beside Val. "I did call Doctor Beckett," he added. "He's going to make a house call here in about an hour. Muirne should have wrapped up her business with AFI by then, and she'll get a medical checkup, like it or not. But she's right. We want to get the AFI registration and patents out *now*."

Lugh rubbed his eyes with the palms of his hands. "We knew the announcement of our product was going to be exciting. Just not this exciting."

"Aye. I never should have underestimated Connor Gilgan," Aiden maintained bitterly.

"You had a better bead on the man than we did." Jacob looked up from his report for the first time. "You and Val," he amended with a glance to his partner. "I should have taken your intuitions more seriously. We might have been able to protect Muirne better."

"All's well," Aiden assured him. "I'm impressed with your work."

Jacob grunted and returned to his screen.

All's well. The words sat uneasily in Val's brain. She felt hollow and jittery and off-balance. Every time her thoughts strayed back to Abhaile Farm, the doors of memory snapped firmly shut. She was too tired to think about that. She wasn't ready to think about the things she had done and how they had made her feel. So she shut the door. Maybe it was her absolute exhaustion, but it seemed there was a picture on that door. A painting of a woman in red. A woman holding a spear.

The post-interview yips were getting to her head.

"Val?"

Val jumped and looked up at Lugh. The Donnehy brother was watching her curiously. "You said that Shauna *gave* you the keys to that pickup truck?"

"Yes. I think she didn't have much faith in Gilgan's men." She chewed her lip thoughtfully. "I hope Connor doesn't realize she helped us. If they're willing to kidnap and drug and threaten Muirne, I can't imagine how nasty they might get with a woman like Shauna." *A woman nobody might miss,* she thought, suddenly sad.

Not that she had *too* much sympathy for the woman who had beat her little sister all the way to the police station. Still, Muirne had called Shauna bright—and Val wondered how much more Shauna could be if she were allowed to be more than Connor Gilgan's dirty secret.

"If the Gilgans turn her out, I'm sure we'll hear about it from Nancy," Lugh suggested—a little naively, in Val's opinion.

The airlock door gave off a pneumatic hiss as it swung open. Muirne strode from the chamber, tugging the hem of her scrubs back into place after the full-body scan. She looked around at the assembly, her face drawn and tired, but her satisfaction unmistakable.

"All done, my dear?" Aiden asked.

"All of it." Muirne nodded. "Patents filed and confirmed, final formulas compiled and secured. Human trials begin early next week. Normally I hate filing patents before a formula is fully vetted, but..." She crossed her fingers. "I've got a good feeling about this one."

"Aye, the project's been blessed from the start," Lugh agreed dryly. "Nothing but rainbows and lucky charms from the beginning."

Muirne only gave her brother a tired smile. Then she turned to the Americans. "Ya really saved our bacon tonight."

Jacob had apparently finished his initial report. He closed his laptop and slipped it into his bag. "That's the job, Miss Donnehy."

"I'm going to arrange a continued relationship between Viking Inc. and Vanguard," Lugh promised. "To keep our security protocols up to date. Can't have this happening again. Don't get me wrong, I thank God you were here, but hopefully, we never need to see you mad Yanks in the flesh again."

Jacob chuckled. "No offense taken. In fact, I'd be much

obliged if you never mentioned we were here. We like to keep a low profile."

Muirne put her hand to her chest. "Cross my heart. Couple'a mad clowns broke me out of the farmhouse. No idea who. Never saw their faces." She winked.

Jacob's phone vibrated, and he glanced down to read a message. "Plane's fueled and ready for wheels up," he told Val as he pushed to his feet. "Let's go home. I don't know about you, but I'm ready for the weekend."

CHAPTER TWENTY-SIX

Viking Inc., Business Division
Manassas, VA
Friday Morning

The clock said eleven a.m. Val wasn't surprised to see the jarls ready to meet when she and Jacob walked in.

"Oh, we've been sitting on the edge of our seats," Charlie assured her, sliding into a chair across the conference table from Val and Jacob. It was the same chair she had sat in for the Seville debriefing. Val couldn't help but feel her mental shields going up as she braced herself for another barrage of questions. She had tried to catch a few hours of sleep on the plane, but between an unusually high level of turbulence, jetlag, the adrenaline drain, and wonky caffeine levels, she may as well not have bothered. Jacob had slept like a baby, the smug bastard.

"Well, not all of us," Charlie amended with a sly look at her boss, who was sitting in the chair beside her. She lowered her voice as if sharing a secret. "Taggert had a few other things going."

"Making arrangements for my weekly pub trivia tournament," Taggert elaborated. "I needed to call in an alternate."

"Start with the email," Charlie told Hawk.

Hawker tapped the interface of his tablet computer and passed it across the table to Jacob. Val leaned over his shoulder to see a snapshot of a thick manila envelope. It was bulging and tattered at the edges. "Muirne Donnehy" was scrawled on the front in big sloppy letters. There was no return address.

"We got a message from Lugh Donnehy about an hour ago," Hawk reported. "Someone dropped this folder in the Vanguard mailbox."

Val's heart sank. After a week like this, she was inclined to believe that nothing good ever came in unmarked envelopes. Then Jacob swiped to the following picture, and Val's worry turned to confusion. A stack of documents sat beside the deflated envelope, bound together with an old rubber band. The top document appeared to be a photocopy of some kind of tax form, but Val couldn't make out any details because there was a small handwritten note at the top of the stack. She squinted, reading the sloppy handwriting.

Donnehy,

I'm tired of Gilgan's dirty dealings. He's a real wanker. Here's some proof. Tax documents and the like. Connor's planted bugs in your labs. Maybe you or the police will find it interesting. I don't know. I don't care. I'm taking my boy and *we're leaving. Don't look for us. Don't contact us. My lad won't last long but we're gonna enjoy the time we have in a place where it doesn't rain so much.*

Sorry about the mess.

-SD

Val let out a slow breath and took the tablet from Jacob's hands. She stared at the sloppy letters, but all she could see was a fat baby arm reaching up through the thin bars of a crib, and Shauna's thick lips pressed into a sneer of tired disdain. *It's non'ya fookin business.*

"SD," Jacob noted. "Shauna Doyle. Looks like she'd had enough of Gilgan's bullshit." He nudged Val gently, startling her out of her fugue. "You were right."

Val smiled, but there was no joy in it. She handed the tablet back to Hawker. "The woman's a hot mess. Here's to hoping she manages to clean up."

She ignored the look of deep skepticism that spread over Hawker's face.

"It'll take a little time to go through this document dump, but I'll advise the Donnehys on how to proceed once we've got a sense of what it contains," he concluded. "Lugh is very keen on a continued partnership with Viking Inc."

Jacob snorted. "Getting family kidnapped by industry rivals will make most people come running for some good-old-fashioned protection."

Together, Jacob and Val walked the jarls through the events of the last few days. Charlie and Hawker each made notes to fill out Jacob's preliminary report, but Taggert only watched them with a steady gaze and his hands folded in front of him. The jarls asked questions, but the debriefing was far from the knuckle-biting gauntlet Val had experienced after the Seville mission. She had a suspicion that the jarls had made her first debriefing difficult for the same reason colleges front-loaded the toughest courses on STEM majors: to weed out the weaklings.

Or maybe they were ready for the weekend, and she was being paranoid.

"So what now?" she asked once she'd finished telling her half of the story.

"Now?" Taggert pushed back from the table and checked his watch. "Now I go take care of some things. We're handing the Vanguard case off to an IT team. They'll handle it from here. You two did well and established a good working relationship with the client. I say you take the rest of today to go home and get some sleep."

Val about melted with relief. The caffeine had drained out of her system, and she felt she could sleep for a month straight—after getting a hot meal. And a bath.

"Keep your phones on." Taggert took his sports jacket from the hook by the wall and tossed it over his shoulder. "We'll let you know when we've got another assignment or if we need any follow-up on the Global Ventures or Vanguard cases." He tugged a fedora over his head, and in her fatigued state, Val almost giggled. He looked like a private eye that had walked right off the cover of a paperback novel from the fifties. With a wave and a nod, Jasper Taggert was out the door and gone.

Charlie and Hawk packed up their computers.

"What about Cleopatra?" Val asked abruptly.

"Cleo?" Charlie looked up, the corners of her mouth

tugging into a thoughtful frown. "She's still living in your head rent-free, huh?"

"I got a toe twitch." Charlie's eyebrows jumped, but Val was too exhausted to explain why she'd borrowed the saying. Or do much of anything else. "She'll be back," Val promised. "Someone like that... They don't just drop off the radar."

"I'm keeping an eye out for her," Hawker confirmed. Val was gratified to see the sobriety on his sharp face. She believed him. "I think you're right," the jarl went on. "She'll pop up again. I'll call you when she does."

"Thank you." Val pushed herself up from the table. Her head weighed a million pounds. "It's only a matter of time before the Egyptian bitch rears her warlike head."

Jacob was halfway to his BMW when Charlie Evans fell into step beside him. It was all he could do not to jump in surprise. He was a damned good observer if he said so himself, but Evans had a knack for knowing everyone's blind spot.

"How'd it go?" she pressed. Her voice was low and husky, far from the chipper tone she kept in the office under the bright fluorescent lights. The eccentric glasses and cheeky grin disguised a hunter.

Jacob reached his car and turned, leaning on the door as he studied his superior by the warm light of the overhead street lamp. "You mean, how did *she* go?"

Charlie only smiled, showing more teeth than cheek.

Jacob tilted his head up and squinted at the stars, barely visible through the haze of lamplight. "She's bright," he answered finally. "But even a blind idiot could see by now that Viking Inc. isn't exactly a standard consulting business."

"She's on to us?" Charlie feigned surprise.

"She wants in, Charlie. I haven't told her anything. She hasn't asked any hard questions yet, thank God, but I can tell you already, *she wants in*. She *wanted* to go in and retrieve Muirne.

"She was ready to fight me over it, I think. Sure as shit was ready to fight a bunch of Irish thugs. Didn't make a lot of the anxious mistakes I've seen newbies make. She's not going to accept the company line much longer, and I don't want to have to lie to her."

Jacob folded his thick arms and gave Charlie his hardest stare, but it did no good. It never had. Jacob suspected Charlie Evans had been dropped on the head as a baby, and it had damaged precisely one part of her brain: the part that felt social pressure.

Charlie shrugged. "She can ask all she wants. She'll have to wait a little longer for any answers. It doesn't matter if she's James Bond reincarnated. Taggert isn't going to invite *anyone* to the back room after only a week of tryouts."

"You agree with that?"

"I do. We need to know more about her, first."

"Like what? She's already undergone plenty of character tests this week. Her instincts are good. Crude, but good."

"You're a good judge of character, Jake." Charlie patted his arm, making him shift his weight uncomfortably. He knew he was good. He didn't need her reassurances.

"It's why we trust you with jobs like this," she explained. "Your recommendation means a lot, but there are a few things we don't know yet because *you* don't know them, because you *can't* know them. Val's been shot at this week. That can change people."

"You think she'll crack."

Charlie shrugged again. "I'm not betting either way. Hawk's going to keep tabs on her for the next few days. To make sure she's okay. Not suffering from any PTSD or anything like that."

Jacob snorted softly. "Or from cold feet." *Or worse yet, loose lips,* he thought but did not say.

Charlie had a fair point, he had to admit. Viking dealt in many secrets. It would be wise to see how well Val Kearie held her tongue before sharing them with her.

Charlie nodded, showing no hint of shame. "It may be undignified, but yes. For what it's worth, I'm rooting for her."

Jacob snorted. "Of course you are. *You* nominated her."

Charlie's eyes widened in a look of mock dismay. "How dare you suggest I enjoy being right?"

Jacob pulled open the front door of his car. He'd have to insist on parking in the private garage next time. In the measly hour he'd been in the office, Veronica had collected half a dozen spots of bird shit. "Let's hope Val doesn't take it too personally when she realizes you guys are spying on her."

Charlie laughed. "Whether she stays on board with us or not, if she spots Hawker's bugs, I'll give her a damned medal."

Jacob sank into the driver's seat and drew in the deep, comforting scent of leather. "All I'm saying is that Val Kearie isn't a girl who will like having the wool pulled over her eyes." He grabbed the door and nodded goodbye to Charlie. "Leave it too long, and you might lose her."

Home
Manassas, VA
Late Friday Afternoon

Exhaustion had looped back around on itself and become a new form of mania. Val's car, a practical little hybrid, was still parked snugly in its assigned spot in her apartment's garage. There was a bus stop a block from the Viking Inc. office. She had planned on hopping a bus home, but when the lumbering beast rolled to a stop at the corner, she kept going.

What the hell. It wasn't late, home was only about a mile away, and the evening air called to her.

It was a Friday afternoon in early summer and she was strolling down narrow streets lined with pubs and cafés beginning to bustle. She passed one especially popular pub, where the patio was filled to overflowing with college kids. They seemed so young to Val suddenly, like children in push-up bras, high-heeled boots, and sagging jeans. Yet she felt the wild compulsion to join them, hop in line and tear up the dance floor with a parade of faceless, intense partners. Dance, swing, move, fight, fly. It was all the same, and it all sang her name.

She passed the old Rosebud movie theater, advertising its weekend run of films. A week ago, Val would have seen the poster for a showing of the original *Judge Dredd* and decided on the spot that she *must* get in line for the popcorn and tickets right now.

A week ago, she had been a different person. Now the thought of sitting still in the darkness and watching the action from a distance made her want to scream. She veered into the mini-mart at the end of the street and paced the aisles. She wasn't hungry, although her internal clock said it was time to eat. When she saw the cashier staring at her suspiciously, she relented and snatched up a basket. She bought eggs and milk, coffee, and a box of Cliff bars, ignoring the inflated price at the register.

When she was outside again, she realized that absolutely none of it sounded appetizing. What sounded appetizing was meat: rare slices of roast beef, hearty bread, fresh fish, rich glasses of mead, and thick, chewy beer.

Grams would have some of that stuff, Val thought. The old woman lived in the mother-in-law apartment above Dad's garage. She knitted doilies and decorated her living room with ceramic cats and commemorative plates from the Bradford Exchange.

She was also the best target shooter in the family, had an outsized enthusiasm for MMA fighting, and preferred beer and beef jerky to afternoon tea. If Val dropped by unannounced, Grams would welcome her with open arms and fry her up a thick slice of pork shoulder with pan gravy.

It sounded good. Val was tempted. Then she imagined trying to explain her week, her feelings, her *restlessness* to the woman who had been a pillar of her life ever since Mom left, and she came up short. She didn't have the words. She couldn't explain the way she felt to anyone, not even herself.

Angry and restless, she went home to her loft apartment. She put away her scant groceries and found a bottle of mead in the fridge. A few inches of liquid swirled around the bottom. She didn't remember how long ago she'd picked the bottle off the clearance rack at the local liquor store.

She pulled the cork out with her teeth, snatched up the last of a wheel of Brie chilling in her cheese drawer, and sauntered into the bathroom. She closed the drain in the tub, turned on the faucet, and sprinkled in a healthy scoop of scented Epsom salts.

Finally, she sank into a tub of soft, fragrant water, nicely warm but not hot. She alternated bites of creamy soft cheese with sips of her sweet drink, and she could relax.

The past week, with all of its unexpected turns, slipped into some vague void behind her. The entire week's worth of yips settled down like an anxious dog finally given a bone to gnaw.

Val drowsed in the water, swirling in happier memories. Strolling through ancient stone corridors, reveling in the past, arm-in-arm with Muirne, who felt almost like kin. Fighting back-to-back with Jacob, all the terror falling behind fierce joy at having a shield-brother at her side once more.

Fear had no place here.

She must have nodded off in the bath. The next thing she knew, the water was cold, her bottle was empty, her cheese was gone, and her fingers and toes were wrinkled like prunes.

Finally ready for sleep, she crawled out of the tub and slipped into bed, naked and damp.

One final memory slipped to the front of her mind before all went dark. It was the image of a woman, her feet planted on a pile of corpses and her crimson cloak billowing out behind her like bloody wings.

She stared into Val's eyes, and Val stared into a mirror.

Her lips moved.

Then Val was asleep.

EPILOGUE

Gray water faded to mist, and mist faded to sky, infinite and lit from everywhere at once. Waves crashed against sand and stone as the ocean breathed.

Long, slender boats slid out of the distance and sliced across the water, leaving rippling V's in their wake. The prows were curved, high, and proud. Oars rose and dipped into the water, steady as the beat of drums. Steady as the beat of her heart.

Sailors jumped from the boats and waded onto wet sand to drag their ships onto the beach. Tall and hearty men with long braided beards, and broad-shouldered women with their heads bent and backs straining against the weight of dragon boats. All of them worked together.

There was raiding, yes, as much in the past as in the future. But there was trade, too. There was building and there was learning. Fierce Northmen were hungry to know the world beyond their rocky frozen coasts. They looked out over the emerald fields and found slender Gaels looking back at them. Fearful, hopeful.

Time slipped past in confusion. Blurry days, months, and years passed as ragged traders and raiders became settlers and camps became towns.

They left a space for her in their streets and their long-halls. They did not look directly at her or glance her way, but they moved around her, making room for respect and welcome. It was a soft acknowledgment that filled her heart with joy. She was a spirit, and these were her people.

The raucous scream of a raven cut through the mist, and she turned away from the busy little place of men. She drew back out to the beach, to the place where land met the moody sea.

A lone figure walked along the shore, the long shaft of his spear thumping in time with his steady footfall. He was tall, taller than the waves, taller than the sky. His face was shrouded in shadow and mist. Birds followed him like a dark halo.

He came to her and she slid to her knees. The coarse sand was rough on her bare skin.

"You have come." His voice was like the grinding of millstones, though there was a softness that felt almost like affection. "You've slept for so long. I've missed you."

Slept? Confusion. Thoughts slid in and out of her, muddled. *But I've barely closed my eyes, Grandad.*

Was that sound chuckling, or was it the rumbling of the ocean? Or were they both the same?

The understanding came to her all at once. She wasn't sleeping. She was Valerie, and though she might still be safe and warm between her sheets in an apartment in Virginia, this wasn't a dream.

"You can read my thoughts," she stated fearfully.

"And more. There is a reason men still call me the All-Knowing."

"All-Knowing?" She was tired suddenly. She felt like a flesh-and-blood human, dragged from her bed far too early. "Then you know I've had a rough week. I need rest."

"That is your human side speaking. You must conquer her, lest she make you weak."

What?

She looked up and couldn't see his face. She scrambled to her feet, though it did her no good because he was still ten miles tall, and even on her feet she was no closer to his face than she was on her knees. Still, she stood.

"I'm not weak," she insisted. "You may have dragged me out of my bed, and you may have all the knowledge in the world, and you may be older than the moon. But I—I am not weak."

"Be still."

The voice forked down her spine like lightning and rooted her to the world. It pinned her and made every hair stand on end.

"Be still," he repeated. If his tone had softened, she couldn't tell. "I am *Odin*, petulant, beloved child. I am the Magician. I do not make mistakes."

She wanted to argue. Her tongue was glued to the roof of her mouth. She realized that she may be strong, but it was the strength of an ant—mighty at scale but terribly small and fragile.

"You are mud and straw," he announced. "You are soft like unbaked clay—but, aye, yes—you have inside you a great strength. You must allow it to awaken, and grow, and burn."

"I—I don't understand. *What* is in me?"

"Awaken, Val Kearie."

The mist swirled. The sea, the distant longboats, and Odin dissolved into the flutter of dark wings.

"Awaken."

THE STORY CONTINUES

The story continues with books two, *Into the Battlefield,* available at Amazon.

Claim your copy today!

AUTHOR NOTES

AUGUST 9, 2022

Thank you for not only reading this story with these author notes as well.

I have been wanting this book to come out for months!

I just got finished reading book four of this series. I hope you are excited as I am for the other eight books (total of nine) in the series, based on how much I enjoyed it.

Please don't let me down... *Smile, laugh, grin, oh shit!*

My goal with this series was to create something obviously paranormal, but with a lot of realism tossed in the mix. Well, as much realism as your typical thriller.

As a character, Valerie Kearie is similar to Bethany Anne, the first character I wrote in *The Kurtherian Gambit* series.

With Valerie, I get to find out who her new friends are, what she is doing with her new job, and how people will react to her as they encounter Reginlief.

It is more of a slow-burn reveal than my typical books,

so I hope the story engaged you enough with the non-paranormal part. I promise that we keep pulling the shades apart as the series progresses.

The genesis of this story was part "I love the Valkyrie character in the Thor movie. What would happen if Ragnarök wasn't a big deal anymore, and...

What would happen with Odin if Earth just ignored him?

I suspected he might look in from time to time and see how Midgard is doing. When he realizes there are issues with the planet, while not causing Ragnarök, they still could cause a serious problem he might decide to fiddle with a little bit.

He does it by interjecting Reginlief into Valerie's body.

Because nothing can go wrong with that idea, can it? We shall see!

For those who know Bethany Anne, you will see that I replaced Coca-Cola with mead. For every Coke you have a Pepsi, and for mead, the other side is beer.

My desire to try mead got so bad that I tried to find a good mead source in Las Vegas. I didn't find anything locally to suit my needs, and I refuse to try a crappy mead. I was in Europe and tried to find some in Spain, but nothing was local to where I was.

Major downer.

Which is funny because I am not much of a fan of alcohol.

Well, that's not totally true. I drink Drambuie occasionally. Since Drambuie is sweet and mead (supposedly) is sweet, I think I might tolerate it. Plus, Valerie is such a huge fan...

If any of you start drinking mead because of this I'm not sure I want to know about it. ;-)

Before you go too far, don't forget to go pre-order the next book (not like I'll be biting my fingernails with worry that this series isn't going to make sell or anything. Remember, *NINE BOOKS*.)

Talk to you in in book 02!

P.S. – Go pre-order now…. Oh, God…please… (Or set a note to remember to read it in KU…something like that!)

Twelve. Count them…NINE. Just saying. *Man, I hope I'm not the only fan. If you enjoyed the story, feel free to leave a review and let me know. Eventually, I'll drink mead and relay that here in the author notes!*

Ad Aeternitatem,

Michael Anderle

If you want to, you can read a couple of short stories that I am sharing in my STORIES with Michael Anderle newsletter here:
https://michael.beehiiv.com/

CONNECT WITH THE AUTHOR

Connect with Michael Anderle

Website: http://lmbpn.com

Email List: http://lmbpn.com/email/

https://www.facebook.com/LMBPNPublishing

https://twitter.com/MichaelAnderle

https://www.instagram.com/lmbpn_publishing/

https://www.bookbub.com/authors/michael-anderle

BOOKS BY MICHAEL ANDERLE

Made in United States
North Haven, CT
14 May 2023

36568816R00195